S0-ABB-524

She was rappelling down the cliff face

across the narrow valley from his hiding place when Kel spotted her.

She was a perfect target, hanging against the pale rock face as she made her way slowly down to the ledge. It was a drop of about forty feet, and he found himself admiring her courage. It was a dangerous climb at the best of times, made even more dangerous by the ever-present possibility that one of the eagles would return and find her looting the nest.

But she would get away with it. Getting away clean was what Jordon Walker did best. "Just ask my brother," he whispered under his breath.

Except that was impossible, he reminded himself with hostility. Because Alec was dead.

And the woman who'd killed him was, even as Kel was contemplating the irony, within easy range of his own rifle. Smiling grimly, he held her in the cross hairs of the scope. *You're mine, lady.*

Dear Reader,

When two people fall in love, the world is suddenly new and exciting, and it's that same excitement we bring to you in Silhouette Intimate Moments. These are stories with scope and grandeur. The characters lead lives we all dream of, and everything they do reflects the wonder of being in love.

Longer and more sensuous than most romances, Silhouette Intimate Moments novels take you away from everyday life and let you share the magic of love. Adventure, glamour, drama, even suspense—these are the passwords that let you into a world where love has a power beyond the ordinary, where the best authors in the field today create stories of love and commitment that will stay with you always.

In coming months, look for novels by your favorite authors: Barbara Faith, Marilyn Pappano, Emilie Richards, Paula Detmer Riggs and Nora Roberts, to name only a few. And whenever—and wherever—you buy books, look for all the Silhouette Intimate Moments, love stories with that extra something, books written especially for you by today's top authors.

Leslie J. Wainger
Senior Editor and Editorial Coordinator

NAOMI HORTON

Dangerous Stranger

SILHOUETTE·INTIMATE·MOMENTS®

Published by Silhouette Books New York

America's Publisher of Contemporary Romance

If you purchased this book without a cover you should be aware
that this book is stolen property. It was reported as "unsold and
destroyed" to the publisher, and neither the author nor the
publisher has received any payment for this "stripped book."

SILHOUETTE BOOKS
300 East 42nd St., New York, N.Y. 10017

DANGEROUS STRANGER

Copyright © 1992 by Susan Horton

All rights reserved. Except for use in any review,
the reproduction or utilization of this work in
whole or in part in any form by any electronic,
mechanical or other means, now known or
hereafter invented, including xerography,
photocopying and recording, or in any information
storage or retrieval system, is forbidden without
the permission of the publisher, Silhouette Books,
300 E. 42nd St., New York, N.Y. 10017

ISBN: 0-373-07425-5

First Silhouette Books printing April 1992

All the characters in this book have no existence
outside the imagination of the author and have
no relation whatsoever to anyone bearing the same
name or names. They are not even distantly
inspired by any individual known or unknown
to the author, and all incidents are pure invention.

®: Trademark used under license and
registered in the United States Patent and
Trademark Office and in other countries.

Printed in the U.S.A.

Books by Naomi Horton

Silhouette Intimate Moments

Strangers No More #323
In Safekeeping #343
Dangerous Stranger #425

Silhouette Romance

Risk Factor #342

Silhouette Desire

Dream Builder #162
River of Dreams #236
Split Images #269
Star Light, Star Bright #302
Lady Liberty #320
No Walls Between Us #365
Pure Chemistry #386
Crossfire #435
A Dangerous Kind of Man #487
The Ideal Man #518
Cat's Play #596
McAllister's Lady #630
No Lies Between Us #656

Silhouette Books

Silhouette Christmas Stories 1991
"Dreaming of Angels"

NAOMI HORTON

was born in northern Alberta, where the winters are long and the libraries far apart. "When I'd run out of books," she says, "I'd simply create my own—entire worlds filled with people, adventure and romance. I guess it's not surprising that I'm still at it!" An engineering technologist, she presently lives in Nanaimo, British Columbia, with her collection of assorted pets.

Dedicated to:

the Conservation Officers of the
B.C. Ministry of the Environment (Nanaimo);

Edward,
at the Canadian Wildlife Service (Qualicum Beach);

Robin Campbell,
whose love for the orphaned, the injured, the abused
and the sick led him to start the North Island
Wildlife Recovery Association (Errington, B.C.),
a nonprofit organization made up of dedicated
volunteers responsible for the medical and surgical
care, rehabilitation and release of wild animals.
Thanks, Robin.

Prologue

She was rappelling down the cliff face when he spotted her from his hiding place across the narrow valley. He caught her in the cross hairs of the rifle scope and held her there, smiling a little.

She was a perfect target, hanging against the pale rock face as she made her way slowly down to the ledge. It was a drop of about forty feet from cliff top to ledge and he found himself admiring her courage. It was a dangerous climb at the best of times, made even more dangerous by the winds whipping through the narrow canyon and the ever-present possibility that one of the eagles would return and find her looting the nest.

That had happened yesterday. She'd been over in the Tals'it Valley, hanging a thousand feet above the valley floor as she was now with nothing but a cobweb of nylon rope and a few crumbling handholds in the cliff face between her and death. The eagle had come swooping out of the sun like a fighter pilot, talons extended, shrill scream of rage echoing against the stone. The woman had crouched down, trying to protect her face and head as she'd inched away from the huge nest, and Kel had found himself holding his breath, drawn into the drama of the scene without even wanting to be.

But she'd gotten away with it. The eagle had sideslipped away finally, riding the winds like a kite, and the woman had scampered back up the cliff untouched.

But then, getting away clean was what Jordon Walker did best.

"Just ask my brother," he whispered under his breath, still watching her through the scope. "Just ask Alec."

Except that was impossible, he reminded himself with hostility. Because Alec was dead.

And the woman who'd killed him was, even as he was contemplating the irony, within easy range of his own rifle.

Smiling grimly, he held her in the cross hairs of the scope. *You're mine, lady,* he told her with cold certainty. *And before I'm through with you, you're going to wish you'd never even heard of Dr. Alec Davies....*

Chapter 1

The bullet hit the rock face of the cliff about a foot from Jordon's left ear and ricocheted into space with a whine.

She dropped like a stone, hugging the cliff. An instant later the crack of the rifle shot echoed and reechoed down the narrow valley and she found herself thinking a little inanely that had the shot found its mark, she'd have been dead before she even heard the retort.

She probably wouldn't hear the next one.

Frantically she tried to get some slack on her ropes to allow herself some maneuvering room, knowing even as she did it that there was no point. She was a perfect target, tethered to the cliff face by a thread of nylon with a five-hundred-foot sheer drop below her and not even a blade of grass for cover. The ridge she was clinging to ran for about twenty feet to the left, angling upward slightly, and at the end was the huge eagle's nest that had brought her down here in the first place.

The nest wouldn't provide much cover but some was better than none, and she started inching her way toward it.

Only then did she realize that if whoever was shooting at her had wanted to kill her, he'd have done it by now. It had been a full two or three minutes since the first shot—plenty of time to have corrected his aim and tried again.

So they were just trying to scare her.

Again.

And succeeding, she thought grimly, wiping her sweat-slick palm on her denimed thigh. That was what...the third time?

Problem was, how much longer were they going to settle for just trying to frighten her off? Sooner or later they were going to realize that their scare tactics weren't working, and they were going to start getting more serious in their efforts to drive her away.

Jordon swallowed and adjusted her climbing rope again to give herself more slack. She tried not to think of who might be across the valley watching her, holding her steady in the cross hairs of his rifle, his fingers even now tightening on the trigger....

Maybe she *should* just say to hell with it. This wasn't the only job in the world.

Except, she added a little more grimly, someone with her reputation pretty much took what was offered and considered herself lucky. There were not a lot of jobs out there for troublemakers.

She shrugged her shoulders under the climbing harness, trying to ease the knot of tense muscles there. They'd tightened in anticipation for the next shot...which, she was fairly sure by now, wouldn't come.

She shuddered and eased herself to her feet, standing on the ledge for an unsteady moment or two while she got her breath back and checked her ropes. Her heart was still hammering against her ribs and she swallowed again, daring a quick look over her shoulder, knowing she wouldn't see a thing but turning to look anyway.

The mountainside across from her glowed a rich brocaded green in the slanting rays of the afternoon sun, still and wild and beautiful. There were a thousand places in that tangle of forest and rock where the sniper could be hiding. He could be watching her right now....

Just as he'd been watching her for the past week or more. Watching and following. She didn't even know when she'd first realized he was there. More than anything, it had just been a growing awareness of not being alone: footsteps paralleling hers, more sensed than heard; shadows where there shouldn't have been any; flickers of movement that would catch her eye, only there'd be nothing there when she looked.

Whoever he was, he was damned good. A professional tracker, if the skill with which he could follow her through these mountains was any indication. And he was as stealthy as one of the big golden cougars she occasionally glimpsed slipping soundlessly through the dappled shadows.

He'd been around her trailer at night, too. She'd awakened at least twice in the past week, hearing something big moving around outside in the darkness. But of course there had been nothing to see, just a blurred footprint one morning in the mud under her bedroom window. It was not much, but it was enough to make her sleep now with the loaded rifle beside the bed.

What he wanted was anyone's guess. There were too many people to even count who found her work with the eagles a threat for one reason or another.

But there was one thing she *could* be certain of—whatever the identity of the shadowy stranger following her, he was trouble she didn't need.

And suddenly, out of nowhere, she felt the old panic rise—that cold, mind-numbing fear of being trapped, of not being able to get away. She fought it, knowing it was illogical, knowing that she wasn't in any real danger. Knowing that the sniper was probably long gone and that she still had a job to do....

But logic didn't have a thing to do with it. She wanted to be off this exposed cliff face and back up on solid ground again and nothing else mattered—not the job, not the eggs, nothing. Quickly she checked her ropes and then started up the jagged face of the cliff, trying not to think of who might be crouched there in the shadows across from the valley, watching. Of the perfect target she made....

Kel hit the clearing at a dead run. Breathing hard, he slowed to a lope and headed toward the trail angling off the small meadow, the one that ran toward the cliff. He scanned the clearing and trees surrounding it with a skillful eye, knowing he was wasting his time. Whoever had taken that shot at her was long gone by now. But the old habits had kicked in the instant the rifle shot had cracked out across the valley and he'd seen the woman drop.

His heart had stopped at that moment. Not with shock, but with rage. Rage at being cheated out of what was rightfully his, at having spent two months tracking her down and then—just when she was his—having her snatched out of his grip by some trigger-happy idiot who probably didn't even know who or what she was. She was *his,* damn it!

The thought made him smile grimly. Killing Jordon Walker wasn't what he had in mind, of course. The only reason he'd had his own rifle trained on her was because he'd left his binoculars in the truck and the hunting scope was all he'd had with him.

In truth, he didn't even want her falling off that damned cliff—not before he had some time with her, anyway. For one thing, a quick clean death like that would be altogether too good for her. Alec had suffered for two long years. He wanted Jordon Walker to have time to *think* about that. Time to understand fully the implications of what she'd done. Time, maybe, to even explain why.

Yeah, Kel thought angrily. He wanted that. If nothing else came out of this hunt, he wanted to know why—why she'd done it, why she'd been able to walk away afterward and continue on with her life as though nothing had happened, while Alec—

He caught the thought before it went any further.

He found her battered, mud-caked old Bronco a few minutes later. She'd parked it at the head of the secondary trail that led out to the cliff edge. It was filled with bits and pieces of climbing equipment and scientific paraphernalia and junk, but he gave the contents of the vehicle only a cursory glance. It was the bullet holes in the windshield that interested him. There were three of them, evenly spaced, just to the right of the driver's seat.

He fingered one of them curiously. They weren't new. Had been there a week, he estimated. Maybe more.

Then he saw the other ones.

Swearing under his breath, he squatted on one heel and ran his fingertips lightly over the spray of holes running across the driver's door and extending up and along the hood. They *were* fresh—so fresh that the ancient green paint was still flaking away from the edges.

He glanced around quickly, the spot midway between his shoulder blades prickling slightly, and eased a taut breath between his teeth. This hadn't been in his plan—what little plan he'd had, anyway. He'd thought it was going to be simple: come up here with that cover story he and Hollister had concocted, find the woman, watch her for a while...and after that? He hadn't even thought it through that far.

But it sure as hell hadn't included *this*. He touched one of the punctures again thoughtfully. Obviously he wasn't the only enemy Jordon Walker had.

Swearing again, he eased himself to his feet, and it was only then—only when he started to turn toward the trail— that he realized someone was behind him.

She'd come up as silent as a cat on the soft moss and pine needles carpeting the clearing under the trees, and Kel's heart gave a distinctly unpleasant thud as he found himself staring into the barrel of her hunting rifle. She was standing maybe thirty feet from him, legs braced, eyes narrowed and cold as they met his, and she held the rifle with the white-knuckled determination of someone who's not entirely comfortable with guns but knows how to use them.

And she could use that rifle—he had no doubt of it. It was aimed in the general area of his chest and at thirty feet, she didn't have to be much of a marksman to blow a hole in him the size of his fist.

"Now just take it easy," he said very softly, holding his arms away from his body. "I didn't do this." He nodded his head toward the Bronco.

He realized then that she hadn't seen the damage and he stood very still as she cat-footed out and around him to get a better look at the driver's side of the Bronco. Her eyes widened very slightly when she saw the bullet holes stitching the door and hood, and Kel saw her pale a bit.

She looked at him again, her gaze taking in the rifle dangling from his right hand, and Kel drew in a careful breath. "I know what you're thinking," he told her quietly, "but you're wrong. I didn't do this, and I didn't take that shot at you a few minutes ago, either."

Her head lifted slightly, eyes challenging. "How did you know someone shot at me?"

Easy now, Kel advised himself. She was frightened and shaken up and getting more suspicious by the minute. "I was watching you. From across the valley." He grinned engagingly, trying to look suitably sheepish. "I . . . uh . . . saw you rock-climbing, and stopped to watch. You're . . . well, you're pretty easy to watch, if you don't mind my saying so."

She did. Kel watched her eyes narrow and tried not to stare at the barrel of the rifle as it lifted ever so slightly. He wiped the grin off his mouth and tried to look nervous.

It didn't take much acting. "Look, I'm sorry. I thought I was alone out here. When I saw you on that cliff face, I just stopped to watch, that's all. I didn't mean anything by it. Then I heard the shot and saw you fall, and figured you'd need—"

"Just who the hell are you and what are you doing out here?" There was more impatience than fear now on her face, and Kel eased out another tight breath. Play it straight, he told himself calmly. There's no way she can suspect a thing. "My name's Kel Stuart," he lied easily. "I'm with the U.S. Fish and Wildlife Service and I've just been assigned to help the local—"

"U.S. Fish and Wildlife?" Her eyes never left his. "You're a little lost, Stuart. You're in British Columbia. And under Canadian jurisdiction."

"Yeah, I know that. I'm part of an international task force that was set up a couple of years ago," he said, telling her what she already knew. "There's been a lot of poaching going on up here and—"

"I know all about poaching," she said shortly. "Harris never said anything about a new man coming in."

He pretended to look relieved. "I'm not working with Harris. Not officially, anyway. I've been sent up free-lance—working undercover. I told Harris not to tell anyone I'm here. Not even you, Dr. Walker." He paused just long enough to let it sink in. "You *are* Dr. Jordon Walker, aren't you? Harris said you were working up here and to keep an eye out for you."

He found himself holding his breath, wondering if it was going to work. Her eyes held his, as hard as agate in the green-tinted sunlight filtering through the tall pines, and he could see her thinking about it, weighing his words, trying to get a feeling for what he was saying.

He suspected he wasn't in any real danger... but then again, he hadn't stayed alive this long by being careless, either. Keeping his expression puzzled and—he hoped—suitably innocent, he stood very still and let her take her time thinking it over.

"If you're really with the FWS you'll be able to prove it," she finally said. "Put your gun down—very slowly—and show me some ID."

"Honey," he said gently, "I just told you I was working undercover." Then, as her eyes turned even cooler, he gave a resigned shrug. "Okay, okay... in my left boot." Trying to ignore the rifle trained on his midsection, Kel leaned his own against the Bronco. "Come to think of it, how do I know you're really who you say *you* are?"

"You don't. But I'm the one holding the gun."

"You have a point there," Kel muttered with a very real jab of irritation. Usually he was the one who had the advantage of surprise, of firepower. He didn't like being on this end of a standoff one bit, but there wasn't a lot he could do except swallow his pride and do as she wanted. Not making any sudden moves, he knelt slowly and tugged up the leg of his jeans, then fished inside his leather boot for the ID card Hollister had gotten made up for him.

He'd hoped he'd never have to use it. It wasn't exactly a forgery, but it wouldn't hold up to a lot of official scrutiny, either. Not that he had to worry. Hollister had pulled enough strings to get him in here more or less legally, and Walker had no reason to suspect anything.

He straightened and held the ID toward her, but she gestured with the rifle and he tossed it onto the ground near her feet. Kneeling cautiously, and never taking her eyes—or that damned rifle barrel—off him, she retrieved the plastic card.

She looked down at it. Turned it over. Stared at the photograph on it, then up at him thoughtfully.

His stomach pulled tight and he found himself having to fight to hold her gaze. She hadn't recognized him so far, but that was to be expected. He hadn't been at the trial in person, and the photographs the newspapers had used had been old ones. He'd still been in uniform back then, too, his hair regulation navy length, and newspaper photos were notoriously bad. But there was always a chance that Alec had shown her more recent ones of his older brother, boasting, perhaps, of Kel's exploits in any one of a half-dozen Middle East conflicts.

If they'd ever been that close, he found himself thinking, watching her. If it had ever really gone that far...

Her eyes caught his in that instant, and Kel slammed his mind down across the thoughts, not risking letting something in his expression betray him. He gazed back at her calmly, praying that if she did see something in his eyes she'd think it was just the normal unease of a man with a gun pointed at him.

There was a moment—just a heartbeat of time, really—when Jordon could have sworn she knew the man standing in front of her. There was something about the shape of his mouth, the narrow bridge of his nose that—

Alec Davies.

She shuddered violently, feeling shaken and sick. He didn't look at all like Alec, of course. It was just her own imagination, seeing similarities where there weren't any, taunting her with echoes of things she'd sworn to put from her once and for all.

She gave another little shiver, then threw off the feelings angrily as she again examined the plastic ID card the stranger had given her. It looked legitimate enough. And Harris *had* said he was going to ask for more government help. So odds were that Kel Stuart really was who he said he was.

And the fact that he was just a little too big and a little too sure of himself didn't add up to anything. Neither did the fact that she didn't like the way he looked at her.

She didn't like the way any man looked at her. Not any-more. Not for nearly two years, anyway, since—

"Did you see who it was?" Without preamble, she flicked the rifle's safety back on and cleared the chamber, then slung it over her shoulder by the webbed strap. "Presuming it *wasn't* you shooting at me, anyway."

Stuart's eyes held hers for a watchful moment, as though wondering if she were trying to trick him, then he relaxed and smiled faintly. "The shot came from high on the west slope—that's all I can be sure of. We can go up there if you like and look around. See if we can find the shell casing or something else that might give us an idea who—"

"Waste of time." She took a few steps back into the shadows and picked up her discarded climbing gear, then carried it toward the Bronco. She was tired suddenly, ex-haustion washing through her in the aftermath of fear. "A shell casing won't prove anything, even if we did find one. And there won't be anything else. There never is."

The man nodded thoughtfully. "You make it sound as though this happens fairly often." His glance drifted to the three bullet holes gracing the windshield of the Bronco.

"Too often," Jordon said shortly, dumping her gear into the back of the Bronco. Her hands were shaking and she clenched her fists, feeling rage and panic and despair well up through her like something black and ugly. It wasn't going to stop here, something whispered at her. It wasn't going to stop until they drove her off. Or killed her. . . .

"What are you going to do now?"

Jordon glanced around. Stuart had one hand braced on the windshield of the Bronco and was leaning casually on his outstretched arm, watching her, his expression curiously closed and private. He'd been watching her the entire time she'd been loading her gear, Jordon realized, and for some reason it made her feel uneasy. Almost as though she were under suspicion.

She shrugged the feeling off and turned away, collecting the rest of her equipment. ''I'll report this to the RCMP, although it's a waste of time. Then I'll tell Harris, for whatever good *that* will do. Then I'm going to go home and have a stiff drink and a hot bath and try to forget about it, and tomorrow I'll come back out here and try again.''

''And if the shooter tries again?''

She hadn't wanted to think about that. Not looking at Stuart, she shrugged as casually as she could manage and fished around in the pocket of her cotton jacket for the keys. ''I have a job to do, Stuart. Getting shot at seems to come with the territory.'' She spared him a humorless smile. ''Hang around here long enough and you'll find that out for yourself.''

''You're shaking.''

It was true, Jordon realized a little stupidly. She was trembling like an aspen and the harder she tried to stop the shivers racking her, the worse they became. ''Yeah, well, being used for target practice does that.''

''I think,'' Kel said slowly, ''that I should drive you into town. You're pretty badly shaken up, and I don't like the idea of your going back alone.''

''I can take care of myself just fine,'' Jordon assured him flatly as she climbed into the Bronco and slammed the door closed. A cloud of dust lifted lazily in the golden sunlight, hanging between them like a veil, and for a moment, seeing the tall stranger's face through it, she was again reminded of Alec Davies. It was one of those bizarre tricks of sunlight and shadow and it lasted for no more than a heartbeat, but it was enough to nearly shatter what was left of her self-control.

She jabbed the key into the ignition and turned it. The engine kicked over with no more than its usual sputter of protest and she breathed a sigh of relief. Then, more out of defiance of her own fear than anything else, she turned her head to look straight at Stuart.

He was still standing beside the Bronco, watching her with an oddly thoughtful expression on his face, and she found herself looking at him intently. But it *was* just Stuart standing there, features a little too rugged, eyes a little too hard, skin a little too tanned and wind-roughened to ever be mistaken for Alec Davies. He'd been much more conventionally handsome, his narrow features more clean-cut and even, his dress and voice and even the way he held himself as precise and fastidious as the razor-sharp mind on which he prided himself.

Impatient with her own demons, she shook them off and put the Bronco into gear. "I don't like people watching me, Kel Stuart," she said coldly, meeting his gaze evenly. "So from now on, do your undercover work on some other mountain."

Not bothering to wait for an answer, she let out the clutch and headed the vehicle up the narrow, rutted trail that led back out to the main road.

And Kel, left in a cloud of dust, simply watched her as she roared away. He could have pressed it, asking for a ride back out to the road where he'd left his truck. Maybe even offering to follow her into the RCMP headquarters to verify her report of the shooting. Could even have asked her out for dinner . . . a drink . . . then back to his room at the lodge for a nightcap. . . .

He smiled grimly, starting on the long walk back to his truck. He'd spent the past five months thinking about what he was going to do when he found her, and for a while he'd fantasized about actually making love to her. About staring down into her eyes while she lay under him, begging him to make it good for her, and telling her flat out who he was and why he was there. The idea held a bitter irony that still hadn't entirely lost its appeal, and he found himself wondering idly if he could go through with it.

Hell, most men would give their eyeteeth for a night with her. Even now, with that fabulous mane of hair cut short and the formless, baggy clothes and no makeup, she was enough to make a man's mouth water.

There would be a rightness to it, that was certain. An innate justice. And justice was the one thing that Alec still deserved.

"I don't like this at all," John Harris was saying impatiently. "That's the third time this month someone's taken a shot at you, Jordon. This is government land, remember—get yourself killed on it, and *I'm* the one who has to fill out forms and try to explain to the bean-counters what I was doing letting you wander around out there in the first place!"

"Your concern warms my heart, John," Jordon told him dryly. "The Mounties were almost as concerned when I told *them* about it. Except Corporal Peterson added that since I saw fit to ignore their repeated warnings and continue my studies, they were more or less washing their hands of me. So if I 'get myself killed,' as you both so charitably put it, he'll just write me off as an accident and close the file."

"Can't say I blame him," Harris grumbled. "You're a pain in the neck, Walker. That group you *work* for is a pain in the neck. The situation up here is turning from bad to worse—it's like an armed camp out there now. Your tree huggers are trying to get the area turned into a forest preserve, the loggers want it thrown wide open to the lumber companies, the poachers are killing anything that moves, the local Native groups are claiming it as aboriginal land and want *everything* off it and my department is in the middle of it!" He threw his hands in the air. "It's nuts!"

"I know you Ministry of the Environment boys and the RCMP are run off your feet trying to keep things from breaking into all out warfare up here, John, but I don't care about politics. World First hired me to do an in-depth study on the eagle population up here, and that's all I'm doing."

Harris gave a grunt. "Except the results of that study are critical, and you know it. If World First can prove that poor logging practices are hurting the eagle population, it'll be one more point in favor of turning this part of the country into a forest preserve. And if those government leases aren't renewed for logging, a lot of people up here are going to be hurting. You're a prime target for a lot of anger."

"World First recommends limited lumbering operations in the valley, John. Balanced land use has always been an option."

"*Limited.* And closely monitored. The big lumber companies have had things their way up here for too long to take that kind of interference kindly, Jordon. They'll fight to the bitter end."

"Maybe it's time the big companies moved out and made room for the smaller operations that *are* more conservation-minded."

"And the First People's Congress? They say all this territory belongs to *them* because England never negotiated treaties with the coastal Natives when this land was first settled by the whites. They don't give a damn if the logging is done by big companies, or little. They want us out, period."

"Just the militants," Jordon reminded him patiently. "The moderates in the Congress make it quite clear they want to live in harmony with the white people up here—they simply want fair compensation for the use of the land. Which I think is only reasonable, if you ask me, considering this *is* their land and our honorable forefathers *did* just walk in and take it without so much as a thank-you."

"For someone who isn't interested in politics, you've got a pretty damn high soapbox."

Jordon grinned. "So you don't know who might be shooting at me."

"Oh, I've got lots of ideas. Take your pick—logger, poacher, Indian chief. For that matter, it could be a left-over hippie who thinks you're with Drug Enforcement and is trying to protect his pot field.'' He looked at her for a long moment, silent, the little frown between his brows telling Jordon that whatever he was thinking, it wasn't making him happy. ''Or—'' he offered thoughtfully ''—if we're covering all the bases, it could even have something to do with that trouble you had at the college.'' He looked embarrassed, a faint wash of pink running up into his hairline. ''I mean, it's *possible*.''

Jordon sat very still, keeping her face inexpressive. ''Possible, maybe,'' she said tightly, ''but unlikely. It happened over two years ago.''

John squirmed uncomfortably, not meeting her eyes. ''You ruined his career, Jordon. A man...umm...might not handle that...too well. He...umm...well, he could have been brooding over it. Maybe it got to him, finally, and—''

''I didn't ruin Alec Davies's career,'' Jordon said with precision. ''He managed that all by himself when he raped me. And it didn't hurt his career at the time at all. My lawyers couldn't put a case together, we lost the trial, the college board swept it under the rug and I was asked to continue my doctoral studies elsewhere.'' She heard the brittleness in her voice and fought to control it, taking a deep breath.

John's face had gone a painful red and he was staring at the papers on his desk intently, obviously wishing he'd never brought the topic up. Jordon looked at him for a moment, forcing herself to relax, to release the fierce, hot anger pulsing through her. ''I'm sorry,'' she said quietly. ''Davies lost his chance at department head because he was drinking too much, not because of the trial. He came out of that looking like a hero.'' Another deep breath and she was able to unclench her fists, fingers aching. ''I met your new man today. Stuart?''

Relief swept across John's face and he leapt at the change of topic. ''He's not my man, precisely. In fact, I never have

found out exactly what department he's with—or even who
sent him. He just turned up a few days ago with a handful
of official papers and a badge and said he'll be working undercover for the next couple of months and not to tell anyone he's here.'' He stopped, concern suddenly mirroring in
his pale blue eyes.

"It's okay," Jordon assured him. "Stuart told me all
about it himself.''

"He did?''

Jordon felt a smile tug at the corner of her mouth. "Well,
I *was* holding a gun on him at the time.''

John raised an eyebrow, then he shook his head and held
both hands up as though in surrender. "I don't even want
to know about it. Just do me a favor—keep an eye on your
back, and if you shoot someone out there make sure it's not
a government agent. Anyone else, and it's a matter for the
RCMP, not me. I hate paperwork.''

Jordon smiled as she walked to the door. A visit with
John Harris always left her feeling better, and today was no
exception. Even if he couldn't help her, he made her laugh.
And there weren't many people these days who could do
that. Or, keeping her reputation in mind, many who even
tried.

A sudden thought hit her and she paused, one hand on
the doorknob, and glanced around at John. "No one ex-
pects me to work with this Stuart, do they? I mean, I've
been the one screaming the loudest about the poaching and
demanding they send more people in to stop it. So your department or whoever's behind him doesn't think I'm going
to hold his hand while he's out here, do they? Because I—''

"Stuart's strictly a lone wolf," John assured her seriously. "If you want the truth, I don't even know what he's
supposed to be doing—infiltrating, making arrests, or just
fact-finding.'' He gave her a rueful smile. "I'm the last
person to find out what's going on in my own backyard,
Jordon. The people who approve and run these interna-

tional operations figure we're just a bunch of small-town hicks, so they tell us as little as they can get away with.'' He shrugged. ''Suits me fine.''

''Well, next time you see him, tell him to stay away from me, all right? I don't need him drawing attention to me or where I'm working—I've got enough trouble with poachers trying to kill my birds without some hotshot secret agent leading them right to the nests.''

''Consider it done.'' John's gaze held hers for a moment, a faint hint of color glazing his fair cheeks. ''I...umm...if you're going to be in town later, would you like to go out for supper or something?''

The undisguised hopefulness on his round, pleasant face made Jordon's heart drop, but she forced herself to smile casually. ''It sounds nice, John, but I've got to pick up some supplies and get back up to camp before dark—you know what it's like driving that road at night. It's even worse since the mud slide. I have to pick my way around the holes and rocks and torn-up trees, and there's always a chance more of it washed out in this afternoon's rain.''

The hint of red in John's cheeks deepened, but he held her gaze stubbornly. ''You could always stay in town overnight and go back up in the morning. I have...'' His courage nearly failed him and he swallowed. ''Well, I have a spare bed at my place. It's a rollaway cot, actually, but...well...you could...''

''I really appreciate it, John, but I can't.'' Jordon said it as gently as possible but she still felt a little jab of guilt as the hopeful glow in his eyes went out.

''Yeah,'' he said quietly, ''I guess not. I understand, Jordon. Maybe some other time.''

''Maybe, John. Thanks.'' And with that, she fled.

As hard as she tried to dismiss it, guilt nagged at her all the way down the corridor of the drab government building that housed the Ministry of the Environment offices. There was no reason—no real reason—for her not to have gone.

It was just John Harris, after all, sweet and funny and even cute in his own way. And harmless.

In spite of herself, Jordon had to smile. *That* certainly didn't have anything to do with it. Two years ago, during those endless sessions she'd had to sit through because her lawyer had insisted on it, the rape counselors had gone on and on about how she'd have to learn to deal with her mistrust of men, perhaps even a fear of them, a mistrust of closeness, of intimacy. But that hadn't been a problem for her.

Alec Davies hadn't been a stranger. He hadn't leapt out of the shadows of a dark street and held a knife at her throat. He'd been her professor, her mentor, the chairman of her doctoral committee. She'd come through the ordeal hating *him,* not men in general. So she hadn't turned John down because she was afraid of him. It was just that she couldn't handle a relationship—regardless of how innocent—and her work, too.

Besides, it wouldn't be fair to John. If she went out with him this once, he'd expect her to go out with him again. And as innocent as his offer of a spare bed might be today, the time would come when it wouldn't be as innocent. It wasn't as though that bothered her or anything—John was certainly a nice enough guy—but she wasn't interested in him romantically. And men sometimes took even the most innocent actions and words the wrong way and turned them around and saw things that weren't there.

She shivered for some reason and found herself thinking suddenly about Alec Davies. *Tease.* That's what he'd called her—on the stand, and under oath. He'd called her other things, too. Worse things. But that had been the one that had hurt her the most. She'd seen the male jurors glance at her speculatively, had known what they were thinking. Every man knew about women who teased, Davies's lawyer had reminded them with a knowing little smirk. Was there a man in the courthouse who hadn't been beguiled at least once in his life by a pretty woman promising more than she intended to deliver?

Another shiver ran across Jordon's shoulders and she shrugged them impatiently under her heavy cotton jacket, pushing the memories away. Romance would have to wait awhile, she thought with a faint smile as she gave the big glass door at the front of the building a shove and stepped outside. She had just about enough trouble right now trying to get her study done without falling off a mountain or getting shot while doing it. Not to mention trying to stay one step ahead of the poachers who saw her eagles as nothing more than something to be butchered for their feathers and talons.

The rain earlier that afternoon had left the air cool and moist and it smelled of wet earth and tidal flats and forest, and Jordon paused for a moment to take a deep breath of it. The small town spilled across the rocky flanks of the mountains ringing the bay, a rough scatter of buildings rambling down to the water in crooked tiers, and Jordon could look out across an array of roofs to the harbor.

The small fishing fleet was in and there seemed to be a lot of activity at the Native-run salmon cannery just to the east of the government wharf where the blue-and-white RCMP cutter and float plane were tied up, rising and falling on the incoming tide. A huge cloud of gulls swirled and dipped above the cannery wharf, their cries filling the air, while beyond them a couple of sailboats were sidling into the marina and the small cruise boat that carted tourists out on whale-watching forays or out to the sea lion rocks was just chugging up to its dock.

Out beyond the mouth of the bay, the outer islands rose against the sky. Untouched so far by the depredations of logging, they were verdant and wild, half-hidden by mist, and they lifted from the water like ancient temples, the last outpost of some mystical otherworldly kingdom where elves and faeries were a common sight, and magic ruled the day.

Smiling at her own whimsy, Jordon walked down the handful of steps at the front of the building and followed the concrete sidewalk around to the parking lot. There were a couple of muddy RCMP cruisers parked close to the door, one of them with a cracked windshield—one of the hazards of driving graveled roads—and the other with a recent scrape and dent along its driver's door. Jordon wondered if it had been an accident, or if someone had deliberately sideswiped it. The violence between local environmentalist groups, loggers and militant Native-rights activists had been escalating rapidly over the past couple of months, and the understaffed, overworked RCMP detachment was run off its feet trying to keep the lid on things.

Harris's green Ministry truck was parked to one side, sitting high on its heavy-duty axles and big rough-terrain tires, and as Jordon walked passed it to where she'd parked her mud-caked Bronco, something made her stop.

Frowning slightly, she walked across to the truck curiously. Harris had taken the tailgate off, probably to more easily carry the Ministry canoe on one of his trips upriver to check the fish ladders and hatchery, and the wide truck bed was littered with clumps of mud and dried grass and leaves. And blood.

Jordon stared down at it. It was dried now, but the big irregular-shaped stain on the bottom of the truck bed was definitely blood. And a lot of it. Curious, she stepped nearer and pulled a tuft of coarse rust-brown fur from where it was caught under the rough edge of the hinge plate. Black bear.

Hit by a logging truck, more than likely.

Or killed by poachers, Jordon thought angrily as she turned toward her Bronco. Black-market bear pelts brought premium prices in the southwest states where they were sold as legal hunting trophies to unsuspecting tourists, and the heart and other internal organs could be sold to the Asian market for up to eight hundred dollars a gram—the same price as heroin.

She didn't realize someone was standing by her Bronco, waiting for her, until she was halfway there. And by that time it was too late—there was no way she could pretend to be going somewhere else. No way, either, to pretend she didn't see them.

Bud Murdoch was leaning against the side of the Bronco, arms crossed, a broad grin splitting his bearded face as he watched her walk toward him. His brother was sitting on the hood, long legs swinging, his narrow features alert and slightly predatory. A lank strand of dark, unwashed hair hung across his eyes.

"Well, if it ain't the prettiest gal in the whole valley. How you doin', Jo-Jo?"

Jordon ignored him. "Get off my truck, Rolly."

Rolly broke into a sly smile, giving his head a toss to flip the hair out of his eyes. "Give me a kiss and I will."

Bud gave a whoop of laughter. "Can't kiss him without kissin' me first, though. How about it, Jo-Jo? Just a little one?" He planted a large, dirty finger on his cheek and leaned forward slightly. "Right here. How about it?"

Jordon eyed the two of them in disgust. "The bars close early?"

"Don't be like that, Jo-Jo," Bud said in a hurt voice. "We're just bein' friendly. Ain't that right, Rolly?"

"That's right," his brother said with a smile. "How come you're always so unfriendly to *us*, Jo-Jo? We've never done nothin' to you—" the smile widened "—yet, anyway."

"I told you to get off my truck." She looked back at Bud, who was still leaning indolently against the door of her Bronco. "You're in my way."

He stared back at her with measured insolence, letting his gaze drift to her breasts. "How come you're always hidin' that pretty little body of yours, Jo-Jo? I figure you've gotta have somethin' mighty spectacular under all them layers of clothes, the way you keep hidin' it."

"I asked you to get out of my way," Jordon said in a cold, precise voice. "I don't have time to stand here and—"

"Sure you do," Rolly said softly, jumping down from the hood and coming around behind her. "Come on, Jo-Jo...you have time for us, don't you?"

Jordon tried to slip from between the two men, but Bud moved to block her and she wheeled away from him, her throat suddenly dry. "Don't you come near me."

"We've always got time for you, Jo-Jo," Rolly said with a suggestive smile. He stepped toward her and Jordon recoiled against the Bronco. "Come on, Jo-Jo. You work too hard. You need a little time off to relax."

Bud's laugh was unpleasant. "Rolly an' me can help you relax, Jo-Jo."

Trapped—she was trapped between them and the Bronco and there was no escape. They loomed over and around her, blocking the sky, jostling against her, hands reaching, smiling faces closing in, and Jordon felt reason and sanity slip as a black uprush of sheer panic exploded through her. She could hear—not Bud's voice, softly coaxing—but Alec Davies, could smell the spicy scent of his after-shave, could feel the cold, hard edge of the lab bench across the small of her back as she tried to move away but couldn't, trapped there...

She heard a scream rising through the air like a knife blade, brittle with terror, and realized, vaguely, that it was her own voice. Heard, too, footsteps running through gravel, a snarled epithet, a shout of warning from Bud that ended in an explosive grunt of pain.

Rolly gave a piglike squeal of alarm and suddenly he, too, was gone, snatched away from her by unseen hands. There was another oath, harsh with anger, then the unmistakable sound of bare knuckles hitting bone, a yelp of pain, a heavy thud as someone slammed against the Bronco beside her and bounced off it to land in the gravel at her feet.

Fists pressed against her ears, eyes squeezed shut, Jordon concentrated on drawing in each breath and releasing it, teeth clenched fiercely against a second scream clawing at her raw throat. The blinding panic kept sweeping through her in wave after wave and it was taking every ounce of strength she had to not just succumb to it completely, knowing if she did she'd founder and drown in it and be lost forever....

Chapter 2

If he touched her, odds were pretty good that she'd lose it completely.

Breathing heavily and rubbing the knuckles of his right hand—bruised and cut from connecting all-too-solidly with Rolly Murdoch's teeth—Kel knelt beside Jordon. She was crouched alongside the Bronco, eyes squeezed shut, arms across her face as though to protect herself from a blow, and he swore under his breath.

Her fear washed around him like something tangible and he reached toward her without even thinking about it, the instinct to calm her, reassure her, catching him by surprise. Luckily, he caught himself in time and drew his hand back.

"It's okay, Jordon," he heard himself saying quietly. "It's just me—Kel Stuart."

Why the hell he was wasting his time, he didn't know. This wasn't any of his business. And his sudden urge to play hero didn't make much sense, either. This was the woman who'd killed Alec—had been responsible for his dying, anyway—and just why he was hunkered down beside her in

BIG SUMMER READ

Summer Reading At Its Best

In July, Harlequin and Silhouette bring readers the Big Summer Read Program. Heat up your summer with these four exciting new novels by top Harlequin and Silhouette authors.

SOMEWHERE IN TIME by Barbara Bretton
YESTERDAY COMES TOMORROW by Rebecca Flanders
A DAY IN APRIL by Mary Lynn Baxter
LOVE CHILD by Patricia Coughlin

From time travel to fame and fortune, this program offers something for everyone.

Available at your favorite retail outlet.

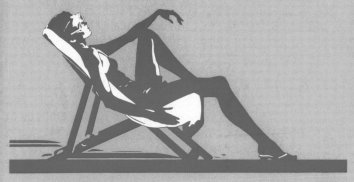

FREE GIFT OFFER

With Free Gift Promotion proofs-of-purchase from Harlequin or Silhouette, you can receive this beautiful jewelry collection. Each item is perfect by itself, or collect all three for a complete jewelry ensemble.

For a classic look that is always in style, this beautiful gold tone jewelry will complement any outfit. Items include:

Gold tone clip earrings (approx. retail value $9.95), a 7½" gold tone bracelet (approx. retail value $15.95) and a 18" gold tone necklace (approx. retail value $29.95).

FREE GIFT OFFER TERMS

To receive your free gift, complete the certificate according to directions. Be certain to enclose the required number of Free Gift proofs-of-purchase, which are found on the last page of every specially marked Free Gift Harlequin or Silhouette romance novel. Requests must be received no later than July 31, 1992. Items depicted are for illustrative purposes only and may not be exactly as shown. Please allow 6 to 8 weeks for receipt of order. Offer good while quantities of gifts last. In the event an ordered gift is no longer available, you will receive a free, previously unpublished Harlequin or Silhouette book for every proof-of-purchase you have submitted with your request, plus a refund of the postage-and-handling charge you have included. Offer good in the U.S. and Canada only.

MILLIONAIRE Sweepstakes !

As an added value every time you send in a completed certificate with the correct number of proofs-of-purchase, your name will automatically be entered in our Million Dollar Sweepstakes. The more completed offer certificates you send in, the more often your name will be entered in our sweepstakes and the better your chances of winning.

PRO1

a parking lot with his knuckles all bruised and cut from defending her honor was something he hadn't even begun to figure out yet.

"I—I'm all right."

Her soft voice brought him to with a jolt. She'd let her arms fall to her sides and was gazing beyond him, to where Rolly Murdoch lay sprawled in the gravel. "What... happened?"

He let her struggle to her feet without touching her, somehow knowing being touched was the last thing she wanted. Frowning, she brushed her short, wind-tousled hair back from her face, looking at Rolly's prone body again, then up into Kel's eyes. "That was you. I heard footsteps...."

"Yeah." He bit the word off, getting more irritated by the moment with her sudden vulnerability, by the way it was affecting him. He didn't give a damn about this woman or anything that happened to her, and yet he found himself wanting to reassure her, to comfort her. She was good—*damned* good! A man would have to be made of rock to withstand the bewildered fear in those huge dark eyes, would find himself slipping strong protecting arms around her and whispering promises before he even knew what had hit him.

Her expression changed suddenly and Kel wheeled around to face Bud Murdoch, who was on his feet now, weaving slightly. Fists clenched, he glowered at Kel sullenly.

"Don't even think about it," Kel advised him in a low voice. Murdoch teetered unsteadily, obviously torn between coming in swinging and making a wise, if humiliating, retreat. Kel nodded toward Rolly. "Pick him up and take him home. And both of you stay the hell out of my way from now on."

"You'll pay for this." Trying to keep one eye on Kel, Bud started to pull his brother to his feet. "You don't hit my brother 'n' me without payin' for it."

"Yeah, yeah." Kel gestured impatiently. "Get out of here. And if I find out you've been bothering Dr. Walker— or any other woman around town, for that matter—I'll find you and finish what I started today. Understand?"

Bud mumbled something unintelligible, half carrying and half dragging his brother across to the truck and shoving him inside. He got behind the wheel and a moment later tore out of the parking lot in a cloud of dust and flying gravel.

"They won't forget this." Jordon's voice sounded stronger. She was still pale and shaken, but there was a healthy glint of anger in her eyes as she watched the Murdochs' truck roar away. Then she turned her gaze to meet Kel's. "I'm sorry you got involved. They can cause you a lot of trouble if they decide to get even."

"I can handle it."

She managed a flicker of a smile, then drew in a deep breath and stepped away from the Bronco, staggering slightly. Without even thinking about what he was doing, Kel caught her upper arm to steady her and she recoiled with an indrawn breath. *"Don't!"*

"Take it easy." Startled, Kel stepped back. "Are you sure you're all right, Dr. Walker? Do you want me to—"

"And *stop* calling me Dr. Walker! I'm not a doctor of anything!" Her voice cracked and she bit down across the words, closing her eyes. "Damn." She swallowed, taking another deep breath, and when she opened her eyes they were calmer. "I'm . . . sorry. That's hardly the way to thank a man who's just come charging to the rescue."

"You've had a hell of a day," Kel said simply.

She gave a gasp of what might have been laughter. "Yeah."

"Are you sure you're all right?"

She nodded, still looking a little pale. "I'm fine. Although I'm glad you came along when you did."

She looked up at him just then, with a shy, sweet smile that took Kel so by surprise he just stared down at her, finding himself wondering a little inanely how anyone so innocently beautiful could be guilty of destroying a man...

...And caught the thought with a silent oath, annoyed at how easy it was to get all caught up—lethally caught up—in that web of potent sexual magic that surrounded her like subtle perfume. "I was in the neighborhood," he growled, even more annoyed at how she kept catching him off guard. "Those two dolts are harmless enough, I guess, but they can't seem to get it through their thick skulls that I'm not interested."

Kel didn't say anything. Was that what she'd told her lawyer two years ago? *Dr. Davies is harmless enough, I guess, but he can't get it through his thick skull that I'm not interested.*

Except she had been interested, according to Alec's testimony. Damned interested. She'd teased and flirted her way around him for nearly a year and then, when he'd made it plain that he didn't want her, that she couldn't buy the recommendation she needed from him with sex, she'd accused him of raping her. The ensuing scandal and trial had ruined Alec... and had left her unmarked.

He wondered if she even knew Alec was dead.

Or cared.

He turned away from her abruptly and started walking toward his truck, not trusting himself to say anything. One wrong word and any advantage he'd hoped for would be gone.

"Thanks again," Jordon called after him. "I... umm... maybe I'll see you around."

The smile flirted around the corners of his mouth and he looked around at her, holding her gaze challengingly. "Oh, I think there's a real good chance of that, Jordon Walker. A real good chance."

A couple of days later Jordon was still thinking about her encounter with Stuart. It had been pelting all day, one of those classic West Coast storms when the rain comes down in seemingly solid sheets, ice-cold and whipped every which way by the wind. She'd taken one look out the steamed-up window of her trailer and had decided to stay home and get caught up on paperwork.

Home was actually what was left of an old logging camp that had been deserted when the company had pulled up stakes and moved a couple of years previously. It didn't consist of much, just a clearing punched out of the bush near the floor of the valley with an old yellow construction trailer and a couple of wooden shacks that had once been used to store equipment.

The trailer was small but in good shape, and Jordon found herself getting more and more attached to it as time went by. She had plenty of water, compliments of a sluice system that kept a huge holding tank filled with ice-cold lake water so crystalline clear that it was like glass. There was a temperamental diesel generator that kept her in electricity and a plentitude of steaming hot water, and a small propane furnace to banish the damp and cold. And there were days when it occurred to her that she'd never been happier.

She'd been here for nearly seven months now. It was hard to believe.

Jordon stretched, stiff from sitting at her small desk entering research data into her journal, and after a moment she got up and wandered across to the stove. She filled the kettle and put it on, then walked across and pulled the door open.

The whole world had vanished in rain and fog and she stared at the sheets of blowing rain whipping past and drew in a deep breath of cold, wet air. She could hear the wind in the tall pines surrounding the trailer, rising and falling like the sound of surf, but the clouds had settled in so low that she couldn't see anything. Ordinarily, the view was spectacular, the deep valley sprawling out in front of her, a sharp

V notched against the sky, and the vast, green-cloaked mountains rising above and around her like sentinels.

Or guardians, she sometimes found herself thinking.

It was safe here. Safe and comfortable. No one looking sidelong at her, eyes speculative; no one shoving a microphone into her face and demanding a *statement;* no one trying to say something sympathetic and getting themselves all tangled up in the words and just making things worse. No two-in-the-morning, breathy, obscene, faintly threatening phone calls. No hostile letters from old alumni disapproving of her behavior.

Up here she had been able to put it all behind her. To almost—*almost*—forget.

Idly, she leaned against the door frame, staring out into the rain. Strange how things worked out. Two years ago she'd been on the fast track, working hard for a doctorate in microbiology that would have led simply and naturally into the lab research she'd always thought she wanted. If anyone had suggested to her back then that one day she'd be clambering up and down sea cliffs to band baby eagles and lugging twenty pounds of scientific gear up fifty-foot fir trees to weigh and measure a nestful of eggs, she'd have laughed outright.

And yet, now, she knew she never wanted to do anything else. Spending twelve-hour days cloistered in a lab with a dozen other scientists, fighting tooth and nail for research grants, being pressured to produce and publish or suffer the consequences...she couldn't imagine ever having wanted it. It had been the dream of someone she couldn't even remember being now.

Strange, too, that it had taken Alec Davies to show her the way out.

It had been no more than a blink of time to him, just a few minutes taken out of an otherwise ordinary evening. Yet for her, those same few minutes had changed her life.

The kettle started to whistle and Jordon shrugged away from the door frame and closed the door, then turned to walk back into the kitchen. She dropped a tea bag into the cup and poured boiling water over it, leaning one hip against the counter as she poked at the bag with a spoon.

What was he doing now? she found herself wondering. The last she'd heard of the brilliant Alec Davies, he'd lost out on his long-coveted position as department head and was still teaching. He undoubtedly blamed her for that. Had she kept her mouth shut about the rape as he'd told her, he'd have been a shoo-in for the position, but the board of regents had shied away from the publicity and had decided to go with staid and predictable over brilliant but controversial.

Publicly, they'd hinted that Davies had turned the position down, saying he didn't want any suggestion of wrongdoing to taint the college in spite of the fact that he'd been cleared absolutely of the charges made against him. Privately, Jordon had always wondered if her accusations had touched a nerve after all, if perhaps the esteemed Alec Davies hadn't been in trouble before and this was the board of regent's way of gently—and privately—slapping his wrist.

Jordon maneuvered the tea bag out of the hot water and tossed it away, then added a splash of milk and carried the cup to her desk. Davies was probably still walking the campus like the revered young god he pretended to be, followed by a trail of wide-eyed and suitably awed young acolytes who hung on his every word. Just as she once had.

And odds were that he was still hand-choosing one of the brightest—and prettiest—to work privately with him. Maybe even staying late with her at night as they worked on her "special" project, gaining her trust, making her laugh, making her feel special and alive and fabulously gifted. And then one night after everyone else had gone home and there was only the two of them, trusted mentor and trusting student, turning on her as he had on Jordon and—

Hot tea slopped over the rim of the cup and across her hand, and she swore, shaking her wrist furiously. Droplets of tea splattered across her notebook and she swore again, staring at it in frustration.

Damn it. She thought she was over the worst of it by now. She'd still dream about it once in a while and wake up screaming, but even that didn't happen very often anymore.

It was Kel Stuart. The memories had only started haunting her again after he'd turned up.

It was something about his eyes. Something about the way she'd caught him looking at her....

She gave her head an impatient shake and wiped the tea off her notes with her sleeve, trying to concentrate on what she'd been doing.

Nests. Of the sixteen eagle nests she'd mapped out since she'd been up here, fourteen of them were being used and all of those but one had recent activity—eggs either near hatching, or young birds already hatched. Eleven of those nests were accessible, if you didn't mind hanging over cliffs on ropes or clambering around the upper reaches of moss-laden, bug-infested trees, praying you didn't put your weight on a rotted branch at the wrong moment.

It was perfect eagle country up here—wild, isolated rain forests completely cut off from civilization, cloud-hung mountain ledges, white-water rivers filled with spawning salmon. Except that civilization was creeping ever closer, usually in the form of the big logging companies that wanted to strip the coastal valleys and off-shore islands of their bounty of towering, thousand-year-old trees.

And it was here that the war between the environmentalists and the forest industry was coming to a head.... With her caught in the middle, Jordon thought gloomily. Her studies on the eagle population up here weren't conclusive yet, but whichever way it went, people were going to be unhappy.

The only people who seemed to be unaffected by it all, in fact, were the damned poachers.

Frowning, she smoothed her topography map and with the point of her pencil traced the trail she'd taken yesterday until she found the tiny circle she'd drawn earlier. Nest Seventeen.

Or it would have been. There were eggs in it—two as far as she could tell—but they were doomed. She'd found what was left of the male eagle at the base of the huge gnarled fir where the nest was located, feet and head gone, stripped of his feathers. They'd caught the female in a leg-hold trap set out on the top of a nearby rock outcropping, using a rabbit as bait and hiding the jaws of the steel trap with fir branches. She hadn't died easily, but in the end she'd been no match for the poachers and their clubs.

Even thinking about it made the rage and frustration well up through her. They'd been young birds, and the big nest they'd taken over had been empty since she'd started her study. She'd been watching them for the past month with a sense of almost proprietary satisfaction, as pleased to add another nesting pair to her study as she was by the simple fact they were there at all, alive and healthy and obviously in their breeding prime. She'd been watching them half out of scientific curiosity and half out of sheer pleasure, as delighted as a new mother when the first egg had appeared in the nest, anticipating the day when the chicks hatched....

She looked at the small circle on the map for a moment longer, then angrily, deliberately, drew an *X* over it. Two nesting eagles in their prime, and they were dead—and for what? So some tourist in Hong Kong or Tokyo could buy an "authentic American Indian war bonnet," or some businessman could wear an eagle talon on a thong around his neck to improve his sexual prowess.

Maybe Stuart could help get it stopped. Jordon closed her eyes and rubbed her temples, listening to the rain hammer against the metal skin of the trailer like small, angry fists.

One agent against an entire ring of poachers didn't sound like good odds, but there was something about Kel Stuart that made her think he could take care of himself.

She smiled slightly, thinking of him striding in to do battle with the Murdoch brothers. Most other men in town would have done the same thing had they been driving by, but the fact that it had been Stuart seemed somehow important. Although she couldn't quite say why, she decided thoughtfully. Except that there was something about him ... something she couldn't quite put her finger on....

She winced slightly, wondering what he must think of her. She'd lost it that afternoon—really lost it. It had been over a year since she'd had a panic attack that severe, in which the terror had just swept over her and she'd stopped functioning.

Frowning, she stared down at the map. The attacks started right after the trial, and for a while they'd been so bad she'd all but been a prisoner in her own apartment. But she'd mastered them finally, and until the other day she'd thought the attacks were over for good.

It made her swear and she shook the mood off impatiently, pulling her chair nearer to the desk, determined to get back to work. The first thing she had to do was put together a report on the two eagles at Nest Seventeen and get it to Kel Stuart. It wouldn't do much good—two healthy eagles were dead and their eggs, too inaccessible to retrieve and incubate, were doomed, the poachers long gone—but at least it gave her a sense of getting something done. And maybe Stuart could find a clue out there that would get him on the right track. Anything was worth a try.

Damn it all, it just didn't add up.

Kel slammed the cupboard door closed and stood looking around at the interior of the small, compact trailer impatiently.

Who are you, Jordon Walker? he asked her silently. Where are your secrets? Where are the hidden things I want to know?

He'd broken into her trailer about an hour ago and had gone through every damned cupboard and closet and hadn't turned up a thing that would give him the answers he wanted.

She lived neat; that was one thing it hadn't taken him long to figure out. The trailer was standard construction-trade issue, with two bedrooms—one outfitted as a well-equipped lab—across one end and a small living room at the other, with a kitchen and bathroom in between. Yet she lived and worked here with very little clutter, her personal things as tidily kept as the books and notes in the tiny dinette across from the kitchen that she was using as an office.

What few personal things she had. Frowning, Kel pulled open the small closet again, looking at the handful of no-nonsense work shirts and jeans hanging there, the row of work boots and sturdy walking shoes lined up underneath. He hadn't expected evening gowns, but most women liked to have something pretty and feminine on hand, just in case.

The drawers in the small dresser had yielded nothing more exciting than a few plain cotton bras and panties, and he'd noted—with some irritation—that her cache of cosmetics consisted primarily of insect repellent and sunscreen.

It just didn't add up. Like the way she'd reacted to the Murdoch brothers a couple of days back. They'd corralled her against the Bronco, but they hadn't had time to do more than bully her a bit, from what he'd seen as he'd driven up.

And yet she'd been scared silly—not shaken up, not a little unnerved, but out-of-her-mind terrified, for no reason at all. And that had been the same woman who—only a few hours before—had scarcely turned a hair at having someone take a potshot at her with a hunting rifle, and had held him at bay not too many minutes after that, as cool as ice and in complete control of the situation. Not the type of woman, in short, who'd be bullied easily.

Kel frowned. He didn't like things that didn't fit. His job in the navy had been to tie up loose ends—to ensure that conquered dictators stayed that way, that insurrections that had been put down stayed down. Cleanup, they called it. Although the work itself could get pretty dirty at times. No one talked about it much—his hadn't been the high-profile battles that garnered all the good airtime or earned him interviews with pretty blondes on nightly news shows. He'd been part of that large shadowy "other" military machine, the one no one really wanted to know about.

And he'd learned, after nearly eighteen years of it, that everything had a cause and an effect. It was understanding that—understanding how to look for truth behind the lies, the patterns of untruths and deception, of what *appeared* to be versus what really *was*—that made him so good.

Which is why he knew something wasn't right here.

He closed the closet and walked back into the small bathroom again, wanting to find—*needing* to find—something that fit the image he'd had of her for all these months. The medicine chest above the sink held the usual array of things: two bottles of painkillers, one for headaches, the other for menstrual cramps, hand lotion, unperfumed soap, shampoo, cold tablets. He was relieved to see a razor on the lower shelf and he smiled to himself. At least she shaved her legs... one small female vanity that made him feel better. There was a small bottle of perfume beside it and he picked it up, noticing that it hadn't even been opened.

Damn it, Jordon Walker, what are you trying to do to me?

He hadn't figured on finding her living up here in sequins and black lace, but even in the most rough-and-ready situations, most women retained at least some of the fripperies of their sex. In fact, it had been his experience in the navy that the more stringent and difficult the assignment, the more defiantly the women assigned to his unit held on to at least one or two reminders of their femininity—a pair of tiny gold earrings, a tube of lipstick, a pair of lacy non-government-issue briefs. Just small things, more symbol than necessity.

But with Jordon, it was almost as though she was deliberately rejecting anything that reminded her of the outside world. Anything that reminded her she was a woman.

The thought made him frown and he lifted the perfume to his nostrils, idly breathing in the faint scent of honeysuckle.

The Jordon Walker who had accused his brother of rape had been every delicious, seductive inch a woman. Kel still had videotapes of the newscasts—that thick mane of curling black hair tumbling around her face and shoulders in silken disarray, her make-up perfect, her trim but lush little body shown off to perfection.

At the trial she'd worn sedate business suits and high-throated dresses, but they'd only emphasized her slender hips and those go-on-forever legs and the high, firm outline of her breasts. The TV cameras had loved her, caressing her near-perfect features as though she were a high-fashion model, catching every nuance of her sidelong glances, every swing of her hips, every movement of her head and reckless toss of her hair.

The media had eaten it up: Beautiful Teaching Assistant Accuses Boss Of Sexual Shenanigans On Floor Of Lab. There were other headlines, too, more innuendo. Rumors that he and Jordon had been lovers for years, that she was blackmailing him for drugs, that he was blackmailing her for sexual favors.... It had gone on for weeks.

Then the jury had brought down their verdict, the charges against Alec had been dropped, Jordon had vanished from sight and it had been over.

Except it hadn't been over at all, Kel thought bitterly. Alec had started drinking. The college powers that be decided he wasn't fit material for the department chair he'd coveted. His marriage started to break up. And finally, almost two years later, he rented a seedy motel room in a bad part of town, downed three-quarters of a bottle of cheap bourbon and shot himself.

Kel put the perfume back and closed the cabinet, gazing at his own reflection in the mirror for a moment. Gray eyes met his, faintly accusing. *You might have been able to have prevented it,* something seemed to whisper at him. *Maybe if you'd paid a little more attention to him, or if you'd stayed to take care of him after Mom died instead of running off to join the navy or if...*

He turned away abruptly and walked toward the kitchen. She'd be back soon. And getting caught in here would put paid to any hope he had of getting her to trust him, to open up, to tell him—in her own words and without knowing who he was—exactly what *had* happened between her and Alec.

But whatever that was, he found himself thinking as he pulled the door open and stepped outside, he was starting to have the feeling that it wasn't going to be as cut-and-dried as he'd hoped.

The eagle came in screaming, talons outstretched, its cry of rage echoing and reechoing off the cliffs.

Jordon flattened herself against the cliff face and tried to shield her face with her arm as the huge bird's shadow swept over her. And then it was by, the curved sickles of its talons missing her by a hairbreadth. Buffeted by the backwash of its massive wings, she swore and scrambled along the ragged ledge to where her climbing rope dangled in the sun, promising escape.

There was another harsh, fierce cry and then the other eagle was there—the female this time—golden eyes glinting in the sun as she swept in, rolling slightly to bring her powerful feet and claws into play. Swearing breathlessly, Jordon ducked.

A heartbeat too late. The tip of the eagle's wing smashed into the side of her head, tearing off her unsecured climbing helmet, and Jordon was flung against the cliff face like a rag doll. She skidded toward the crumbling lip of the ledge, scrabbling for a handhold, and for a moment she really thought she was going over.

Then her foot lodged against something solid and she got a purchase with the fingers of her right hand and she clung there, dizzy and sick. Nearly eight hundred feet below her the ocean seethed and boiled around the bottom of the cliffs and its roar seemed to fill the air around her. One slip, that's all it would take... one slip and she'd be over the edge, falling, falling....

Her right shoulder was bleeding badly. It was starting to hurt now, too. The big male had come in behind her without warning—she'd been trying to get a leg band on one of the hissing eaglets when a shadow had suddenly moved across her and she'd heard the whisper of wind in feather, felt the draft from the one strong downbeat of his wing. But before she'd had time to react he'd hit her with one outstretched foot, his razorlike talons slicing through her jacket and shirt and into the flesh beneath.

Thank God he hadn't been able to hook that talon into her clothing or he'd have pulled her off the ledge and she'd be lying on those jagged, surf-swept rocks below her right now. As it was, maybe she'd just postponed it. How was she going to get up that rope to safety?

Tears of pain stung her eyes and she felt dazed and disoriented, her ears still ringing from the blow on the side of her head. Thank God she'd released the chin strap on her helmet, she thought dizzily, or she'd have followed it over the cliff for sure. Alec Davies had taught her that. It was ironic, in a way, that he should be responsible for saving her life now when he'd done so much to destroy it....

Blindly, she groped along the ledge until she found the dangling rope and she fumbled with it, trying to secure the clips to her harness. At least then she wouldn't have to worry about falling . . . even if she passed out, she wouldn't fall.

The rope trembled in her hand and she looked up stupidly, blinking back tears. Something moved against the sky, just a flash of white, and Jordon went cold.

Someone was up there.

Her stomach pulled tight with sudden fear and she squinted against the brightness of the sky, heart hammering. It would be the easiest thing in the world to release her rope where she'd secured it at the top . . . all he'd have to do was loosen the knot and her own weight would do the rest.

It would look like an accident—that was the perfect part. The RCMP would find her gear at the cliff top and figure she'd failed to secure her own rope properly, and maybe— if they felt like taking the time—*maybe* they'd search for her body.

Although there wouldn't be much point. The undertow along this stretch of coast was renowned for not giving up what it took. There were a thousand little inlets and coves where she could be washed up and never found, a dozen underwater caves that could claim her without anyone ever knowing.

And then, suddenly, someone appeared at the top of the cliff. It was a man, that's all she could tell, and he rose against the sky like a monolith, silent and still. The sun was in her eyes and she couldn't see who it was, had her mouth half open to call to him when he bent over and she could see the flash of metal in his hand.

A knife. . . . He was going to cut her rope!

There was a rattle of stones above her and a small avalanche of pebbles and loose dirt, and when it cleared she looked up to see someone rappelling down the cliff face toward her.

Hugging the wall, Jordon pulled herself as close to the nest as possible, flinching at a malevolent hiss from one of the young eaglets as it spotted her. It struck at her savagely and she wrenched back, nearly crying out as she hit her shoulder on an outcrop of rock. And in the same heartbeat she saw the big male eagle sideslipping toward the cliff again, his scream of rage ripping the warm morning air like a chain saw.

He swooped in like a Valkyrie in full battle cry, huge wings churning the air around her as he tried to drive her away from the nest, neck outstretched and that terrible curved beak slicing through the air as he struck at her again and again. There was an oath from somewhere behind her and a muffled *pop,* and suddenly she and the nest and the attacking eagle were enveloped in a blanket of thick, choking smoke.

Something grabbed the back of what was left of her jacket and she gave a muffled squeak, gagging on smoke, and tried to crawl away.

"Quit fighting me," growled a vaguely familiar voice. "I know it probably goes against your principles or something, but I'm *trying* to save your damned neck!"

An arm caught her around her middle and hauled her upright, squeezing the breath out of her, and by the time she'd stopped gasping and coughing and had enough of her wits collected to start fighting properly, there didn't seem to be much point.

Stuart.

"What are *you* doing here?"

"Rescuing you," he said through clenched teeth. "Again. Put your arms around my neck and hang on—and don't knee me, or I'll damned well drop you and let you find your own way up."

"But—but—what did you *do!*" She looked around frantically, trying to spot the eagle through the thinning smoke.

"Smoke bomb. Used for cover. Or for a distraction. Ready?"

"But you can't possibly climb up there and carry me at the same—ooph!" This last was just a gasp as he put his hands on her waist and lifted her against him firmly.

"Shut up," he said very calmly, looking down into her eyes, "and hang on."

Jordon opened her mouth to protest, then snapped it closed and wrapped one arm around his neck and the other up under his right shoulder, locking her hands together, and tried not to look down as he started up the cliff. She was safe enough, she knew that—she'd spent days in climbing school learning exactly this sort of rescue technique, and Stuart obviously knew what he was doing.

He climbed easily and quickly, using the ropes, the steel pitons and rings she'd already embedded in the rock face and the natural footholds of the cliff with an effortless skill that could have come only from years of practice. Pressed tightly against him, she could feel every shift and ripple of muscle in his chest and belly and thighs as he worked his way upward and she tried to ignore the intimacy of their embrace, very conscious of the movement of his right thigh between hers as he braced himself, the pressure of his arm across her back, the heat of his breath against her throat. He hadn't shaved in a while and his cheek was stubbled and rough against hers, the touch compellingly masculine, and he smelled faintly of soap and wood smoke and good clean sweat.

And it felt good, she realized with a little shock of recognition. It had been well over two years since she'd been this close to a man—since she'd wanted to be this close—and the experience was decidedly . . . nice.

"Almost there. You okay?"

Jordon nodded, not trusting her voice as her heart did a flip-flop at the innocent touch of his lips against her ear. This was getting a little crazy, she told herself a trifle desperately. This was no time to be thinking thoughts like these. Especially about a man she scarcely knew. She'd hoped it

would happen sometime, this wonderful little frisson of
sexual awareness that had been absent for so long…but this
was *not* the time.

And then they were at the top and they clambered over the
lip of the cliff and lay there, panting, in a tangle of ropes,
Jordon's shoulder aching so badly now that it brought tears
to her eyes.

She crawled away from the cliff edge and sat up, releasing her climbing harness, and looked at her rescuer.
"You're…good at this sort of…thing."

Kel struggled to his feet, breathing heavily. "I used to be."

"You used smoke on my birds." It was only then that
Jordon realized she was shaking too badly to stand. Kneeling, shoulders hunched, she closed her eyes as tremor after
tremor ran through her. "You shouldn't have used smoke on
my birds. Who knows what effect it's going to have on
them. They might not even come back to the nest and then
the…the eaglets… Oh, damn!" A surge of tears came up
out of nowhere and she had to use every bit of willpower to
keep them under control. "Damn! E-every time you s-see
me I'm f-falling apart!"

To her surprise, he seemed more concerned than angry.
He dropped on one knee beside her and gently—very gently—pulled her blood-soaked jacket and shirt away from her
shoulder. "Maybe because every time I see you, someone's
trying to kill you," he muttered.

"H-how bad is it?"

"You're sure as hell not going to be doing any climbing
for a few days. And it's bleeding like a son of a gun."

"Oh…."

Kel gave Jordon a sharp look. The wound on her shoulder wasn't that bad, but she'd had a scare and had lost a fair
bit of blood, and shock sometimes did strange things to
people. "You're not going to faint on me or something, are
you? It's a mile and a half to where I left the truck—and I
don't want to have to carry you out."

"I don't faint," she retorted with some hostility. "And if I'm keeping you from something important, Stuart, just leave. I can take care of myself."

He had no doubt about that. She'd taken care of herself pretty well for the past two years while Alec's life fell apart one day at a time. Not really wanting to, he thought of the feel of her against him—warm and feminine and deliciously soft—as they'd come up the cliff, wondered if Alec had ever held her that close, had ever—

"Get this jacket off," he growled. He sat back on his heels and started to strip off his own cotton chambray shirt.

"I said I can—" She stopped abruptly, her eyes widening as she watched him unbutton the shirt. "W-what are you doing?"

Her voice sounded thin and scared and as he watched the fear surface in her eyes, Kel felt a cold uneasiness touch the back of his neck. And suddenly, for no reason he could put his finger on, it seemed important that she not be afraid of him. "I need something clean to put on your shoulder," he said quietly, "and my shirt's all I've got. Unless you've got a better idea...."

Her wide dark eyes searched his and Kel forced himself to hold her gaze without so much as blinking, keeping his mind blank, not thinking of anything at all. Concentrating on the sprinkle of freckles across the bridge of her nose and the odd color of her eyes, not quite brown and not quite green but something in between, as rich as cut velvet, and the smudge of dirt on her cheek and—

"Sorry." She shook her head as though to dispel whatever she'd been thinking and started to slowly, painfully, pull off her jacket. "You... It's just that sometimes you remind me of... of someone, and I... Never mind."

Kel drew in a slow, careful breath. She was talking about Alec, he was certain of it. And it was an opening, of sorts. But for some reason he suddenly realized he didn't want to follow it up. Not at the moment. It was something about what he'd glimpsed in her eyes for just that split second when they'd met his. Not fear. Something else. Something worse. It had been pain and hurt and betrayal and a hundred other things, and—under it—the panicky look of something trapped.

He pulled his shirt off and started tearing it into strips. "This person I remind you of. He a good friend?"

"No." She shuddered.

"Someone you work with?"

She looked at him then, a cool, over-the-shoulder assessing look that held none of the earlier fright, and Kel cursed himself. If he gave himself away now he may as well forget about ever uncovering the truth. "This is pretty rough-and-ready, but it'll do the trick." He held up the makeshift bandage, pretending not to notice the way she was looking at him. "Don't take this the wrong way, but you're going to have to take your blouse off."

Her gaze held his for a heartbeat longer, still wary and a little mistrustful, then she just nodded, shoulders slumping, and started painfully struggling out of the loose-fitting shirt.

Kel helped her finally, trying not to touch her, but as he eased the shirt off her torn shoulder his fingertips brushed warm, satiny flesh and his stomach gave a twist. She sat there quietly with her back to him, the loosened shirt pulled down to bare her shoulders, and Kel swore under his breath and started bandaging the gash.

It was deep and ragged, and although it wasn't bleeding as badly now, he knew that any movement would set it off again. She flinched as he eased the blood-soaked strap of her bra down over her shoulder and laid the folded pad of fabric over the gash, pressing it down firmly.

"Can you hold that for a sec?"

She nodded and reached around to hold the dressing in place as he started securing it with the long strips he'd torn from his shirt. "Okay, that's got it—you doing okay?"

She nodded, not saying anything, but he could see a sheen of perspiration along her upper lip and could tell by the way her breathing caught now and again that he was hurting her even while trying not to. Carefully he wrapped the strips of fabric around her shoulder, crisscrossing them and pulling them as tightly as he dared, trying his damnedest to keep his mind on what he was doing and not on the smooth, satin sweep of her bare back or the tantalizing swell of her left breast above the loosened fabric of her bra, or the downy soft hair at the nape of her neck, or—

He corralled his treacherously undisciplined thoughts finally, thinking with a kind of weary despair that things weren't going at all the way they were supposed to. When he'd planned on getting close to her, this wasn't what he'd had in mind. He was supposed to be getting her to talk, not taking care of her. He should be demanding that she tell him why she'd accused Alec of raping her, what she'd wanted— better marks, a good recommendation on her doctoral project, revenge. Or maybe just the satisfaction of knowing that she could destroy a man with just a handful of words.

He stared down at the nape of her neck and wondered if this is how she'd done it...if she'd put temptation this close to Alec, if he'd stood behind her and had been as tempted as Kel was right now to lower his mouth to the soft skin, to touch her....

"Are you finished?"

Her voice brought Kel back to the present with an unpleasant jolt. He eased himself back onto his heels and carefully drew his hands from her. "Put your shirt on and let's get moving. The sooner you get to a doctor and get that shoulder cleaned up, the less chance of it getting infected."

Chapter 3

All in all, it was a completely wasted day. It took them nearly four hours to get into town, then Jordon spent another frustrating hour at the hospital while an overly serious young doctor stitched up her shoulder and gave her a tetanus shot and antibiotics and a dozen other things, as well as a ten-minute lecture she did *not* need to hear on the perils of pestering the local wildlife.

By the time she met Stuart in the waiting room she was in an evil mood, and Stuart—to his credit—took one look at her and hurried her outside and into the Bronco without a word.

He did, however, take a long, hard look at her once they were in the truck, frowning as though he didn't like what he saw. "You sure you shouldn't stay in town tonight? The doc said there's always a chance of infection from a cut from a wild animal. And your place is a hell of a long way from help if—"

"If you don't want to take me home, just say so," she said heatedly. "I had to take a week-long first-aid and wilderness survival course before World First would even *give* me this job, so I can take care of myself!''

"Just asking," he muttered, starting the engine. "You got those painkillers he gave you? And the antibiotics?"

"You're worse than my mother!" she said, fuming. "I don't need looking after, and I don't need—"

"Lighten up, Jordon," Kel drawled. "I'm on your side, okay?"

Jordon gave him a hostile glare, then subsided into silence. Until, finally, she sighed and gave him a grudging sidelong look. "Sorry." He didn't say anything, and she sighed again. "It's just that I shouldn't have been around that nest when I knew the adults were nearby. And I had no business unclipping my safety line. It was getting in the way and I figured... It was just plain stupid, all right? *That's* why I'm mad—because I feel like an idiot. And I don't like hospitals...."

She fought down a shiver. Even with Stuart's protective presence beside her, it had taken all her willpower to sit waiting quietly in the emergency room. Just the smell made her stomach knot, bringing back those nightmare memories of the emergency ward the police had taken her to after she'd reported the rape, of the impersonal way she'd been poked and prodded and examined, of the brutally frank questions they'd asked, of the undisguised skepticism in the police officer's eyes when he'd glanced over the medical report afterward.

She did shiver then, violently, and Kel looked over at her. "You sure you're okay?"

She nodded.

A smile tipped up one corner of his mouth. "Ever give any thought to taking up another line of work?"

She had to smile then, in spite of the ache in her shoulder and the fact that her head was splitting and she felt scruffy and dirty and worn-out. "That's a strange question coming from an undercover government agent. Are you telling me you've never been in a tight spot?''

"Plenty of them," Kel replied quietly, strong-arming the Bronco around a pothole. "But I get paid for it. From what I can tell, you're up here on a do-good government grant that barely covers the cost of bullets and bandages. I doubt that bunch of tree huggers you work for bothered to tell you that you'd be up against poachers, irate out-of-work loggers and other assorted crazies when they offered you the job of a lifetime." He gave her a lazy glance. "Tell me I'm wrong."

"My study is financed by a group of wealthy conservation-minded citizens, not the government, and I doubt any of them has hugged a tree in his life. Neither, for that matter, have I."

"I stand corrected." He grinned at her and thrust his wadded-up denim jacket into her arms. "Stick that under your head and get some sleep. That shot the doc gave you is going to kick in pretty soon now, and you're going to feel like you've been hit by a truck."

It was a prophetic statement. By the time Kel had driven up to her trailer, had tucked the Bronco in under the trees and had cut the engine, Jordon felt as though she'd been run over not by just one truck, but by an entire fleet of them. Big ones.

As she opened the door of the Bronco and stepped out, she rubbed the bruise on her right temple where her climbing helmet had struck her. It was dark by now and the night air was crisp and cold and tart with the pungent incense of pine and fir. The mountains seemed to crowd close, black silhouettes humped against the edges of the world, and the strip of sky that ran the length of the valley was blazing with stars, so sharp and bright they seemed close enough to touch.

"One hell of an isolated little spot you've got out here," Kel muttered, coming up behind her. "Aren't you nervous living up here alone?"

"It's one of the things that attracted me to the job." Jordon took a deep breath of cold air, feeling it clearing her head, then started toward the trailer. "That was before this business with the loggers started, though. And before we started having so much trouble with poachers." She smiled slightly. "I worry about it once in a while, but unless I can convince my eagles to start nesting on the roof of the town hall, I don't really have a choice."

"You need a dog."

Jordon had to laugh. "I've thought of that, too. But a dog's a lot of responsibility, and I don't know how long I'm going to be up here. Or where I'll be going when I'm finished with my study."

She fumbled with her key, trying to unlock the door of her trailer, and in the next moment Kel took it from her fingers and did it himself. When the door opened, the battery-operated lantern mounted on the far wall clicked on and Jordon squinted against the subdued glare and stepped inside.

"No electricity?"

"I have a generator, but it's so noisy I usually just use a camp lantern for light. I use propane, mostly."

"And you really like being stuck up here in the middle of nowhere?"

He sounded so seriously perplexed that Jordon had to smile. "It's peaceful and quiet, and nobody bothers me. There are worse things than being alone, Mr. Stuart. Much worse."

His eyes held hers in the glare from the lantern, looking troubled and a little skeptical, then he gave another of those noncommittal grunts he seemed so fond of and stepped up into the trailer, shepherding her ahead of him.

"You have anything to eat in here?"

"I'm not hungry."

"I am." He walked by her and stepped into the small kitchen.

Jordon watched him in astonishment as he started to pull cupboard doors open. "Now, look here, Mr. Stuart, I—"

"Just Kel," he told her calmly. "And you're not going to begrudge me something to eat, are you? I saved your tail this afternoon—and my truck's still where I left it before I found you on that cliff. So—" he looked around the cupboard door at her, smiling congenially "—unless you want to drive me all the way out to that cliff tonight, you've got yourself a houseguest."

"But—"

"Clam chowder sound good?" He took a couple of tins out of the cupboard, then started rummaging under the counter until he found her cache of pots and pans. "You look beat—why don't you get into bed, and I'll bring you some soup and a sandwich."

"I—you—we . . ." It was as far as she got before she ran out of steam, and she let her shoulders slump with sheer exhaustion as she watched Kel make himself at home in her kitchen. "Please, Kel. It's late and I'm tired. Take the Bronco—you can bring it back in the morning and we can—"

"The sofa will do fine. If you have an extra blanket, that's great if you don't, I'll do without." He gave her an engaging grin. "Hell, Jory, it's not like I'm making a move on you or anything. Although," he added with a disconcertingly shrewd gaze, "I'll admit I wouldn't turn down an offer to some company for the night if you . . . uh . . . were so inclined."

Jordon didn't know whether to laugh or throw something at him. She was torn between outrage at the fatuous expression on that smug, handsome face, and utter astonishment at how easy he made it sound—as though he was perfectly used to having women throw open their bedroom doors at a moment's notice, even women he'd only just met.

For that matter, maybe he was.

"I think you've got me confused with someone else," she said in a brittle voice, knowing she sounded like a complete prig but not giving a damn. "I don't know what you've heard about me around town, Kel Stuart, but you can put your fantasies on ice. Now get out of my trailer and leave me alone."

Something shifted deep in Stuart's eyes. He looked at her for a long moment, thoughtful, perhaps even a little speculative. His face was heavily shadowed by the light cast from the lantern above him and for a moment his features looked lean and predatory and just slightly dangerous.

And then, in a heartbeat, it was gone. He gave a snort of rueful laughter. "Hell, I'm sorry. I didn't mean anything by it. I mean, I *did*—you're a beautiful woman and I'm a pretty normal man, with all the weaknesses that come with it— but..." He shook his head, giving a quiet laugh. "I'm digging myself deeper with every word. Look, I was way out of line. And I apologize. It was just a... Call it a whim. Or wishful thinking."

There was another expression in his eyes now, something a little more basic, a little more wistful, and in spite of herself, Jordon felt her anger slowly start to trickle away.

"There's another reason I'm staying here tonight," Kel said suddenly, his face serious. "That shoulder's going to start hurting like hell once the painkillers wear off, and you're going to want to take some of those pills the doc gave you. They're going to make you drowsy and slow you down, and I don't like the idea of your being out here, alone and hurt, with the Murdoch brothers and God knows who else prowling around."

She should be ordering him out, Jordon knew. The last thing in the world that she wanted was Kel Stuart sleeping in her home, invading her privacy, crowding her. And yet, in some logical, matter-of-fact part of her mind, she knew he was right.

He seemed very close suddenly, so close she could distinctly feel his warmth, could smell the fresh piney scent of his clothes and skin, and he rose very tall and broad-shouldered in the narrow confines of the hallway where she was still standing.

And then he was reaching toward her, putting gentle hands on her shoulders. "Come on, lie down while I—"

"Don't!" Pulling back sharply, she threw her hands up to hold him at bay. And realized even as she said it that she was being silly, that he hadn't meant anything by it. "I'm sorry," she whispered. "I don't like being crowded...."

"So I've noticed." Kel thought of that afternoon in the parking lot when the Murdoch brothers had cornered her. Was that what had happened then? "Something like claustrophobia?"

"Something like . . . that." She shivered.

And again, as he had before, Kel found himself wondering . . . wondering what had happened to this woman to put that kind of fear in her eyes, wondering if it had something to do with Alec. Wondering, too, if perhaps she wasn't just a consummate actress and he more gullible than he'd ever thought possible.

Except no one could fake the kind of panic he'd seen when he'd rescued her from the Murdochs. And there was something about the weariness in her eyes that made him doubt she was faking now.

He stepped away from her very carefully, giving her room, and nodded toward the bedroom down at the end of the corridor. "Why don't you try to get some rest? You're safe with me here, Jordon." He smiled ironically, more for his benefit than hers. "Safe *with* me, for that matter."

Now what? he thought irritably as he walked back into the kitchen and started opening cans.

It had all worked out better than he could have planned it. He was exactly where he wanted to be—close to her, alone with her. And she was vulnerable, trusting him, too distracted by pain and drugs to be able to lie to him for long.

So why the *hell* was he pussyfooting around her as though she were made of glass?

He'd hunted her down to get some answers, to force her to tell him the truth. He wanted to hear the words come from her own lips, to look into her eyes when she said it—with no witnesses, no judge, no jury. Just the two of them. Alone.

Well, there were just the two of them. And they were alone. And instead of sitting her down and damned well making her tell him what he wanted to know, he was in here making soup.

He swore and dumped a tin of clam chowder into the saucepan and stirred the mess angrily.

He hadn't had a real plan—he could see that now. He'd come out here after her simply because something had driven him to it, some need to see her, confront her.

Why? Hell, he still didn't know. All he *had* known was that he had to see her—watch her, talk to her. Observe was maybe a better word. He hadn't even known what he was looking for, what he was going to say to her when they finally came face-to-face.

Maybe he was just looking for proof, he thought grimly. Proof that she *was* guilty. That, in the end, Alec had been an innocent man unfairly accused, a man wronged. A man driven to kill himself not out of guilt or shame but out of despair.

It was about twenty minutes later that he filled a bowl with steaming chowder and carried it and a spoon down to the bedroom. Jordon had pushed the door almost closed and he rapped on it with his knuckles, waited a moment or two and rapped again. Nothing.

"Jordon?" He nudged the door with his foot, waiting for her to tell him to either come in or stay the hell out, but there was still no response. Frowning, he pushed the door all the way open and stepped into the sweet-scented darkness of her bedroom.

It took a second for his eyes to adjust, although he already knew his way around from the last time he'd been in here. Recalling that, the way he'd handled her private things, had poked through the corners of her life, he felt a little jab of guilt that he forcefully ignored. "Jory?"

She was on the bed. Fully dressed, although she'd gotten one boot off before sleep had ambushed her, and had managed to unbutton her blouse most of the way down. It gaped slightly, giving him a view of her flat stomach, the smooth skin of her breasts against the pristine white of her bra.

"Damn." He stood there for a moment, part of him telling himself to get out, now, before she awakened and saw him standing there looking at her, and another part telling him even more impatiently that he should find a blanket and cover her with it so she didn't get chilled in the night.

In the end, practicality won out. He looked around for a place to set the soup, then bent down and unlaced her remaining boot and slipped it off, praying she was sleeping soundly enough not to notice. Getting her out of her torn, bloodied shirt was trickier, but he did it finally, managing with only moderate success to keep his mind on what he was doing and not the velvet of her skin, or the outline of her nipples against the soft cotton of the bra, or of the way she smelled—of pine trees and fresh air.

It wasn't that she was a woman, or even that she was a virtual stranger, that bothered him—but that it was *this* woman. And that he was noticing things about her and feeling things that unsettled and disturbed him. It wasn't supposed to be like this, he told himself grimly. He wasn't supposed to find himself almost *liking* her.

The dressing on her shoulder was very white against her skin and he checked it quickly, making certain it was secure and wouldn't come loose if she became restless in the night. Then he took a deep breath and swiftly unfastened her khaki slacks and eased them over her hips, thinking idly that men had gotten themselves arrested for less.

Or accused of rape.

It made his mouth tighten and he tossed the slacks aside carelessly, then pulled the quilt up from where it was folded across the end of the bed and covered her with it, tucking it around her shoulders.

He stared down at her, troubled by things he couldn't even pin down, and found himself tracing the curve of her cheek with his eyes. You're a mystery, Jordon Walker, he told her silently. You're the only person alive who knows what really happened—the only person alive who can tell me everything I want to know.

She looked too delicate and innocent to be guilty of ruining a man's career and marriage . . . of destroying his life. Burnished by starlight, her hair glistened on the pillow and her face, in repose, was serene and breathtakingly beautiful. Small wonder Alec had—

Had what? Something cold wound its way up Kel's spine and he gazed down at Jordon thoughtfully. Was it possible that she hadn't lied? Could Alec actually have raped her?

The thought chilled him to the bone and he swallowed, sickened by the thought of anyone brutalizing the fragile woman lying asleep in the starlight. It couldn't be true. Not Alec.

But hell, just how well had he known Alec really? They were brothers, but in blood only. They'd never had a damned thing in common, had never played together, had never shared their dreams or fears or yearnings. Had never really even talked except for the usual social pleasantries once they'd reached adulthood. They'd written now and again, at birthdays and at Christmas. Alec's wife, Sharon, had stayed in touch better than Alec had, but her letters had just been about the children and Alec's work, pleasant uneventful updates about report cards and skinned knees and Alec's most recent academic successes.

The truth was that he'd never really known what Alec had been thinking, what he'd dreamed about, what had been important to him outside his work. There may have been demons lurking in that dark head...demons that could have driven him to—

Kel wheeled away with a soft oath, refusing to even think about it. *Tomorrow*, he silently told the sleeping woman as he pulled the door almost closed behind him. Tomorrow you're going to start opening up.

She awakened in moonlight.

It poured through the window beside her bed like silver fire, and she lay there and listened to the roar of frogs. The moon was three-quarters full and it lit the sky, backlighting the tall firs surrounding the trailer. The trees' ragged boughs dipped and swayed in the breeze and she watched the shadows dance on the far wall, moving in strange rhythmic motions as though to some eerie music only they could hear.

Her shoulder ached and she was stiff and sore. Wincing slightly, she struggled to her feet, thinking idly that those pills Saunders had given her must have really knocked her out—for the life of her she couldn't remember taking off her clothes and crawling under the quilt.

Saunders's idea of revenge, probably. He'd wanted her to stay in the hospital for a day or two, just to make sure the wound on her shoulder didn't turn septic.

Jordon shivered slightly. She'd take her chances. Even the thought of staying in that place overnight made her break into a cold sweat. All she had to do was close her eyes and she could see the impatience on the doctor's face that afternoon two years ago, could hear the sarcasm in his voice as he'd told her his exam hadn't turned up any conclusive evidence other than the fact she *had* had sex within the previous twenty-four hours. But had it been rape? His eyes had told her he thought otherwise. That she was just another woman with a bad case of morning-after regrets and a grudge to bear.

Frowning, she rummaged around until she found her slacks, and dug in the pocket for the bottle of painkillers. She shook one into her palm, hating to give in but also knowing it was silly not to. She had work to do: work she couldn't get done on an hour or two of restless sleep.

Shivering slightly in the cool breeze coming in through the open window, she pulled on the man's woolen work shirt she used as a robe, breath hissing as she maneuvered her injured arm into the sleeve, then buttoned the shirt as she walked down to the kitchen.

There was no need to light one of the Coleman lamps. Shafts of pale moonlight speared the night, sharp-angled pillars of silver that gave the dark corners a hint of something darker and made the familiar outlines of the furniture alien and a little foreboding.

She ran the tap, got herself a glass of water and swallowed Saunders's capsule. Then, restless, she padded into the living room to stare out the big window that looked down the valley.

It was all shadows and moonlight out there, too. The mountains rose on either side of the valley like two-dimensional cutouts, and between the trees, the bit of visible sky was confettied with stars. It looked so peaceful. Protective, almost. A person could disappear into the night, could become just another anonymous shadow that could come and go without notice.

She thought idly of Kel Stuart and the way he'd looked at her that afternoon, his eyes hooded and speculative and secret. What had he heard about her, she wondered? Even if he hadn't recognized her name—and there was no reason he should—there were people in town who knew her background and would be more than happy to fill him in. Maybe that was why he looked at her in that slightly predatory way—maybe he was just estimating his chances of enjoying some of what she'd given Alec Davies.

"Bastard," she whispered, not even knowing which of the two men she meant. Tears flooded her eyes unexpectedly and she squeezed them closed and pressed her forehead against the cool glass of the window, trying to hold the tears back.

But they spilled anyway, and finally she just let them fall, feeling the despair wash through her, wondering when it was ever going to end. When she'd ever be free of Alec Davies's ghost...

Across from her, lying silent and unmoving in the deep shadows cascading around the sofa, Kel watched.

He'd been asleep until a few minutes ago and hadn't known what had wakened him at first. But then Jordon had come drifting silently through the moonlight and he realized that some instinct he wasn't even aware of had stirred him.

At first, he thought his suspicions had been right after all, that she'd come slipping through the moonlight, all polished smooth flesh and silken hair, to take him up on his offer of a shared bed. And he'd wondered for a split second what his reaction was going to be.

But then, in the same heartbeat, he'd realized that she didn't even know he was there. So whatever it was that had her up wandering around at three in the morning, it wasn't seduction.

It made him wince slightly. He'd come on to her that evening just to see what she would do—giving her a chance to play her sweet little games on him just as she had with Alec. Except it had backfired badly. The surprised hurt on her face had cut him to the quick and he'd felt like a damned fool standing there, wondering savagely if he'd been testing her or testing *himself* ... and what, if anything, he'd managed to prove.

She was still standing at the window, staring out across the valley. The loose-fitting man's shirt she was wearing came to midthigh, and he found himself gazing at her long smooth legs with lazy approval, enjoying the play of moonlight on flesh, on the tantalizing glimpse of upper thigh the curved shirttail allowed him. She had her elbows planted on the windowsill so the fabric pulled, and he couldn't help but notice the way it molded around her taut little bottom.

No two ways about it, he thought idly: Jordon Walker was one hell of a fine-looking woman.

And it was only then that he realized she was crying. Silently, with no more sound than a swallowed sob, the tears trickled down her cheeks, unheeded, almost as though she wasn't even aware of them. But it was the expression on her face that made his breath catch, the look of sheer desolation and loneliness and a weary, sad despair.

He was on his feet before he even thought about why, rolling from under the blanket and walking across to her, barefooted and silent. "Jordon?"

He realized his mistake the instant the word was out of his mouth. She catapulted back from the window with a startled exclamation, hand clutching the throat of the shirt.

He swore impatiently, realizing she couldn't see him clearly in the shadows. "Jory, it's me—it's Kel."

"Wh-what are you doing here!"

"You told me I could stay... after I brought you home. Don't you remember?" Not quite the truth, but not quite a lie, either.

"No." She sounded confused and mistrustful, and Kel realized she probably didn't remember even half of the trip back up here. Prayed she didn't remember not taking her own clothes off and putting herself to bed. "Yes," she muttered after a moment, almost grudgingly. Furtively, she wiped her eyes. "But I didn't think you meant it. You scared me half to death!"

"Your shoulder bothering you?"

"No." Her gaze slid from his and she turned away, giving her eyes another furtive swipe with her hand. "I just . . . nothing."

"The mysterious stranger again," Kel said offhandedly, knowing by the quick look she gave him that he was right. "Do I really look like him?"

"No." Jordon shivered. Her heartbeat had slowed to almost normal by now and she was starting to feel distinctly silly. She had no idea how she hadn't seen Kel lying on the sofa when she'd come into the room. But she hadn't, and when she'd heard the quiet voice behind her and had turned and seen his face, narrow and dangerous in the darkness, it hadn't been Kel at all but Alec Davies, and—

She took a deep breath, looking up at him. "You don't look like him at all actually. It's . . . You remind me of him sometimes, that's all. You know when you think you see something out of the corner of your eye and you turn to look at it—and nothing's there? It's like that. It just catches me sometimes."

"Want to talk about it?"

Oddly enough, she got the feeling that he really meant it. She found herself looking at him curiously, wondering if he'd always been this tall and broad shouldered or if it was just something about having him in her trailer in the dead of night that made her notice it more. Wondering, too, if he'd always had that intriguing little scar just under his left eye, and why she'd never noticed how strong and clean-cut his features were.

An interesting-looking man, this Kel Stuart.

And he was gazing down at her as though some of the same thoughts were on his mind.

Their eyes met and locked, and it was like stepping off a cliff without a safety line. Her stomach gave a lurch and she blinked, knowing by the way the skin tightened at the outer corners of his eyes that he'd felt it too. Had recognized it for everything that it was, had known that *she'd* recognized it.

And for the life of her she didn't know what surprised her more—feeling that odd little sizzle of sexual awareness at all, or knowing that it had been spontaneous and utterly unexpected for both of them.

It made her feel better somehow, knowing he wasn't making a play for her because of something he'd heard. Whatever his expectations, at least they were based on nothing more sinister than normal male hormones.

In spite of herself, she had to smile as she turned away and walked toward the kitchen. "No, I don't want to talk about it. It's three in the morning, for one thing. And you wouldn't be interested."

She glanced around and found Kel watching her thoughtfully, and even though he was standing in more shadow than moonlight, she could tell he was frowning. "Is there anything you need? An extra blanket? Pillow?"

"No."

He sounded oddly distracted, as though he were thinking about something else all together, and Jordon just nodded. "All right. Good night."

"Yeah . . . yeah, good night."

It was the sound of a shot that woke her. Close, and very loud.

Then there was another shot, this one sounding as though it came from inside the trailer, and in the distance she could hear someone give a startled shout.

Jordon was out of bed and moving before she was even fully awake, grabbing the heavy woolen work shirt hanging on the knob of the closet door with one hand and groping for her rifle with the other.

Except it wasn't there.

Heart hammering in her throat, she looked around the small room wildly, her mind spinning as she tried to remember where she'd left it.

The Bronco. She'd left it in the Bronco....

"Get down!" Her bedroom door exploded open as Kel hit it at a dead run, and before she could do more than give a yelp of surprised protest he'd grabbed her by the arm and had wrenched her down to the floor. "You're a perfect target standing in front of the window like that, damn it! Are you trying to get yourself killed?"

Jordon clung to the floor, breathless with shock. "What's happening?"

"I don't know." Kel eased himself onto his knees. "Stay down."

Even if she'd been inclined to move—which she wasn't— the look he gave her would have changed her mind, and it was only then that she realized he was carrying a gun. He got to his feet, looking lean and capable and dangerous in the grayed dawn light, and she swallowed, not daring to move as he crossed to the window. Cautiously, he moved the curtain aside with the barrel of the gun and peered outside.

After a taut moment or two he swore under his breath and let the curtain fall closed. "It looks clear, but you'd better get dressed—there's always a chance they'll be back and we'll have to fight our way out of here. And stay away from the window until I get back!"

"Back?" Her voice was thin and breathless. "You're not going out there!"

"Don't worry—I can take care of myself." He gave her a reassuring grin. "Hang on to this—" He pressed the small gun into her hand. "If I'm not back in half an hour—or if you hear or see something you don't like—get in the Bronco and light out for town, fast. And *don't* stop to look back."

Jordon nodded, watching as he started for the door, moving like a shadow. "Kel—" She swallowed, her fingers tightening on the shirt. "Be careful."

"Always." Again, there was a flicker of a reckless smile. "Remember what I said about staying away from the windows. Better yet, just stay right where you are until I get back."

She didn't, of course. The minute Kel was out of the room, Jordon was on her feet, pulling on her jeans and the shirt and a pair of socks with more speed than caution. Her shoulder responded with a jolt of pain that made her swear, but she gritted her teeth and ignored the ache, grabbing up the gun and her boots and heading down the hallway for the living room.

Stopping only long enough to put her boots on and hastily lace them, she tiptoed across to the big window and peeked out cautiously.

There was nothing out there. The sun was up by now and it spilled golden warmth down the sides of the mountains, touching the tops of the big firs across the clearing. Something moved in the shadows under the trees and her heart gave a leap, but in the next instant Kel appeared, pausing for an instant at the edge of the clearing and gazing around intently.

He carried her rifle like a man used to handling weapons; Jordon thought of the way he'd moved when he'd come into her room—swift and silent and deadly, taking charge in the way of a man who is comfortable issuing orders—and used to having them obeyed.

The kind of a man they needed up here, she found herself thinking. Maybe Kel would be able to do what the others hadn't, and bring the poaching to a stop once and for all.

If they didn't get him first, she reminded herself grimly. And her with him.

He was walking back across toward the trailer now, loose limbed and watchful, and Jordon felt some of the tension across her shoulders ease. It was strangely comforting seeing him out there prowling the dangerous perimeter of her small world. There was something about the way he carried himself, the way he moved, that told you he could take care of himself in a tight situation, and he radiated a deadly competence that she found distinctly reassuring.

Besides which, she admitted with a tiny inward smile, he was also just plain easy to watch. He'd pulled his jeans on in a hurry and they gaped where he hadn't bothered buttoning them, and they rode low enough on his narrow hips to cause her a moment or two of concern as she watched him stride toward her. Sunlight spilled across his wide shoulders and down his chest, catching sparks in the dark hair matting his chest and flat belly, and for the first time since she'd met him, Jordon found herself noticing—really noticing—how ruggedly handsome he was.

Enough to make a woman look twice, she decided thoughtfully. Not that she was remotely interested—she'd come up here to get herself untangled from the web spun by one man, not to get herself entangled in another. But the fact she could look at him and find him appealing was in itself a healthy sign. She'd worried about that. Worried that she'd never be able to let a man near her again, never want to be touched, held, loved. That every time she closed her eyes all she'd see would be Alec Davies's face, would feel only his hands on her, rough and impatient, would hear only his voice, his harsh breathing....

Chapter 4

Enough. Jordon cut the rest of the memories off with a skill born of experience, turning away from the window and going across to the door to open it. Kel's head shot up when she stepped out onto the top step and although he didn't say anything, she could see impatience flicker across his strong features.

"All clear?"

"Do you ever do what you're told?"

"Did you find anything that would tell you who it was?"

"No." He held her gaze steadily. "But I think it's time you told me what you're really doing up here. I've met South American dictators with fewer enemies than you."

She blinked. "You know what I'm doing. I'm working with World First to—"

"Lady, I may have flunked biology in high school and the only eagle I know anything about flies at Mach 2, but I sure as hell recognize a stirred-up hornet's nest when I step in it." He strode up the three shallow steps and shouldered by her. "You are one major lot of trouble."

There were probably a dozen smart-alecky answers to
that, Jordon thought as she followed him into the trailer,
but she couldn't think of even one at the moment. Probably because everything he was saying came just a little too
close to the truth for comfort.

Kel was making coffee when she walked into the kitchen,
and after watching him for a moment, she decided to retreat to the chair by her desk in the little dining nook.

"John Harris says you've got a doctorate in microbiology or something. How the hell do you get from that to
fighting poachers in northern B.C.?"

"I wondered why you kept calling me *Doctor* Walker."
She smiled faintly, rubbing at a scratch on the tabletop.
"I'm not a doctor of anything—I didn't finish my degree.
And I didn't come up here to fight poachers. It was just a
job. *Is* just a job."

He cast her a speculative look. "Dropout, huh."

Jordon was silent for a moment. "Something like that."

"Second thoughts, or did you run into trouble of some
kind?"

Jordon's eyes narrowed slightly and she looked at him for
a long moment, wondering what he knew. Or thought he
knew. "Just what are you getting at, Stuart?"

He looked around at her, his face and eyes guileless.
"Nothing. I just thought you might have run into money
trouble, that's all. Or had a problem with your research
project or something. That could explain why you're up
here risking your neck putting together a paper on eagles."

He was either a consummate actor, Jórdon thought a little irritably, or he really didn't know about her. Not that
there was any reason to think he should. The incident with
Alec Davies had changed *her* entire life, but on a larger scale
it had really been just another small, sordid scandal that
hadn't even hit the newspapers outside the state.

She forced herself to smile carelessly, shaking off her
suspicions. "Nothing so altruistic. I came up here for the

money." Which wasn't entirely untrue. Her court costs and
most of her lawyer's fees had been paid out of a fund put
together by local women's groups, but there had still been a
lot of expenses. Although that wasn't the real reason, she
reminded herself. What she'd wanted was the solitude, in-
visibility....

"And the pay's that good."

In spite of herself, Jordon had to laugh. "Actually, the
pay's terrible. I came up here because it was a job—and jobs
are hard to find when you've dropped out of college with
three-quarters of a doctorate in microbiology and no skills
to speak of." And a reputation for accusing your fellow
workers of rape, she added to herself with a hint of bitter
humor.

It still didn't make any damn sense, Kel thought impatiently. If she'd accused Alec of rape to get even for some
imagined sexual slight, or to blackmail him into giving her
a passing grade on her research thesis or just to stir up
trouble in the department, it had backfired on her. She'd
destroyed her entire career along with Alec's, throwing away
six and a half years of college and two honors degrees in the
space of a single day.

And why? She must have gone into Alec's doctoral program with the usual dreams. Hell, Kel had seen her marks,
had read her files. No one put in the kind of intensive work
that marks like that required without a pretty clear set of
goals.

So what in God's name had Alec done—or not done—to
justify the kind of anger that would make a woman throw
all of that away, to trade in six and a half years of dreams
and a chance at some of the crack research jobs in the
country, in order to band eagles in the middle of nowhere?

"So what is it that you're doing that's got so many people bent out of shape?"

"Most of the logging that's done up here is on land that
the timber companies lease from the government. They've

been leasing the land for years with no questions asked, but now people are starting to demand some input as to the type of logging that goes on.''

"Clear-cut versus selective," Kel put in, glad he'd done his homework. "Clear-cutting's cheaper—you just go in and mow everything down, taking out the timber you want and leaving the rest to rot. Selective means taking the timber out literally tree by tree. It also means being careful not to damage the stuff you leave behind, which all takes time. And costs a hell of a lot."

"There are arguments on both sides, some valid and some not. Conservationists maintain that clear-cutting destroys the soil stability and the water runoff patterns, and that the land—and forest—never fully recover."

Kel started rummaging through the small propane fridge. "And what's that got to do with eagles? Are their nesting areas being destroyed?"

"That's certainly part of it. But the big problem is silt. When clear-cut logging is done in a major watershed area, the ground cover is taken off and major erosion takes place when it rains. The creeks and streams become heavily silted with soil carried down by seasonal runoff—the streams often change course or get blocked completely, and the fish die. And it's seriously affecting the salmon population. They come into the rivers and streams to spawn—except where a lot of clear-cut logging's been done. There the streams are so badly silted and contaminated that the salmon die. Local fishermen have been blaming the decreased catch on clear-cutting, and the logging companies blame the fishermen for overfishing."

"Who's right?"

"Both, more than likely. But the salmon runs *are* down, there's no arguing that. And since salmon are a major food source for coastal eagles, it's affecting the hatch. The egg count seems to be down and—" She caught herself. "Sorry,

I just assume everyone knows what I'm talking about. And is interested."

Kel had to smile. When she talked about the great birds, her face became as animated as a child's, and it was impossible not to get caught up in her excitement. And almost as hard to remember that this was the cold, calculating woman who had destroyed his brother. "So you're saying that the eagles are laying fewer eggs, or just hatching fewer?"

"Both. And from the analyses I've been doing on stomach contents, it's clear that salmon is making up less and less of their overall diet."

"So why does this have people shooting at you?"

"It may not." She shrugged. "But if my study proves that clear-cut logging is adversely affecting the eagle population up here, it's one more argument against renewing the logging leases. If the leases aren't renewed, a lot of people are going to be out of work."

"Can't the leases be renewed on the condition that no clear-cut logging be done?"

"Sure. But the big timber companies say they can't do selective logging and not lose money."

"Is that true, or is it just industrial blackmail?"

Jordon shrugged again. "I don't even pretend to be an expert. I know clear-cutting *looks* bad—there are valleys up here that look like they've been bombed, with not even a twig left standing and so much timber left lying around it's hard to believe it's all legitimate waste. And I also know that the streams *are* being silted up, and that as well as affecting the salmon run it's also polluting some of the rubbing beaches."

Kel raised an eyebrow, and Jordon smiled. "Killer and gray whales come in to shelving beaches and rub on the gravel and sand to dislodge parasites. But a lot of the bays are so polluted with silt and runoff debris that the whales aren't coming in anymore, and the biologists aren't certain what effect it's having on the whales' social *or* physical well-being. The tourist people aren't happy, either—they take boat tours up close to the whales, and they see *their* business going down the tubes.'' She shook her head. ''Everything's so intertwined up here…trees, water, salmon, eagles, whales. Affect one thing, and it just goes down the line like tumbling dominoes.''

''I don't see how scaring you off is going to change anything,'' Kel said thoughtfully. ''The conservation movement is pretty active in this part of the country. If you leave, they'll find someone else.''

''Of course. But when your livelihood's being threatened, you strike out at the most obvious target—and at the moment that seems to be me.'' She managed a rough smile. ''To be honest, I can't even blame them. But sooner or later the loggers and the conservation people and the Native groups and everyone else up here are all going to have to sit down and *talk*. And in the meantime, I am not going to be run off!''

''The logging companies aren't the only ones targeting you,'' Kel said thoughtfully. ''From what Harris says, you've been raising hell with the Ministry of the Environment about the poaching. The more noise you make about that, the more heat you're putting on the poachers—and these guys play rough.''

''Believe me, I know more about it than I ever wanted to.'' She shuddered. ''I found six elk last week. They'd been shot with what looked like a machine gun, then cut up with a chain saw—antlers and hearts gone, the rest left to rot.'' She looked at Kel, her eyes bleak. ''I thought when I came up here I was leaving the violence and ugliness behind. That everything would be pristine and clean and…pure.'' She smiled faintly. ''But I guess no matter how far you go, it's still there.''

Kel found himself frowning. *No matter how far you go…*

He gave himself an impatient shake and pulled the fridge door open again. ''You're out of milk.''

"You'll have to use powdered. I was supposed to go in to town to pick up supplies today, but..." She shrugged and got to her feet. "I'm going to have a shower, then I'll drive you up to Hanging Rock Ridge so you can pick up your truck. You've wasted enough of your time on me, between playing paramedic yesterday, and Wyatt Earp this morning."

Kel looked around but she was already halfway to the bathroom, and he swore under his breath. He'd gotten invasion plans out of enemy soldiers faster than he was getting information out of her! "Don't get that dressing on your shoulder wet," he called after her.

She mumbled something he didn't catch and he swore again, as much at himself as at her. Nothing was going the way it was supposed to. He should have had the whole story by now. *Would* have had the whole story if people would quit shooting at her long enough for him to ask the damn questions. Between rescuing her from irate eagles and hauling her back and forth from the hospital and charging off after this morning's yahoos, he wasn't getting a lot of time to do what he'd come up here to do.

He heard the truck before he actually saw it. The growl of its engine brought him to the window instantly, eyes narrowed, gun in hand, wondering what in hell was going to happen now. Maybe the loggers, the poachers and the entire Natives' Rights Coalition had banded together and were coming up in a frontal attack, deciding to do collectively what they'd failed to do individually.

In spite of himself, Kel had to smile. He'd met a lot of women in his life, but none who attracted trouble quite like this one. She was a fighter; that was the problem. She was tenacious and idealistic and stubborn to a fault. It was almost as though she was trying to prove something, as though there was some need in her to make a stand, regardless of the consequences.

Was she the kind of woman who'd take an innocent man to court on a rape charge, even knowing she couldn't win? Or the kind who'd stand up to a guilty one in the face of the same odds?

The truck door opened, a man got out and Kel swore again. When he'd looked at this area on his map a couple of months ago, he'd thought it was going to be just Jordon Walker and him and a million square miles of nothing. Instead, it was like rush hour in downtown Manhattan!

He got to the door at the precise instant Jordon's guest did, and he pulled it open even as John Harris was lifting his hand to knock.

Harris gaped at him in surprise, then tried none-too-successfully to look glad to see him. "Stuart." Juggling a cardboard carton filled with groceries, he gave Kel a curt nod, trying to peer past him into the depths of the trailer. "They said down at the general store Jordon had radioed in an order of supplies yesterday but hadn't picked them up. I...uh...figured she hadn't much felt like it after her accident, so took a chance and brought them up."

"I'll tell her." Kel took the box from Harris's hands before the startled man could stop him. "Thanks."

Harris stood rooted to the top step, his face stubborn. His gaze kept slipping past Kel's shoulder, searching the shadows. "Is she...uh...here?"

For a rash moment Kel was tempted to lie through his teeth and tell the other man that Jordon was off counting eagles or some damn thing and to come back tomorrow. But he swallowed his impatience, realizing that, in the long run, trying to get rid of Harris was going to cause more problems than it solved. "She's having a shower," he growled ungraciously. Turning away, he carried the groceries into the kitchen, leaving Harris standing at the door.

Harris came inside after a moment. He wandered uneasily into the kitchen and Kel gave his head a jerk toward the stove without stopping his search through the box. "Help yourself to coffee."

"Where…ummm…are the cups?" Harris asked stiffly.

"End cupboard." Kel unearthed a carton of eggs with a grunt of satisfaction. Then, giving Harris a sour look, he added, "you want something to eat?"

"No."

Harris's voice was clipped and Kel looked up at him, finding the other man eying him with subdued hostility. He met Harris's glare evenly, then turned away with studied carelessness and dug an onion out of the box of groceries. So that's the way it was.

Kel found a knife in one of the drawers and started chopping up the onion, trying not to smile. Poor Harris. He'd come charging up here to play hero only to find that some other man had beat him to it. And not just any man, either, Kel thought with amusement. A half-naked man, unshaven and uncombed and obviously just out of bed, feet bare, jeans still unbuttoned. One who knew his way around the kitchen with the air of someone who'd been here for a while.

And all the while, in the background, the sound of the shower. And the knowledge—recognized by both but acknowledged by neither—that Jordon was in there right now, naked and wet and slippery with soap.

He should have been ashamed of himself for torturing Harris like this. But for some reason he felt in no hurry to assure the other man that he'd spent the night virtuously alone on the sofa. And that even if he *had* been inclined to share Jordon's bed, she hadn't been in any condition to make it worth his while.

Let him stew about it for a while longer. If he and Jordon were an item, she'd clear it up soon enough. And if they weren't, it was none of Harris's damned business what had happened up here last night.

As if at a signal, the shower went off and a couple of minutes later Jordon came out, rubbing her wet hair with a towel. "I thought I heard a—John!"

"Hi, Jordon." Harris's smile was so wide it made Kel's mouth hurt just to look at it. "I heard you'd banged yourself up pretty bad yesterday and thought I should stop by and check on you." He gave Kel a glare. "I didn't realize you had company."

"Kel drove me home from the hospital last night," she said offhandedly, either not realizing she was leaving the statement open to a lot of misinterpretation or simply not caring.

"Honey, you didn't get that dressing wet, did you?" Kel grinned, enjoying himself just a little too much. "Maybe I should have another look at it."

Jordon gave him a peculiar look. "It's all right." Still looking puzzled, she glanced around at John, then back to Kel.

"How does an omelette sound?" Kel asked guilelessly. "Harris brought us some groceries."

Jordon's look was a little more calculating this time, as though she'd finally figured out the cause of the tension between he and Harris and wasn't too sure she liked it. "An omelette sounds fine. *If* you're sure you've got the time."

"All the time in the world," Kel assured her with another grin. "Harris, sure you can't join us?"

Harris's mouth was sullen, and he made a show out of looking at his watch. "Maybe another cup of coffee, then I've gotta roll."

"Is there any chance you can drive Kel up to Hanging Rock?" Jordon asked. "He left his truck up there yesterday when he brought me down, and it would save me a trip."

"I'd be glad to," Harris said with swift satisfaction, obviously cheered by the prospect of getting Kel as far away from her as possible. "I'll drop in on my way back if you like. Just to see if you need anything."

"You might want to radio the RCMP and have *them* drop by later," Kel put in deliberately. "We had visitors about six this morning."

Harris's eyes narrowed. "What happened?"

"Nothing," Jordon said quietly. "They just—"

"They took a shot or two at the trailer—didn't hit anything as far as I can tell, but I don't know if that was intentional or because they were lousy shots. They weren't expecting me to be here, obviously, and I caught them off guard when I returned fire. I may have hit one of them." He looked around at Harris. "If you see someone in town with a hole in him, you might want to ask where he got it."

"Damn it, Jordon, this is getting serious!" Harris was tight-lipped and pale. "You've got to call it quits. That's all there is to it. I know that study you're doing is important, but it isn't worth getting killed over."

"I am not backing down," Jordon replied with a distinct edge in her voice. "What I'm doing up here is important. Those *eagles* are important."

Kel have her a curious look. Her fierce defiance just didn't make sense. There were a thousand other places she could go to escape the media circus that Alec's death had created—she didn't have to stay up here getting shot at.

Frowning, he reached across the counter and picked up the bottle of antibiotics that Dr. Saunders had given her yesterday. The whole thing just didn't add up. And it bothered him more than he liked to admit.

Maybe because the Jordon Walker he'd found wasn't the same Jordon Walker he'd been expecting and it threw him off balance. Or maybe just because it made him wonder about things . . . things he didn't like having to think about too much. Other things that didn't add up. Things about Alec . . .

"Here." He stepped across to the table and took one of Jordon's hands in his, turning it over and dropping two red-and-white capsules into her open palm. "Down the hatch. Antibiotics—two of these suckers four times a day, remember?"

"And that's another thing," Harris muttered, watching Jordon as she dutifully swallowed both capsules with a mouthful of coffee. "From what Doc Saunders said, you were damned lucky yesterday. What happened, anyway?"

"There's a big nest on a ledge just off Desperation Point that I've climbed down to a couple of times with no problem. The chicks are at that age when both adults are hunting full-time to feed them and I thought I could get down, pop bands on the chicks and get back up before one of the parents got back, but . . ." She shrugged, wincing as though she'd forgotten about her shoulder.

"Eagles aren't anything to mess around with."

The warning was a little unnecessary in Kel's point of view, considering Jordon was the expert. "At least they aren't shooting at her," he said with an edge to his voice. "Still no idea who could have been taking a potshot at her the other day?"

"Some logger probably. Who knows?" Harris's look suggested he'd be just as happy if Kel minded his own business. "But it just reinforces my opinion that it's time to pull the plug on this study of yours, Jordon. It's too dangerous up here."

"I don't believe it's loggers at all," Jordon said quietly.

"I'm inclined to agree," Kel said, surprising himself slightly. "Poaching activity is really stepping up out here, based on previous reports and what I've seen over the past week. I found three bear carcasses up by Hanging Rock yesterday morning—gutted and mutilated."

Jordon shuddered. "I found two grizzlies a couple of weeks ago—nothing missing but their paws and some entrails." She looked at John. "That bear you had in the back of your pickup the other day—had it been killed by poachers too?"

Harris frowned slightly. "How did you know about that?"

"I noticed the blood when I walked by the truck in the parking lot, and when I took a closer look I found a tuft of bear fur." She looked up at Kel just then, her eyes dark with anger. "What I'd like to know is what your people are doing about it. Maybe you're good at what you do, but there's only one of you—and two dozen of them, armed with assault weapons and helicopters and night-scopes and tons of Asian and Far East money behind them. The black market in illegal animal parts like elk horn and bear gallbladders and eagle feathers is around two hundred million dollars a year. What chance does our wildlife have against *that?*"

Kel hesitated slightly, feeling a jab of guilt. Technically he wasn't up here looking into the poaching at all—but for a completely illogical moment, he found himself wanting to assure her that he would do his best to put a stop to it. "The...department does the best it can," he finally hedged.

"Well, maybe it isn't enough," Jordon said angrily. She got to her feet and walked across to the sink, tossing out the dregs of her coffee and rinsing the mug. "Look, don't bother with that omelette. I'm not hungry. And I have work to do."

It was fairly clear that she thought both of them should be doing the same thing, and Kel swallowed an oath. There was no way he could avoid going with Harris. For one thing, he needed his truck. And for another, he doubted Harris would just drive off without an argument and leave him and Jordon alone. Besides, he didn't have any kind of a plausible excuse for staying... aside from saying he was uneasy about leaving Jordon alone. Which wasn't entirely untrue, he was annoyed to realize, but which wouldn't carry much weight with Harris *or* with Jordon. It would just get them both suspicious, and he couldn't afford that. Not yet. Not until he had the answers he'd come after.

"Give me a couple of minutes to get dressed and I'll be right with you, Harris," he drawled, making it sound a lot more intimate than he needed to. The glower on Harris's face was everything he'd hoped for and Kel turned away and headed into the living room with a private smile, not knowing why he got such a charge out of taunting the guy. He was harmless enough.

"I probably never did get around to thanking you properly for helping me yesterday," a quiet voice said behind him.

Pulling on his shirt, Kel turned to find Jordon standing there, frowning slightly. The early morning sun coming through the window fell around her like melted gold and he couldn't help but notice the things it did to her eyes and still-damp hair. He tried not to pay too much attention to the way the shirt and jeans fit her trim little body. Or to the way she was looking up at him, small oval face serious, those dark thickly lashed eyes holding his with disturbing intensity.

"Don't mention it," he said easily. "Maybe I'll drop by for coffee some evening if I'm in the area."

To his surprise, the corners of her mouth tipped up in a shy half smile, and she nodded. "All right. I'd...like that."

But it gave him absolutely no satisfaction, Kel realized with a kind of savage anger. If anything, the hesitant way she'd agreed made him feel like a thief whose victim has just handed him the key to the house. It was almost *too* easy. And there was something about the entire thing that just plain left a bad taste in his mouth.

"Keep the damn door locked when you're in here," he growled, not even looking at her as he shouldered by. "Don't open it unless you know who's on the other side, don't go out—for any reason—without your rifle, and for God's sake if you're going to be wandering around in the bush, keep one eye on what's going on behind you. And don't trust *anybody!*'' He didn't know why he added that last, but it sounded like good advice, all considered.

"Does that mean you, too, Mr. Stuart?" Her voice held a hint of amusement.

Kel stopped at the door of the trailer and looked around at her, tempted for one angry, confused moment to put an end to all the games then and there. "Damn straight," he said softly, holding her gaze with a hint of deliberate challenge. "You just never can tell about people, Jordon Walker. You never can tell." And with that he pulled the door open and strode outside and down the steps, leaving John Harris and Jordon staring after him in surprise.

If she hadn't seen it with her own two eyes, Jordon mused a few minutes later as she watched John Harris's half-ton pickup rattle its way back up the rutted path to the road, she'd never have believed it. They'd been sparring like two buck deer in rut, shaking their antlers and pushing and shoving, each trying to outmuscle the other without actually trading blows. And just because of her.

It made her smile. Didn't men ever grow out of that sort of thing?

Laughing, she walked back into her trailer and closed the door, feeling better than she had in days. Strange, what a little male jealousy could do for a woman's ego. She'd always prided herself on being practical-minded when it came to men, but there was no denying that having two of them tussling over her did amazing things for her self-confidence.

She found herself wandering into the small bathroom and eyeing her damp hair in the mirror above the vanity, wondering if she should let it grow out again. Cutting it had been one of those impulsive, angry gestures that had accomplished nothing in terms of real benefits. She'd done it herself after having watched a film clip on the late-night news and seeing herself caught in the unrelenting lens of the news camera, her thick long hair sweeping around her shoulders.

It had looked lush and seductive and sexy, and she'd gone into the bathroom with a pair of shears and had hacked it off then and there, damned if anyone was ever again going to accuse her of using physical attractiveness to get what she wanted. She'd thrown all her makeup out that same night, pitching everything into a paper bag and carrying it down to the trash chute in her apartment with tears streaming down her face.

She'd shown up at her lawyer's offices the following morning in a baggy jogging outfit, a scarf wrapped around her ruined hair and her eyes still swollen from a night's worth of angry, hurt tears. He'd had a fit—not without reason, considering they were supposed to be in court that afternoon. He'd had his secretary make an emergency appointment for her at a nearby hairstylist, followed by a quick trip to the makeup counter and clothing department of a downtown department store.

It had been for nothing anyway. The damage had already been done by then, the jury ignoring the fact she'd gotten two honors degrees in science through brains and hard work, concentrating instead on Davies's testimony that he was a poor overworked and utterly innocent man whose reputation was being besmirched by the sexually rapacious teaching assistant he'd spurned. He had the name and the power of the university behind him; she had nothing but her own word. And in the end, the truth had counted for nothing.

Jordon met her own eyes in the mirror, forcing herself to hold her own faintly accusing gaze. It's no good blaming only Alec Davies, she told herself brutally. It was as much your fault as anyone's that he got off. You should have reported the rape immediately. You shouldn't have showered, shouldn't have thrown your clothing away, shouldn't have... Oh, hell, there were so many things she'd done wrong. She should have fought him off when he first grabbed her. Should have started screaming her head off. Should have...should have...should have!

Swearing, she wheeled away from the woman in the mirror and stalked into the bedroom. Well, she hadn't. Hadn't fought, hadn't screamed, hadn't done a dozen things right. But then she'd hardly had a lot of experience with rape. It wasn't something they taught you along with biology and calculus. Although, based on the horrifying stats she'd been reading about campus and date rape, maybe they should start.

It was too late now to be worrying about it, anyway. The whole thing was long over and done with, and she was getting on with her life—as Davies undoubtedly was getting on with his—and she was, if not exactly wiser, a good deal less trusting. And obviously the whole mess hadn't damaged her very badly or she wouldn't be thinking about Kel Stuart as much as she was.

She stopped in front of her dressing table and ran her comb through her hair, fussing with it for a moment, then allowed herself a small smile. Admit it, Walker, she taunted herself gently, there's something about that man that's hard to resist. And maybe it's about time, after nearly two years, that you came out of your shell.

Kel was still on her mind a couple of days later.

She'd half expected him to drop in for that cup of coffee he'd mentioned, but he hadn't. And she was starting to admit that she was disappointed.

Not, heaven knows, that she had any right to feel anything. She knew nothing about Kel—he could be married for all she knew, with a wife, six kids and a dog back in...well, wherever it was he was from. Or—

"Snap out of it," she told herself with a wry smile, adjusting the focus on the high-power binoculars. She was lying belly-down on a patch of damp grass on the cliffs

overlooking the sea, watching a nest in a lightning-sundered
pine on a tiny island just offshore.

It was just a rock, actually, a pinnacle of gray stone jut-
ting out of the sea, sheer-sided and girdled with breaking
waves and foam, its top tufted with a bit of sedge grass and
a bush or two and the one ancient, gnarled tree.

There were—as far as she could tell, anyway—an almost
unheard of three chicks in the nest, and the two parents were
kept busy, working nonstop to feed them. It was a perfect
nesting site. The old tree grew in a cupped hollow, sheltered
on three sides from all but the worst storms, the open side
facing the mainland, and it was impossible to reach unless
you happened to be an eagle.

One of the big bald eagles had come swooping in just
minutes before and was still in the nest, and she fixed the
binoculars on it, not even bothering to pretend that she was
filling in the detailed form on the clipboard at her elbow.
She'd started out making notes on estimated size and weight
and wingspread, and the number of feeding trips each parent took and so on...but for the past half hour she'd just
been lying here in the sun enjoying the birds and the solitude and the view.

The last week had been a vacation of sorts, her torn-up
shoulder keeping her from doing any serious clambering
around trees or cliffs. Instead, she'd hiked right to the end
of the Tals'it Valley until walls of sheer, cold stone had
stopped her, spotting two new nests on the way. She'd spent
the rest of the time lying quietly in hidden spots with binoculars and her clipboard, making copious and meticulous
notes on most of the newer nest sites and the birds using
them.

The sun soaked into her like hot butter and Jordon
yawned, knowing she was going to fall asleep if she stayed
there much longer. Behind her, Lamehorse Creek burbled
and chuckled its way to the cliff edge, where it dropped the
hundred feet to the sea like a veil of fairy dust, wind blown

and rainbowed with sunlight. It sounded cool and welcoming and Jordon rolled over and sat up, fighting another yawn.

She shoved the binoculars into their worn leather case, then got to her feet and walked across to where she'd left her backpack leaning against a rock by the stream. She tucked the binoculars into a side pocket and the clipboard and notes into another one, then pulled out the plastic container holding her lunch.

She ate it sitting cross-legged on a flat rock that jutted out into the rambunctious water of the creek. Jordon was lulled by the sound of water caressing stone and the hot sun across her shoulders. The water was as clear as expensive crystal and she sleepily watched it frolic over and around the jumbled rocks of the streambed, letting her mind wander until temptation got the better of her and she stripped off her boots and heavy socks and scooted to the edge of the rock so she could dangle her feet into the water.

It was surprisingly warm and she smiled and kicked her feet through the bubbles, letting her head fall back so her upturned face was toward the sun, eyes closed.

She heard the slight scuff behind her but didn't think anything of it until a shadow fell across her. "You make just about the prettiest damn target, sitting there, that I've seen in years."

The voice startled her so badly that she was on her feet before she was even aware of moving, fighting to keep her balance on the slippery rocks on the bottom of the creek as she turned clumsily to see who was behind her.

Kel smiled down at her a little maliciously. "Scare you?"

"Of course you scared me, you idiot!" She put her hand on her chest, her heart jackhammering so badly it made her head spin. "Damn it, what do you think you're doing!"

"Good." He reached down and caught her wrist and unceremoniously pulled her back up onto the sun-warmed rock. "Maybe it'll make you pay a little more attention to what the hell's going on around you. You've been perched out on this rock with your back to the trees and your rifle a good dozen steps away for the past twenty minutes.''

"There's nobody out here, for crying out loud," Jordon replied testily, her pleasure at seeing Kel again offset by her annoyance at having been taken so completely off guard. She sat back down on the smooth rock indignantly. "Even the poachers don't bother coming this far out. So why are *you* here?''

"Following you," he said cheerfully, his grin almost as warm as the midsummer sun pouring through the trees. He hunkered down on one heel beside her, forearm on his thigh, squinting in the sun. "I've been watching you for the past couple of hours, on and off." He nodded somewhere vaguely behind him where the mountains rose like green-cloaked giants against the sky, tatters of mist caught in their water-runnelled heights. "I ran across your Bronco, fig-ured odds were that you'd be out here on the cliffs some-where, and came looking for you.''

"I thought I'd hidden the Bronco pretty well in that clump of trees." She frowned worriedly. "If you found it, so can the poachers." And if they could find the Bronco they could find her. And the nests.

"Not unless they watched you hide it," he said with a lazy grin. "I was up on Lamehorse Ridge when I caught a flash of sun on something coming along that old logging road you followed in. I thought it might be the guys I've been track-ing for the past three days, so I came down to have a look. And there you were.''

He made it sound as though she were the best thing he'd seen all day, and she had to smile, responding to the warmth in his eyes. She lay back on her elbows and looked at him. "Have you had lunch? I have an apple and a handful of carrot sticks and some trail mix left over.''

"How about a beer and a deli sub?''

"A *what?*" Jordon sat straight up. "You're not serious!"

"I never joke about food," he said with a laugh, wriggling out of the straps on his heavy backpack and resting the pack beside him. He rummaged in it for a moment or two, then pulled out a can of beer, tore the tab off it and handed it to her with a broad grin. "Still cold."

"You're nuts! Are you telling me you hike around with your backpack full of beer?"

"Not as a habit." He pulled out another can of beer and tore the tab off it, lapping spilling foam from his hand, then set the can down while he unearthed the rest of his lunch. Which was, to Jordon's amazement, an honest-to-goodness submarine sandwich, piled with sliced meat and cheese and coleslaw.

He smiled at her expression. "Don't get too excited—it's left over from last night."

"I don't care if it's left over from last month," Jordon said emphatically. "I haven't had a sub for so long I'd forgotten what they look like." Still grinning, Kel wrestled a knife out of his jeans pocket. He opened the big blade, started sawing the sub in half and Jordon groaned. "Or what they smell like!"

"Lettuce is a little wilted." He held up one half and eyed it critically. "It's been in my pack all morning, wedged between the beer to keep it cool . . . watch the mayo!"

A trickle of runaway mayonnaise trickled down Kel's tanned wrist and Jordon reached out swiftly and scooped it up in her fingers, licking them clean with an exclamation of delight. "Heav-en-ly! Now quit teasing . . . gimme!"

Kel laughed as she gathered up the sandwich in both hands and took a bite, closing her eyes with sheer pleasure. "Mmmm . . . fabulous! Wonderful! Incredible! You've saved my life again, Stuart. This even beats rescuing me from that ledge the other day. I definitely owe you!"

"I'm keeping a running tab," Kel said with a grin. He held up his palm and pretended to write on it. "Saving Jordon's life, payment to be negotiated. Quantity discounts available."

Jordon laughed, licking mayonnaise from between her fingers. "No more rescues, I swear. I promised John Harris *and* the RCMP that I'd do my very best to stay out of trouble from now on."

Kel gave a skeptical grunt. "From what I've seen, you don't go looking for trouble—it has a way of finding you."

Jordon smiled very faintly. "Someone else told me that once. Said I had a Don Quixote complex—and that I was going to have to learn that sometimes the windmills tilt back." She took another mouthful of her sub, not really tasting it, thinking idly of Geoff Barnes, the young hotshot lawyer who had taken her case against Alec Davies. He'd been a tilter at windmills, too—the fact that the case got into court at all was more a credit to Barnes than to the solidity of her case.

She hadn't *had* a case...just an accusation. Her word against Davies's...

Chapter 5

"You know, this reminds me of the time I ran away from home when I was eight." Kel took a long swallow of beer, then set the can aside and started untying his bootlaces. "I packed a couple of peanut-butter sandwiches and an apple or two, a road map and a clean pair of socks—my mother *always* told me to take clean underwear when I traveled—and set off to conquer the world."

Jordon laughed. "What part of the world were you conquering?"

"The wilds of Indiana."

Jordon's stomach gave an unpleasant twist. Alec had been from Indiana. Ignoring the feeling, she watched Kel pull his boots and socks off. "What made you decide to run away?"

"Oh, the usual. Another fight with my brother." Kel's smile was bitter, the memory still rankling even after almost thirty years. Strange, how the mind hung on to certain images, preserving them in all their detail with crystalline clarity.

He didn't even have to close his eyes to see Alec's face that morning, his expression triumphant, his eyes taunting Kel to even try and tell the truth and see how far it got him. The shards of broken pottery lay in his memory as sharply as they had on the floor that morning, sunlight turning the dust to gold: the remains of one of their father's most treasured artifacts, brought back from a dig in Belize the year before, and a perfect, priceless example of pre-Colombian art.

Alec had knocked it over, had watched it fall and smash, a strange little smile on his face, almost as though he'd enjoyed seeing the destruction of something so precious. But Kel, of course, had been blamed. Rough-and-ready Kel, too loud and physical and rambunctious for his own good. His father hadn't said much, had simply looked at him with that sad, resigned expression of disappointment that was even more hurtful than angry words would have been. And in the background, Alec's triumphant little smirk.

Kel suddenly realized that Jordon was looking at him curiously, and he grinned carelessly and started rolling up the cuffs of his jeans. "Al—my brother—used to get into all sorts of trouble, and I'd get blamed for—"

"Al?" Jordon's face paled. "Your brother's name is Al?"

Kel cursed his own carelessness. "Alan," he lied, pretending not to notice the unease in her wide brown eyes.

She nodded after a moment, frowning slightly as though trying to shake off a bad memory of her own, and Kel felt his stomach tighten. Then she smiled. "And that's why you ran away."

"Al had broken this incredibly valuable piece of pottery, and I'd gotten the blame. Dad never said anything—he never did. He just looked at me in that way parents have when they suspect someone switched babies at the hospital because you couldn't *possibly* be theirs." He grinned, lowering his feet into the water. "Anyway, I ran away. I got as far as the creek before I got tired, so I sat down and ate my sandwiches and played in the water for a while. A couple of hours later my mother drove up with a picnic hamper. I remember she brought me a hot dog and a piece of apple pie, and we sat in the sun and paddled our feet in the water and talked most of the afternoon.''

''She sounds pretty special.''

''She was.'' The sudden ache under Kel's chest bone caught him by surprise. ''She died when I was ten, but I remember her as clearly as if I'd just seen her yesterday.''

''I'm sorry.'' Jordon's hand rested momentarily on Kel's arm, just a fleeting touch of sympathy that surprised him as much as the pain of the memory of his mother had.

Just as surprising was his own reaction to Jordon's gesture—a curious sense of vulnerability that, for just a moment, he almost welcomed. It felt good having someone care even that little bit. It felt good knowing that someone else was sharing his pain. Having someone else that close to him emotionally wasn't something he was used to. Hell, he'd spent most of his life making sure people *didn't* get that close. Being open meant being vulnerable, and being vulnerable meant leaving yourself wide open to hurt. If nothing else, Alec had taught him that.

''What happened after your mother died?'' Jordon was looking at him, her eyes soft in the sunlight. ''Between your brother and you, I mean.''

Kel's smile was bitter. ''We fought worse than ever. Dad was too busy to pay much attention to us—to me, anyway.'' He managed a wry smile. ''I'd been a profound disappointment to my parents. They'd put off having kids until late in life, and I was supposed to be this clever little guy who could do differential equations in his sleep and invent twelve new ways to save the world by noon. Instead they got a kid who was more brawn than brain—the only scholarship I ever got offered had a football attached, and I was always a hell of a lot more interested in sports and girls than I was in science or literature.''

"And Alan was everything your parents dreamed of."

"In spades." Kel heard the hard edge in his voice, tried to fight it down. "He was the classic child prodigy—he did it all, and did it brilliantly. Could do no wrong, in my old man's eyes." There was a tightness in his belly, and Kel took a deep breath to loosen it.

"How do you get along now?"

"He's dead." He didn't know whether the anger in his voice was at Alec or at himself. Or perhaps it was at the dark-eyed woman sitting beside him, relaxed and carefree in the sun.

It felt strange to be sitting here talking about Alec's death with the woman who had been responsible for his dying, and not even feel the rage he'd have expected. But somehow over the past few days it was as though Alec's death had receded . . . as though the physical miles between here and Indiana had distanced him from his brother as well as from the urgency to right the wrong. . . .

He turned his head and looked at Jordon, finding her sitting altogether nearer to him than he'd realized. She had that kind of smooth olive-toned skin that tans well and the sun had brush-marked bronze highlights across her cheekbones and the bridge of her nose. Her long legs were tanned, as well, and were, Kel decided, just a little too distractingly displayed in the casual khaki walking shorts.

When had he distanced her from Alec, too? he found himself wondering. Sometime during the past couple of weeks his feelings toward her had changed. Gone was the anger and the confusion and the resentment. Even the obsessive need to know *why* had dimmed. He was still curious about her, but in another way now, in a way he was starting to realize had a lot more to do with himself than it did with Alec.

"Don't you get lonely living up here by yourself?" He asked it just to distract himself from the way the sun glistened on her hair, trying not to notice the smooth curve of her neck as she leaned forward a little, the pressure of her breast against the soft cotton of her shirt.

"Not really." She picked up a leaf from the rock beside her and twirled it by the stem. "There are some things I miss—like a deli sub now and again—" she flashed him a smile "—but there are a lot of other things I *don't* miss. Traffic jams. Smog. Lineups. Muggers." Again, there was that flash of humor. "Although I'll take muggers over the Murdoch brothers any day. Mmm...what else." She looked thoughtful. "Users," she said after a moment, her eyes pensive. "That's one thing I don't miss—people who go through life just taking what they want, thinking it's their due just by virtue of their damned superiority."

Kel gave her a curious glance. If she *weren't* talking about Alec, she could have been. He'd been like that, reaching out and taking what he wanted, when he wanted it, and letting someone else worry about the consequences. Or take the blame.

"What about poachers?" he asked. "They're sure as hell taking everything they want."

"Yes, but at least they're an evil you can see. One you can fight. It's clear right from the onset which side of the line they're on—you don't get them confused with friends."

Again, Kel found himself looking down at her curiously. *Just ask her,* something whispered at him. *Tell her who you are and why you're here—why you need to know. Ask what happened between her and Alec...what really happened that night in the lab...in the days, the weeks before....*

"Come on." Jordon slipped her hand in his and bounced to her feet. "Let's go wading!"

"Are you crazy?" Kel gave a bark of laughter, letting her pull him to his feet. "That water's cold!"

"Some big-time heroic secret agent you are!"

Still laughing, Kel allowed himself to be pulled into the effervescent water. To his surprise it wasn't half as cold as he'd anticipated, and it tingled around his bare calves like

champagne. The rocks on the stream bed were smooth and
slippery and he curled his toes into the fine sand, thinking,
very idly, that he had no business enjoying himself this
much. Not now. Not with Jordon....

A school of minnows darted through the shallows in front
of them and Jordon made a wild grab for them, coming up
with nothing but a handful of glittering water. Kel found
himself laughing again, unable to keep himself from noticing how the sun made her eyes sparkle. And how, when she
laughed, the troubled shadows in her eyes seemed to van-
ish.

She seemed relaxed and happy for the first time since he'd
met her, and he found himself getting caught up in it, her
energy and delight contagious. And a moment later he was
beside her, futilely trying to snatch bright arrows of gold
from the water as the minnows flashed around their ankles.

Strange, how things had changed in the past two weeks.
They weren't the same person in his mind anymore, the
Jordon Walker who had accused his brother of rape and this
Jordon Walker. It was incomprehensible that this laughing, dark-eyed woman had been responsible for the trial that
had started his brother's downfall, and, more indirectly, for
Alec's bourbon-fueled decision to take his own life. There
had been more to it than that, Kel knew that now. And
whatever it was, he knew instinctively he wasn't going to like
it.

So maybe that's why he was postponing it. Why he was
content, for just a while at least, to walk barefoot in a
mountain stream with a woman who smelled of sunshine
and fresh air, and pretend that the rest of the world didn't
exist.

Jordon slipped suddenly and half fell against him with a
yelp and Kel caught her easily in his arms; they skated
around on the slippery stones trying to keep their balance,
breathless with laughter. She felt good in his arms, warm
and curved and lithely muscled. And when he finally got

solid footing under him again and she looked up at him, lips still parted with laughter, he found himself dropping his mouth to hers without even thinking about it.

The impulse caught her as much by surprise as it did him, and for half an instant they went motionless, Jordon's eyes wide with sudden alarm only inches from his. And then, before he had time to react, her gaze softened with amusement and she turned her head slightly and the next thing he knew, her lips were under his, and he was kissing her.

He had enough time—a heartbeat, at least—to be surprised at how easy it was. How...right. And then it just didn't matter anymore.

Her mouth was sweet and wind cooled and he lost himself in it willingly, slipping his tongue into the welcoming warmth and finding hers waiting. The scent of her skin filled his nostrils and he tightened his arms around her, wanting to feel her against him, wanting to fill his senses with her. She was kissing him back slowly and languidly and the rhythmic give-and-take of her tongue against his made his belly tighten and he could feel the soft pressure of her breasts against his chest, the strong flex of her thigh muscles against his as she shifted to keep her balance on the slippery streambed.

His body responded with unexpected vitality to the promising pressure of breast and pelvis and thigh and he found himself thinking a little dazedly that things were moving altogether too fast, that in another instant or two she was going to realize how aroused he was and pull away in embarrassed anger. It was too intimate for a first kiss...too much too soon...he should be fighting it.... Except idle good intentions were useless against the onslaught of other emotions as she moved against him, perhaps by accident as the sand shifted under her or perhaps by design, and then he didn't give a damn about anything anymore but kissing her.

As though she sensed the change in him, Jordon shivered very slightly and then she moved against him again, deliberately this time. It was just a tentative touch, as though she were half-afraid of his reaction. But when he pulled her against him firmly she made no effort to pull away, although it would have been impossible for her not to know what was—all too graphically—on his mind.

He tasted her need as part of his, could sense the change in her breathing, the way the muscles in her belly tightened when a pebble moved under his right foot and he shifted to keep his balance, pressing himself against her.

And then finally she drew her mouth from his, closing her eyes for a moment or two as though to catch her emotional balance. "Oh . . . wow."

She touched her upper lip with her tongue, as though savoring the remembered taste of his mouth, and Kel's stomach pulled tight. "Yeah." His own voice sounded more unsteady than it needed to. "I . . . uh . . . would say that about covered it."

She gave a gasp of laughter, her cheeks an intriguing shade of pink, and she eased herself out of his embrace. "That wasn't . . . planned, or anything. Was it?"

"No." *Planned?* Kel nearly strangled trying not to laugh. The only thing he'd planned was forcing her to tell him why she'd set Alec up, and here he was standing up to his knees in mountain water kissing her as though someone had told him it was the last kiss he was ever going to get. "No, sweetheart, it wasn't planned."

He turned and waded back to the wide smooth rock and stepped out of the water, sitting down heavily. Bad move, Davies, he told himself in annoyance. This wasn't part of the plan. This had *never* been part of the plan!

"I didn't mean to scare you off." Jordon smiled a little uncertainly as she stepped up onto the sun-warmed stone.

Grinning, Kel grasped her hand and tugged her down beside him. "You didn't. I was just trying to figure out a way to say I'm sorry. I, uh . . . didn't want to do that. Kiss you, I mean."

"That's real flattering. Thanks."

In spite of himself, Kel had to laugh. "That's not what I meant. I *wanted* to do it—I just don't think I should have."

Jordon looked at him for a long moment, her gaze moving across his face feature by feature. "I'm glad you did," she said very softly. "And in fact," she breathed, turning toward him, "I'd like you to do it again."

Kel found himself reaching for her even as she shifted closer to him, and then she was in his arms again and all his newly sworn good intentions vanished as though they'd never even existed. Her breath warmed his mouth and he parted his lips, brushing them lightly across hers, and a moment later he was kissing her again and a moment after that he gave up even trying to convince himself that it was wrong.

All in all, Jordon mused a long while later, it had turned into an extraordinary afternoon. The sun was soaking into her shoulders and she moved them languidly, feeling more relaxed and lazy than she had in too long to remember.

She turned her head to look down at the man stretched out on the grass beside her, and found Kel watching her through half-closed eyes. His thick dark hair was tangled, as much by her fingers as by the light breeze, and her heart gave an odd little thump as their eyes met. He'd taken his shirt off and his bare shoulders and chest gleamed like gold in the sun and she had to fight the urge to reach out and touch him.

As though knowing what she was thinking, he smiled without saying anything and reached up to rub her shoulders, and she relaxed against the pressure of his hand. They'd spent the entire afternoon like this, talking and laughing or simply sitting in the sun in silence, sharing that special closeness of a man and woman just discovering each other. They'd chased minnows some more, had strolled along the banks of the creek hand in hand and now and again had surrendered to the magic growing between them.

They'd been like a pair of teenagers, unable to keep their hands off each other for very long, their embraces becoming increasingly intimate as the day had worn on, Jordon thought with an inward smile. And so far, to her relief and joy, there had been none of the fear or nervousness she'd half expected.

Kel had been in no hurry, for one thing, showing a restraint she considered remarkable considering she'd all but flung herself at him.

She smiled again, still slightly surprised by her own brazenness. It was the first time she'd taken the initiative like that in her entire life. But after the shock had worn off she'd been very glad she had.

Very glad.

"What are you smiling about?" Kel slipped his arm around her, drawing her down beside him. His teeth glinted in a lazy smile and he brushed a strand of flyaway hair off her forehead, cradling her in his arms.

"Nothing in particular." His chest was warm from the sun and she ran her fingers along the wide sweep of his shoulders slowly, loving the silken feel of his skin. "Just at how things work out, sometimes. I came up here to get away from people and things and—"

She caught the rest, not wanting to destroy the magic by thinking of Alec and the rest of it. Instead, she kissed his shoulder, letting her tongue linger on his moist skin, tasting salt. "Anyway, I came up to do the study for World First so I could be alone and get some thinking done, and almost from the day I arrived things have been crazy. I've been shot at and threatened and now I've met you and have spent an entire day necking up a storm instead of getting any work done, and—"

"Not an entire day." Kel nuzzled her throat. "Just part of a day."

Jordon smiled against his rough cheek, letting her eyes slide closed as his mouth found the soft, downy spot just under her ear and the touch of his tongue made her toes curl. A liquid warmth spilled through her and settled in her lower stomach and she found it difficult to breathe.

And suddenly she wanted more. Wanted his mouth on her shoulder, her breasts, her belly. Wanted to feel his hands caressing her, to feel his body moving against hers, to feel him making love to her....

"Kel." She turned in his arms and slipped her arms around him and he responded with a smile, seeking her mouth with his and finding it easily. She parted her lips to the probing touch of his tongue and started kissing him back with sudden urgency, and he groaned softly as she moved against him, sliding her thigh between his.

"Jordon..." His voice held a hint of warning and she felt his fingers tighten on her back.

"Please," she whispered, not letting herself think about what she was saying, what she was doing, just concentrating on the emotions welling up through and around her. She drew her fingertips lightly down his back and around his rib cage, then up to brush his nipples, hearing his breath catch. "Please, Kel. I...I want you to make love to me."

Kel went absolutely still, wondering for half a moment if she were playing some sort of game. Was she testing him? Testing herself?

Or—and the thought chilled him to the bone—was he testing himself? Testing to see how far he was willing to take it? Was he trying to somehow compete with Alec, even after all these years? To prove that he could somehow withstand her fatal charm when Alec couldn't?

Or was the idea not to withstand temptation at all, but to claim something his brother had had...?

He groaned softly. He thought he'd outgrown that desperate need to compete with Alec, to find something he could do that Alec couldn't. It had ended—he thought—with the navy. In making a life for himself so alien from anything Alec would have chosen that the niche he'd carved out was his alone, the honors he'd piled up undimmed by anything Alec could produce.

"Kel . . . ?"

Jordon's mouth moved against his and Kel swallowed, trying not to think of caressing her and touching her and easing himself down into the enveloping warmth of her body. . . .

"No." He said the word more roughly than he'd intended and cursed himself when he felt her flinch slightly. Taking a deep breath, he gripped her shoulders and eased her away from himself, then sat up. "That's not a good idea, Jordon. I'm sorry."

One look at her face told him how badly he'd handled it. She gave him one stricken look, her cheeks flooding with scarlet, then she sat up and started hastily pulling on her socks.

"Damn it!" Kel raked his hair back with his hand, furious at his own clumsiness. "Look, Jordon, it's not what you think. I—"

"Don't apologize," she said in a thick voice. "I—I can't imagine what I thought I was doing. You're probably married or something and—"

"I'm not married," he said with quiet urgency, realizing he couldn't let it go like this. "Jory, that's not it. Damn it, it's not that I don't *want* to make love to you. It's just that—"

"I said don't apologize! And you don't need to explain, either." She shoved her feet into her boots and stood up, not even bothering to lace them. "I threw myself at you like a love-starved adolescent . . . I don't blame you for backing off. I must be out of my mind to think—" She bit the rest of it off, stuffing the remains of her lunch into her backpack. "Let's just forget it ever happened. After all, nothing *did* happen. It's not as though we have to see each other every day or anything. There's no reason we even have to—"

"Jordon, stop it!" Kel strode across to her and grasped her by the arms. "Listen to me. Put that down, damn it, and listen to me!"

"You're hurting my arms!"

He heard the hint of panic in her voice and swore, releasing her instantly and stepping back. "Jordon, don't run away from me. I want to talk to you. It's important we talk about—"

"I don't w-want to talk!" She gave a gulp, as though around a sob, but to Kel's everlasting relief she didn't bolt. Hugging herself, she stood there miserably, not meeting his eyes. "It was my fault," she said in a ragged whisper. "I thought…" Her voice broke and she squeezed her eyes shut, and Kel felt the muscles across his shoulders tighten.

"Jory?" Carefully, not wanting to scare her off, he took a couple of steps toward her. "Honey, it's no one's fault. We let things go a little further than they should have, that's all. I didn't make love to you because you'd never have forgiven me if I had. Tonight or tomorrow morning or maybe the next day, you'd have hated me for having made it too easy. *That's* why I said no, not because—"

"But that's why I wanted you to," she whispered miserably. "Because it *would* have been so easy. It's been so long, and I thought that if I was with someone I liked, someone I trusted…"

Her voice broke again and she looked up at him, her eyes swimming with tears. "I was assaulted two years ago. Sexually assaulted. I haven't…" She drew in an unsteady breath. "I'm scared I might…not…be able…to. Make love, I mean. So I thought—" She wiped her cheek with her arm. "It seemed so right with you. I felt safe and you seemed…interested."

He didn't want to hear this, Kel thought numbly. Didn't want to think about the implications of what she was saying. "So you mean I was just therapy?" He said the word angrily, using the rage growing within him to keep himself from thinking. Using it to keep himself from walking across and gathering her up into his arms and telling her no one would ever hurt her again.

She looked up at him with shame-filled eyes. "Sort of. It wasn't fair, but…" She let her voice trail off, looking away.

"And I seemed *interested.*" Why was he doing this to her, something inside him demanded. Why was it suddenly so important to hurt her? To drive her off? And what the *hell* was he feeling so guilty about? It had been Alec, the blood drumming in his ears seemed to say. It had been Alec, not him…not *him*…!

And then he was walking away from her without saying anything more, not knowing where he was going, not caring, knowing only that he had to get away. He grabbed up his shirt and backpack and strode into the bush without looking back, stumbling slightly as he pushed blindly through the groping branches, feeling sick and disoriented and so filled with a baseless, directionless rage that he was dizzy with it.

He thought he heard her calling his name, but he ignored her voice, not wanting to think about her lying in Alec's arms. About her screaming, fighting to get away…about that cruel, cold smile Alec always had when he got away with something.

It was too late to help her now. Too late to help Alec. Too late to help even himself.…

"What the hell do you mean, you want out?" Trey Hollister's voice reverberated through the room like a crack of thunder and the big black-and-tan German shepherd lying in front of the fireplace raised his head in alarm.

"Just what I said." Kel tossed back the last swallow of whiskey and wiped his mouth with his hand. "What's the big deal, anyway? You got me in. All you have to do is get me out."

"And the woman?" Trey's eyes flashed in the firelight, his lean face taut with anger as he faced Kel across the room. "You never did tell me what the hell you wanted with her, Davies. I didn't push for an explanation because I trusted you, but we've worked together for enough years that I know you a little too well. Something happened up there." He glared at Kel, eyes calculating. "It scares me, Kel. *You* scare me. I've never seen you like this." He nodded toward the half-empty bottle of whiskey sitting on the table by the bed. "How long have you been holed up in here with that bottle? Two days? Three?"

Kel flushed. "I'm through," he said stubbornly. "I figured I owed it to you to tell you first, that's all."

"You owe me a hell of a lot more than that," Trey growled.

Kel stared across the firelit room at the man who had once been his best friend. The man he'd fought beside in more than one ugly little war, the man he owed his very life to. "Don't push it, Hollister," he said very softly. "I pay my debts, you know that. But not this time. Not this way."

"I'm not talking about Libya. I'm talking about right here. When you asked me to get you a legitimate cover so you could go in where the woman was working, I did it. It was no big deal—I subcontract security personnel all over the world, and the FWS have been using my people for a couple of years now. They'd already asked for more personnel, so when you turned up I just put you on my payroll and everything was jake."

Something in Hollister's voice made Kel's eyes narrow.

"I lost one of my men." Trey's gaze met his head-on. "He was running a sting operation with the poachers operating up around where the Walker woman's been doing her eagle study. They must have broken his cover, and they shot him. Last night, the RCMP found what was left of him.''

Kel swore. ''Who?''

''Jimmie Two Shoes. You met him.''

Kel felt as though someone had just hit him in the stomach. He swore again softly and wheeled away to stare down into the flames muttering in the fireplace. ''He was just a kid.''

''Twenty-six. With a wife and a four-month-old son. I didn't want to take him on—I rarely take on married men, especially when they've got families. It distracts them, makes them vulnerable. But this is Jimmie's land. His people have been here for five hundred years, and he wanted to do something to help protect it. So I broke all my own rules and hired him, and now he's dead.''

Anger and pain ran through Hollister's voice like water, and Kel looked around at him. ''I'm sorry. It's . . . rough, losing kids like that.''

''It's rough losing anyone,'' Trey said harshly. ''And I figure he might still be alive if I'd sent someone in there to back him up like I should have, instead of wasting manpower by sending you in to *play* undercover agent.''

''Damn it, Hollister, don't you lay that kid's death at *my* feet!''

''They're playing life and death up there. I had no business letting my friendship with you get in the way. When the Wildlife people asked for another man, I should have sent in a trained undercover agent with a background in international poaching activities . . . not someone who just wanted a convenient excuse to be in the area so he could spy on a woman!''

It hit a little too close to home and Kel turned away and walked across to the small maple table by the bed. His room at the Caribou Lodge was large by most standards, but it felt small and crowded at the moment, filled with anger. Uncapping the whiskey bottle, he poured a generous amount into the glass, then lifted it and swallowed half, eyes narrowing.

"I'd watch that if I were you," Trey growled from somewhere behind him. "Alec tried to find answers in the bottom of a bottle and it killed him."

"Jordon Walker killed him," Kel flung back, not believing it even as he was saying the words. Jordon had been the prey that night, not the hunter; he knew that now.

"You sure about that?" Trey's voice was measured. "You look like a man who's been facing a few ghosts, Kel. A man who's been forced to look at things he'd rather not know about. If you want to talk about it, I can—"

"I don't have anything to talk about," Kel said angrily, downing the rest of the whiskey in one long swallow. He tossed the glass onto the table and put the cap back on the bottle, twisting it tight as much in defiance of himself as Trey. He turned to look at his friend. "So what are you telling me, Hollister?"

"I want to hire you. Legitimately this time."

It was the last thing Kel expected. "Is this your idea of a joke? Give an old friend a job to keep him off the bottle and off the breadline?"

"You're pushing it, buddy." There was a glitter in his eyes that told Kel that, friend or no friend, Trey's patience was fast nearing an end. "You retired from Special Forces six months ago, and you've got nothing else lined up. I need men—good men who can get out of tight spots with no help and can handle their own in a fight. Men who know their way around high-tech weaponry and terrorism and are used to being out in the field for months on end with no one around telling them how to run the show."

"I just quit one job like that. What makes you think I want another one?"

One corner of Trey's mouth turned up. "I know you, buddy, remember?"

In spite of himself, Kel found himself smiling in return. "We were a good team, once."

"We still could be." Trey's face turned serious. "I mean it, Kel—I could use your help. Someone out there shot Jimmie Two Shoes and hid his body under a deadfall and left him for the crows. I want whoever did it. I'd go up myself, but there's a situation down in Panama I promised to take care of first."

"I don't know the first thing about international poaching," Kel muttered, the muscles across his shoulders tightening. "If I go stumbling around up there not knowing my ear from my elbow I could cause more trouble than I solve."

"You're exactly the kind of man I need up there. You're a new face, for one thing—you're not on anyone's computer. Even if they do run you through a check, your name won't ring any alarms."

"A computer check?" Kel's left eyebrow lifted. "These guys have computers?"

"We're not dealing with a bunch of good old boys taking a few whitetails out of season," Trey said grimly. "We're talking about a massive international black-market trade in illegal animals that turns a hundred million dollars a year and is growing daily. The Asian and Far Eastern markets are especially hungry. They see our wildlife as nothing more than parts—the gallbladder from a black bear can bring ten grand, easy. And that's not all. Bear paws and claws, elk horn, moose antlers, wolf eyes . . . hell, they're butchering anything that moves. Our wildlife is just one big supermarket, and they're shopping with unlimited credit."

"Wolf eyes?" The thought turned Kel's stomach.

"*Jinbu.* In China, they figure if you eat part of a wild animal you'll get its power. So if you eat a wolf's eyes, for instance, you'll acquire the wolf's visual acuity. If you eat its heart, you'll have its courage." Trey's face was hard. "Elk antler and bear gallbladders are ground up into powder and sold to cure sexual dysfunctions. Bear claws are symbols of courage and strength—they turn up in jewelry usually. Most of the jewelry you buy in the southwestern states is perfectly legal, but there's also a steady trade in illegally taken items.''

"Like eagle feathers," Kel said thoughtfully, thinking of the glitter of anger in Jordon's eyes when she talked about the depredations against her precious birds. He thought of her up there right now, unaware that Jimmie's killers were on the prowl. Perhaps whoever had killed Jimmie had been the one who'd shot at her. Maybe she was going to be next....

"You *owe* me," Trey said with soft urgency, perhaps misinterpreting his silence for something else.

He owed Jordon, too, Kel thought wearily. She was up here in the wilds of coastal British Columbia because of Alec. She'd been on the fast track to the good life—a *safe* life—when Alec had turned it all upside down, and she'd run away... from the media, the memories, perhaps even herself. If she died up here, it would be one more thing to blame Alec for. One more wrong that would never be righted, all because Alec had taken the easy way out.

A jolt of anger burned through Kel. Alec wasn't here to protect her, but he was. He couldn't make up for what Alec had done to her, but he *might* just be able to keep her alive long enough to put her life back into some sane, logical order.

Maybe that's what had brought him up here looking for her, he mused ironically. Maybe it hadn't been revenge at all, but simple family honor.

"All right, I'll do it," he whispered hoarsely, rubbing his stubbled face with his hands. "Who do I report to?"

"You're on your own. Carte blanche—whatever you need, you get. As long as you stay more or less within the bounds of the law, the RCMP don't even want to know you're up here until you're ready to lay charges. You'll work in cooperation with John Harris and his people, but only to

the extent that we don't want his men getting underfoot—
he'll be advised to accommodate you in every way. If you
have a problem you can't solve yourself—and there had
better be damn few—you contact me. If I'm not available,
call Washington." Trey grinned suddenly. "The usual
number. Spence O'Dell's in this one. Remember him?"

Kel subdued a shudder. "I remember him. I thought he
was heading up some supersecret agency in Virginia."

"He is. But my people in Washington know how to contact him."

"Does he remember *me?*"

Trey gave a snort of laughter. "I suspect so. That worry
you?"

"I swear to God I didn't know she was his wife."

"Neither did most of the others, from what I heard. But
don't worry about it. They divorced years ago." Trey smiled
fleetingly. "You'll keep the ID I already had made up for
you—it's perfectly legal. Have you got a weapon?"

"Just a rifle I borrowed from Harris."

"I'll contact the RCMP—drop by on your way through
town, and they'll fix you up. They've got the clearances and
paperwork on file. If they don't have what you need, they
can get it within hours. And don't shortchange yourself with
firepower, Kel. The people you're up against have state-of-
the-art weaponry—fully automatic, night scopes, laser
sights—the works. And they're not shy about using them."

"I want Murphy, too." Hearing his name, the big dog
looked up and banged his tail on the floor a couple of times.
"Not for me," Kel added. "For Jordon. She's got half the
countryside on her case about one thing or another—
poachers, loggers, a local Native rights group—and she's on
her own up there. There have been a couple of incidents... just threats, so far, but I'd rest easier knowing she
had Murph with her."

Trey nodded, looking thoughtful. "Have you...uh...told
her yet? Who you are, I mean?"

Kel shook his head, trying to ignore the jab of guilt that shot through him. He didn't want to talk about it. Not yet. Maybe he never would. He looked around to find Trey looking at him curiously, but he just smiled roughly and walked across the room, extending his hand. "Keep your eye on your back down in Panama, Hollister."

"Always." Trey grasped his hand firmly. "You keep an eye on *your* back, too, you son of a gun. And don't get my dog hurt."

"How's Linn and the kid?"

"Which one? She's pregnant again."

"Pregnant?" Kel gave a long, lazy laugh, shaking his head wonderingly. "Never thought I'd ever see the day an old war-horse like you would wind up dandling babies on his lap. Marrying Linn I can understand—hell, if she hadn't already been married to you when I met her, you wouldn't have had a chance! But kids..."

"Families can be pretty great," Trey said with a smile. "Good thing, too, considering the bunch I inherited with Linn."

Kel shrugged a little too casually. "Families are great if you can keep a lot of miles between you."

Trey looked at him for a silent moment, his eyes serious. "Maybe it's time to put all that to rest, Kel," he said softly. "It's just you and your dad now, with Alec gone. And I suspect he needs you as much as you need him—whether you want to admit it or not."

Kel just smiled, slapping Trey on the shoulder and pushing him toward the door. "Get out of here. Next you'll be telling me I should get married again."

"I would if I thought it would do any good." Trey grinned back good-naturedly. "Have a shower and a shave, Davies—you look like hell. And toss that bottle out while you're at it. Go back into the bush with a hangover and the only thing you'll be a threat to is yourself."

* * *

He had a strange dream that night, filled with faces he half knew and a vague, unformed sense of danger that woke him a little after three, soaked with sweat and panting as though he'd just run the four-minute mile. He got out of bed, staggered into the bathroom and stood under the pounding shower until the water ran cold, then he toweled himself off and crawled back between the clammy sheets and dozed fitfully for another hour or two.

And when he awoke the final time, just before dawn, he'd been dreaming of Denise. Their marriage had lasted three years. Long enough for both of them to realize they'd made a mistake. Denise had wanted children, a home—a *family*. And he, Kel thought grimly, had wanted everything but. They'd parted angrily, and Kel found himself thinking idly that in all the years afterward he'd never even come close to marrying again.

Probably never would. He thought of Trey suddenly, smiling a little as he let his mind drift to when he'd been at Trey's home on Vancouver Island. It had been filled with laughter and animals and toys, neighbors' kids wandering in and out, Trey's oldest son from his first marriage there for a day or two with *his* wife and new baby—making Trey Hollister a grandfather, Kel thought with real amusement.

Linn had welcomed Kel into their home as though she'd known him all her life, and their toddler son had clambered into his lap at every opportunity, drooling and laughing. Linn's father, a grizzled old Irish street cop, had flown up from Florida while Kel had been there, and then Linn's sister and *her* husband and two kids had turned up and the place had been like a circus.

And for a little while, Kel thought with a touch of wistfulness, he'd felt as though he belonged. There had been laughter and good food and love in abundance, and it had washed over and through him, filling him, healing him.

He swore suddenly and rubbed his face wearily. Three days' worth of stubble scraped his palms and he winced and sat up, then swung his legs over the side of the bed and sat there in the gloom and chill for a long while, trying to convince himself that he was doing the right thing. He'd told himself that he had to leave, before she found out who he was. That he didn't want to know what had really happened with Alec... knowing already that it was ugly and brutal.

He thought of Jordon in spite of trying not to, remembering how good she'd felt in his arms that afternoon on the cliffs by the sea. Remembering the taste of her mouth under his, the weight of her rounded breast filling his hand, the nipple taut through her bra and cotton shirt, what it was like to cup her smooth little bottom in his hands and pull her against him and tease himself with the softness between her thighs, knowing she wanted him, knowing what it would be like to fill her up and lose himself in her. Remembering—

He lunged to his feet with a rough curse and strode into the bathroom, squinting against the bright light and careful not to meet his own eyes in the mirror above the sink. Just get it over with, he told himself savagely, reaching for his razor and foam. He'd agreed to help Hollister find who had killed Jimmie Two Shoes, and he'd do that and then get the hell back to civilization and try to put Jordon Walker out of his mind once and for all. He couldn't do anything for her. It wasn't his responsibility.

Something moved in the doorway and he glanced around, finding Murphy standing there looking up at him curiously, tail gently wafting. "What the hell are *you* looking at?" Kel muttered, giving the can of shaving foam an angry shake. "Haven't you seen a jerk before?"

Chapter 6

Jordon was out in the shed where the diesel generator was housed when she first heard them. It sounded like someone shouting and she paused, head turned slightly, straining to hear over the clatter and roar of the machine. But the only other thing she could hear was the noisy clamor of crows in the big trees above her and she shook her head after a moment and walked back to the generator.

It had been its usual balky self, requiring a lot of fiddling and fine-tuning and creative profanity before it finally kicked in with an ungracious cough of smoke and fumes. It had finally settled into a steady roar that made the galvanized shed rattle. She wiped her greasy hands on a rag as she glared at the thing, wondering how she'd ever taken things like electricity for granted. In her previous life all it had taken was the flick of a switch, and lights and computers and television sets and all the other niceties of modern life came alive.

Thank heaven for the big propane hot-water tank at least, she thought as she walked across to the open front of the shed. She'd been just about to step into the shower when she'd realized that she'd forgotten to turn the generator on for the night.

And she was half-frozen, she realized in irritation. Instead of bothering to get dressed again, she'd just pulled on her old flannel work shirt before dashing out into the cold, wet night. Under the shirt, she was as naked as the day she was born. And she hadn't even bothered with shoes, and her bare feet and legs were like ice. Why she'd thought the damned generator was going to be anything but its usual obstinate self tonight she had no idea—she should have *known* she'd be standing out here half the night trying to coerce it into running.

For that matter, she was probably just being silly bothering with it at all. It was noisy and foul smelling, and it shattered the serenity with its clattering roar. But the generator was also the only way she could run the outside flood lamps, and lately she was more comfortable with them on all night.

And that annoyed the hell out of her. One of the things she'd loved about living up here was the utter silence at night. She'd lie in bed and listen to the occasional cry of a night bird or the sigh and moan of the wind in the big trees around the trailer and think how safe she felt.

But not anymore. Now she slept fitfully and lightly with the loaded rifle beside the bed, and dreamed of shadows.

There was a heavy mist trailing through the trees, a harbinger of rain, and although she couldn't see them, she knew the valley and mountains were hidden by low clouds, as sodden and gray as old snow. Preoccupied with her thoughts of a long hot shower, she stepped out of the shed and started walking toward the trailer, shivering as icy water squished up between her bare toes with every step, her breath puffing white in the chilly air.

She heard the shouts first and paused, startled by the unexpected sound of voices. Then she saw the truck, a big four-wheel-drive pickup with knobby tires and tons of chrome, bouncing wildly as it careened up the rutted path to her trailer and into the circle of light cast by the flood lamps.

It rocked to a stop and Jordon froze, pinned by the powerful beams of its headlamps like a rabbit in a jacklight. Even half-blinded by the lights, she could see them: three, maybe four men in the cab, two of them hanging out the window with sloppy, drunken grins. And behind them, hanging on to the roll bar arching across the back of the cab, stood another three or four. They were shouting at her now, waving their beer bottles like sabres, but Jordon wasn't listening, her mind spinning in a thousand different directions, all of them edged with panic.

Whoever was driving the truck gunned the engine noisily. Jordon swallowed, her heart pounding like a runaway train, poised between racing back to the false safety of the shed or trying to make a run for the trailer. It was farther away, but the rifle was there...the rifle...she had to get the rifle...!

But even as she gathered her muscles to run, someone gave a rebel yell and the driver of the truck threw it into gear and it leapt toward her, the back end fishtailing on the wet ground, big tires chewing up dirt and grass.

Then it got traction and came careening across the yard toward her, the beams from the headlamps swinging crazily, and even as Jordon sprang toward the trailer she knew she wasn't going to make it. The truck cut her off and Jordon veered away from it, half falling on the wet grass. She scrambled madly to get her feet under her before they could get the truck turned around. The men in the back were shouting instructions to the driver and whooping and yelling at her at the same time, and there was a sudden rifle shot, then a second, and the truck roared as the driver spun it around in a tight circle.

Jordon was on her feet and running hard, hoping to use their momentary confusion to get around them before they realized what she was doing. But someone spotted her as she started to bolt out and around the truck and the driver managed to swing it around and get between her and the trailer again. The men in the back were shouting themselves hoarse and firing wildly into the air, urging the driver on as though he were a bull going for the matador. Then someone remembered the deer lights mounted on the roll bar and turned them on and Jordon recoiled as she was caught fully in the high-powered beams, blinded and disoriented, and she stumbled on the uneven ground and very nearly fell again.

She scrambled to her feet, panting, holding her arm up to shield her eyes from the blinding lights. "What do you want!" she screamed at them. "Leave me alone!"

"Get her!" someone bellowed, giving another rebel yell. "Come on, Joe—get her! Get her!"

The truck rolled menacingly toward her and Jordon stumbled back, praying they were all too drunk to realize that if they simply stopped the truck and came after her on foot they'd catch her in no time flat. Then she was running again, sprinting hard to her left. The truck spun around to follow her, tires spraying dirt and torn-up grass, and the instant it got momentum Jordon doubled back so abruptly that the driver, caught by surprise, went roaring right by her, so close that she could have touched the glossy flare of the truck's fender as it slewed by.

The men in the back set up a bay of alarm and Jordon thought she heard feet hitting dirt behind her but didn't even look around, running as hard and fast as she could. The shed loomed in front of her, wide double doors gaping, and then she was through and into the sheltering darkness.

The lights...get rid of the lights! Panting, she hit the cutoff switch on the generator before she'd even skidded to a stop. It quit with a sputter. Outside, the flood lamps flickered once, then died, and the whole clearing was suddenly plunged into utter darkness.

She heard a bawl of surprise from someone and the truck rocked to a stop, the beams from the headlamps and spots scything the night. Truck doors started slamming and she could make out black figures moving around, silhouetted against the lights from the truck, and Jordon wiped the sweat from her upper lip with her arm and eased herself back into the deep shadows at the rear of the shed.

She couldn't stay in here—even if they hadn't seen her come in, they'd figure it out soon enough. Move, her mind chanted at her urgently. Don't just hide in here until they find you. Move!

But where? There was the trailer, where she had the advantage of a solid lock on the door and the hunting rifle that John Harris—to her everlasting gratitude—had taught her to use and insisted she keep on hand. Her Bronco was parked right outside, but the keys were in the trailer and she didn't have a clue how to hot-wire a truck. And even if she did, there was no way she could outrun them.

No. Better to stay on foot where she had better mobility. And stealth. The trees—that was her one hope. Head for the bush and hide until they tired of the game and took their guns and their liquor and their anger and retreated.

Except how long could she stay out here, barefoot and all but naked? Adrenaline was keeping her warm at the moment, but that would wear off all too fast. And it was going to get cold tonight, perhaps even rain, and she'd be out there in nothing but a shirt, freezing to death....

Licking her lips, she opened the back door in the shed slightly and peeked out. Nothing moved and she squeezed through, fighting to stay calm. That was her one advantage—calm, sober rationality. As long as she didn't give in to panic, she'd be all right.

Something brushed against her bare leg, something furred and alive, and she recoiled with a swallowed scream, nearly falling. Then she sensed more than actually saw movement and glanced around just in time to see a black shadow detach itself from the deeper black of the shed wall just behind her and in the next instant it was *there*, looming so close she ducked instinctively.

But as she turned to run, the shadow stepped between her and freedom and grabbed her around the waist, swinging her back into the deep shadows against the shed. It was a man, and he held her easily, pinning her arms so she couldn't fight. And as she drew in a deep breath to scream, a hand clamped across her mouth and wrenched her head back against a broad, male shoulder.

"Scream and we're both dead," a voice rumbled close to her ear. "It's just the cavalry, honey. It's just me. . . ."

Jordon nearly went limp with relief as Kel's warm breath brushed her cheek and she had to squeeze her eyes shut against a sudden welling of tears, too numbed with fright and surprise to do more than just lean against him. His body heat wrapped around her like a blanket and she shivered violently, and in the next moment he'd turned her in his arms and was holding her tightly against him, his arms shutting out the nightmare.

On the other side of the shed angry voices rose through the night, arguing over who hadn't done what and where she'd gone and whose fault was it, anyway. Someone was in the shed, banging and crashing around in the dark and swearing drunkenly as he proclaimed in a loud voice that she wasn't in there, and then one of his companions started yelling at him to start up the generator while he was at it.

This resulted in more profane crashing around and Jordon could hear him muttering as he tried to get the generator started. She grinned a little inanely against Kel's chest. "He'll never get it going."

"Are you all right? They didn't hurt you, did they?"

Jordon shook her head and nestled closer against him, trying to get warm. "I was out here when they drove up. I c-couldn't get back to the trailer. . . ."

"Probably a good thing they caught you out in the open. You'd have been trapped in the trailer. They could have burned you out or tipped it over or God knows what. You were smart to stay out here."

Jordon just nodded, clenching her teeth together to keep them from chattering.

Kel swore suddenly. "What the hell—?" He ran an exploratory hand down her back and around the flare of her bottom, his oath of surprise just a whisper. "You're not wearing a damn thing under this!"

"I was j-just going to have a shower when I remembered the generator, and I—"

There was a crash just inside the door to the shed and Jordon stiffened, her fingers knotting in Kel's shirtfront. The noise subsided after a moment as whoever was in the shed worked his way back toward the front, and Kel eased her away from him gently.

"Stay here. Put this on—" He pulled off his leather jacket and wrapped it around her and Jordon snuggled down into its warmth gratefully. "Don't move until I give you the all clear, got that?"

She nodded numbly and he gave a low, soft whistle. Something furry brushed against Jordon's bare legs again and she flinched with an indrawn breath.

"Give me your hand." Kel braided strong fingers with hers and whispered something into the darkness, and an instant later a very cold, very wet canine nose bumped softly against her palm. "Murph, this is Jordon. Guard, Murph. Got that? Guard Jordon."

Squinting hard, Jordon could just discern the outline of a large dog in the darkness, catching the glint of his eyes as he turned his head. Then a formidable length of wet tongue wrapped itself around her fingers. "Meet Murphy—he's your new guardian angel."

"But where . . . how . . . ?"

"Stay here," he told her firmly. "If I'm not back in five minutes, light out for the creek—my truck's parked near the bridge, keys under the seat. Get in it and drive like hell. And don't stop for *anyone* until you get to the RCMP, understand me? Not for *anyone!*"

"But—"

"Come on, Murph. Let's give these guys something to think about."

And then he was gone, melting into the shadows as though he'd never been there at all, and Jordon was left staring into the misty darkness at nothing. Pulling the jacket tightly around her, she crept closer to the shed and settled in to wait.

She heard the first shout a couple of minutes later. It was followed by a snarl and then the sound of a large dog worrying something, and the man's voice rose into a squeal of fear. There were other noises then—the sound of breaking glass and a bawl of rage from someone, then three shots in quick, measured succession. The faint light reflected on the trees from the truck spot and headlights went abruptly out, dropping the clearing into complete darkness.

The instant he'd shot out the deer lights on the top of the truck cab, Kel grinned. As far as plans went, it wasn't inspired—drop your enemy into darkness to confuse and intimidate him, then take him out one man at a time—but it was as effective as hell. Murphy seemed to be enjoying himself if the snarling and growling that was going on was any indication, and the effect it had on his prey would have been funny if Kel had been in the mood for laughter. There were shouts of alarm and the occasional shriek of pain and the lot of them were tearing around and crashing into each other noisily, Jordon forgotten in the urgency of getting away from this new and unexpected threat.

He hefted the iron pipe he'd used to smash the truck headlights, tempted to wade back into the fray and wrap it around a couple of thick skulls. But he restrained himself. For one thing, Murphy seemed to be handling things just fine without him. And for another he was starting to realize that the men weren't half as dangerous as he'd first thought. They weren't cold-blooded poachers out for murder and mayhem, just a truck full of loggers from the nearby mill, headed home from the late shift with too many beers under their belts and a lot of cold fear in their bellies. Their jobs were vanishing even as they watched and they were afraid, and Jordon was an easy target for their anger and confusion.

One of the men had managed to get the truck started and was backing it out of the clearing at top speed. Kel called Murphy back as the others realized their only means of escape was getting away without them and they lit out after it. A noisy chase ensued, and as the shouts and oaths faded into the distance, Kel gave his head a shake and went back to find Jordon.

She appeared from around the end of the generator shed and walked toward him, stiff with cold. "Lady, you are turning into a full-time job."

"You're not even half as tired of rescuing me," she muttered as she stumbled by him on half-frozen feet, "as I am of *being* rescued!"

Whistling for Murphy, he followed Jordon to the trailer, trying not to notice how short the tails were on the old shirt she was wearing, and how much long, shapely thigh they showed off as she stumbled up the steps and into the trailer ahead of him. Her legs and feet were caked with mud and bits of dried grass and pine needles and she was shivering so badly he could hear her teeth clattering.

Once inside, he didn't bother saying anything but just planted his hand in the small of her back and propelled her down to the small bathroom. Reaching past her and into the shower, he turned the hot water on full. He pried her fingers off the edges of the leather jacket and peeled it off her, then started matter-of-factly unbuttoning the old flannel shirt, knowing damned well that he was playing with fire but not caring.

He'd sworn, when he'd headed up to her trailer earlier that night, that nothing was going to happen between them, that he had not just a right but an obligation to keep it that way. He was stuck up here with her for the next few weeks— Hollister had seen to that—but there was no need for it to go any further than it already had.

Except he'd known, as he'd held her against him in the darkness, had felt the supple warmth of her, had caught the subtle scent of her hair and skin, that it wasn't going to be that easy. And right now, looking down into the velvet depths of her eyes and recognizing what he was seeing there, he wondered why he'd ever tried to tell himself otherwise.

It was Jordon who stopped it in the end. She caught his hands on the next-to-last button and held them between hers, gazing up into his eyes calmly. She wasn't shivering anymore, and the fright and anger in her eyes had changed to something else, something smoky and primitive that made his stomach tighten.

"This isn't why I came up here tonight," he growled, torn between shoving her away from him and crushing her mouth under his. Wanting and not wanting with the same desperate, savage intensity.

Her mouth sweetened with a smile and she looked up at him through her lashes. "I didn't think you had. In fact, I honestly never expected to see you again."

"I didn't think you would, either," he admitted with a trace of real humor. "I don't understand what the hell's going on here. I'm not looking for complications in my life."

"Neither am I." Her eyes were warm with amusement. "And I'm just as confused as you are, Kel Stuart. We could stop it right now. We could just agree that whatever's happening isn't what we want."

"We could." It wasn't conscious thought that made him reach out and cup her face in his palms, but Kel didn't even bother questioning it. He tipped her face toward him and dropped his mouth over hers and simply luxuriated in kissing her slowly and deeply, meeting the silken thrust of her tongue with his and feeling himself start to slip dangerously near the edge of self-control.

The unbuttoned shirt fell open and Kel ran his hand down her throat to her shoulder, brushing the fabric back, her skin like warm silk to his touch. She gave a slight start when he fit his hand over the heaviness of her breast and he felt the nipple pucker against his palm, sensed more than heard her intake of breath, the way she stiffened almost imperceptibly, and in the next instant Alec's face floated into his mind, sneering slightly.

"*Damn* it!" He pushed her away from him so urgently that she stumbled against the shower stall, her eyes wide with surprise. "I'm sorry," he said through clenched teeth. The shirt hung open and he tried not to notice her small, dark-tipped breasts, the slight curvature of her belly, the dark triangle at the juncture of her thighs. He tore his gaze away and wheeled toward the door, his jaw set. "I'll make coffee."

"Damn you!"

It was just a sob, filled with fury, and Kel flinched as something hit him between the shoulder blades. The bar of soap ricocheted against the wall and went spinning away and Kel turned awkwardly to look at her. "What the—?"

Her eyes were brimming with tears and she was clutching the shirt closed, her face white with anger. "Get out! Just get out of here and don't come back!"

Kel turned the rest of the way around, looking at her in confusion. "Jory, what the hell's the prob—?"

"You've got the problem," she shouted furiously, tears spilling. "I'm *not* damaged goods, damn you!"

DOUBLE YOUR
ACTION PLAY...

"ROLL A DOUBLE!"

Peel off label & place inside

?

CLAIM UP TO 4 BOOKS
PLUS A LOVELY
"KEY TO YOUR HEART"
PENDANT NECKLACE

ABSOLUTELY FREE!

SEE INSIDE..

NO RISK, NO OBLIGATION TO BUY...NOW OR EVER!

GUARANTEED

PLAY "ROLL A DOUBLE" AND GET AS MANY AS FIVE GIFTS!

HERE'S HOW TO PLAY:

1. Peel off label from front cover. Place it in space provided at right. With a coin, carefully scratch off the silver dice. This makes you eligible to receive two or more free books, and possibly another gift, depending on what is revealed beneath the scratch-off area.

2. You'll receive brand-new Silhouette Intimate Moments® novels. When you return this card, we'll rush you the books and gift you qualify for ABSOLUTELY FREE!

3. Then, if we don't hear from you, every month, we'll send you 4 additional novels to read and enjoy. You can return them and owe nothing, but if you decide to keep them, you'll pay only $2.96 per book—a saving of 43¢ each off the cover price.

4. When you subscribe to the Silhouette Reader Service™, you'll also get our newsletter, as well as additional free gifts from time to time.

5. You must be completely satisfied. You may cancel at any time simply by sending us a note or a shipping statement marked "cancel" or by returning any shipment to us at our expense.

Terms and prices subject to change without notice. Sales tax applicable in NY.
©1990 Harlequin Enterprises Limited.

The Austrian crystal sparkles like a diamond! And it's carefully set in a romantic "Key to Your Heart" pendant on a generous 18" chain. The entire necklace is yours free as added thanks for giving our Reader Service a try!

"ROLL A DOUBLE!"

PLACE LABEL HERE

SCRATCH HERE

SEE CLAIM CHART BELOW

240 CIS AELT
(U-SIL-IM-05/92)

YES! I have placed my label from the front cover into the space provided above and scratched off the silver dice. Please rush me the free books and gift that I am entitled to. I understand that I am under no obligation to purchase any books, as explained on the opposite page.

NAME _____

ADDRESS _____ APT. _____

CITY _____ STATE _____ ZIP CODE _____

CLAIM CHART

🎲 🎲	**4 FREE BOOKS PLUS FREE "KEY TO YOUR HEART" NECKLACE**
🎲 🎲	**3 FREE BOOKS**
🎲 🎲	**2 FREE BOOKS**

CLAIM NO.37-829

Offer limited to one per household and not valid to current Silhouette Intimate Moments® subscribers. All orders subject to approval.   ©1990 Harlequin Enterprises Limited

DETACH AND MAIL CARD TODAY!

SILHOUETTE ''NO RISK'' GUARANTEE

- You're not required to buy a single book—ever!
- You must be completely satisfied or you may cancel at any time simply by sending us a note or shipping statement marked ''cancel'' or by returning any shipment to us at our cost. Either way, you will receive no more books; you'll have no obligation to buy.
- The free books and gift you claimed on this ''Roll A Double'' offer remain yours to keep no matter what you decide.

If offer card is missing, please write to: Silhouette Reader Service, 3010 Walden Ave., P.O. Box 1867, Buffalo, NY 14269-1867

DETACH AND MAIL CARD TODAY!

BUSINESS REPLY MAIL

FIRST CLASS MAIL   PERMIT NO. 717   BUFFALO, NY

POSTAGE WILL BE PAID BY ADDRESSEE

SILHOUETTE READER SERVICE
3010 WALDEN AVE
PO BOX 1867
BUFFALO NY 14240-9952

NO POSTAGE
NECESSARY
IF MAILED
IN THE
UNITED STATES

"Damaged...?" Kel stared at her in honest bewilderment. "What the hell are you talking about, Jordon? What did I—?"

"I can see it in your eyes every time you touch me," she sobbed, fighting the tears. Steam from the shower was filling the room, swirling around her, but she didn't seem to notice. "I can see the questions, can see you wondering what really happened. And you're right, I wasn't just 'sexually assaulted.' I was *raped!* But that doesn't make me untouchable! It doesn't mean—"

Understanding hit Kel so solidly that he groaned, stepping toward her. "My God, is that why you think I—?" He swore at his own stupidity, reaching for her. "Jory, that's not—"

"Don't you dare touch me!" She shot by him and was out of the bathroom before Kel could even react, his fingers closing on air as he snatched at her. "Just get out of my life, Kel Stuart! I don't need you!"

Swearing ferociously, Kel turned the shower off and was after her in the next heartbeat, reaching the bedroom door just as it was being slammed shut. He threw his hand up and stopped it, ignoring the jolt of pain that shot from wrist to shoulder. Jordon tried to shove it closed from the other side, but he held it firmly. "Stop it, Jordon—let me in. Damn it, let me in!" He gave the door a push and she stumbled back.

"Do you think that's why I didn't throw you down on the bathroom floor and make love to you just now?" His voice was too loud for the confines of the small room, but he didn't care; he was too angry to give a damn about whether he was shouting or not. "I suppose it never occurred to you that I just might *care,* did it? That I might not want to rush you because I'm afraid of scaring you or hurting you or just letting you talk me into something you're going to regret the minute it's over?"

"Get out!" She looked around frantically as though searching for something to throw. "Get out of here!"

"That's enough." Kel covered the distance between them in two long strides and caught her against him, turning his face away as she started flailing at him. "It's all right, Jordon," he said quietly, ignoring her struggles and simply holding her tightly against him. "It's all right."

She gave up after a moment and stopped struggling, and finally she just relaxed against him, fighting the sobs he could still feel tearing at her.

"Damn it, lady," he growled, "if you think I'm handling you with kid gloves because you were raped, you're right—but not because I think you're damaged goods. It's because I think you're scared to death."

"I'm n-not scared!"

The quavering bravado in her voice made him grin. "Sure you are. And so am I." He rested his mouth against her ear for a moment, trying to get the words right. Knowing that if he didn't, if he left her feeling soiled and undesirable, he'd be no better than Alec. "I'm scared of rushing you, that's all. Scared I'll get too impatient at the wrong moment and take you too far too fast, or that I'll say something that might bring it all back. It's hard for me, too, you know. Hard to keep putting the brakes on when all I can think of when I'm around you is sex—hot and raw, and plenty of it!"

He thought for an instant that he'd gone too far. She stiffened slightly, then he heard her give a stifled gasp of laughter and knew it was going to be all right. "You've got a terrific knack with words, Stuart. Are you supposed to be reassuring me?"

"That's not all I've got a terrific knack with," he murmured against her ear. "And if things were different, lady, I'd have you down on that bathroom floor right now showing you exactly what I mean."

She looked up at him. Her eyes were still wet, the lashes clumped with tears, and her cheeks were flushed and damp. "Crude, Stuart. But effective." She smiled finally, then wiped her cheeks with her fingers, relaxing against him. "And I'm sorry. They talked in my rape counseling group about self-image and hidden anger and all that, and I never paid much attention. I guess I thought it didn't apply to me." She laughed and looked up at him, nestled into the circle of his arms. "Is that really what you think about when you're around me?"

"All the time," Kel growled, thinking idly that he wasn't even lying.

"So you'd do it—take me to bed—if I asked you?"

Kel's heart stopped. "Jordon..."

She gave a wicked little laugh. "Hypothetically speaking, of course."

He couldn't keep from grinning. "Hypothetically speaking, I'd have you down on that bed before you could catch your breath." She just nodded, looking thoughtful, and Kel gazed at her, serious now. "Do you want me to make love to you?" he asked, idly wondering if he'd ever have the willpower to say no.

"Yes." She pulled back slightly to look up at him, her eyes filled with wonder. "But not yet. I—I need to get used to the idea first. Used to you. Used to... wanting, again. It was different on the cliffs—I didn't want you then, just your lovemaking. They were separate, almost. But I've had time to think about it since then. To think about you..."

It was wrong, Kel told himself dimly, gazing down into her soft, loving eyes. Wrong to taunt her with what she couldn't have, what he couldn't give her. They had no future—he could never tell her who he was, and their lovemaking would be fraught with lies.

And yet, some other part of his mind teased gently, what harm could come of it? She wasn't expecting a lasting, lifelong relationship, she just wanted someone to hold her in the night and make the fears go away. Someone to teach her about the magic of her body again, to take away the terror and the shame and the hurt. Someone to show her that it was all right to want, all right to touch and be touched, to feel and need and laugh long into the night.

Except if he managed to convince himself that it was really that altruistic, he reminded himself bitterly, he was a bigger liar than he'd suspected. If he made love to Jordon Walker, it was going to be just as much for his own satisfaction as it was for hers. And where in hell Alec fit into the already complicated equation, God alone knew.

He smiled down at her, then kissed the end of her nose and gave her a gentle shove toward the bathroom. "Get in there before I decide to change your mind for you. I'll have a hot brandy waiting when you get out."

A hint of pink washed across her cheeks and she laughed softly. "You have no idea how good you are for me, Kel Stuart. I never thought I'd be able to even talk about sex with a man again, let alone actually contemplate doing... it."

He grinned down at her lazily, holding her gaze until the blush deepened. "Honey, I don't think just *doing it* quite covers everything I had in mind. I'm past the age where speed and body counts matter... I like the all-night kind— slow and deep and lasting forever."

"Oh." It was just a tiny, breathless sound, and she looked a little dazed.

And Kel, trying his damnedest not to think of what it would be like to step into the shower with her and ease himself into the wet heat of her and make love standing under the pounding spray, turned and walked virtuously out the door.

It took nearly as long for his overheated body to subside as it did for Jordon to get out of the shower, but by the time she came down into the living room, dressed—to his relief—in khaki slacks, heavy wool socks and a bulky knit sweater, he was more or less himself again.

She didn't say anything about what had happened, taking the hot mug of brandy from him with a smile and a moment of warm eye contact that said much more than words could have. Sitting in the big armchair and tucking her feet under her, she sipped the hot brandy and frowned, looking down at Murphy. The big shepherd had walked across to sit beside the chair and rested his chin on the arm and gazed up at her soulfully.

Jordon reached out and started scratching him between his ears. "You don't think they'll be back, do you?"

"Nope." Kel dropped onto the sofa and ran his fingers through his hair, balancing the mug of coffee on his upraised knee. "Not tonight, anyway. Tomorrow night..." He shrugged. "Who knows."

"You think I'm wrong to stay up here, don't you?"

"I think you're putting yourself into a lot of unnecessary danger. Taking a stand on something is fine, but getting yourself killed for all the wrong reasons doesn't make much sense."

"It's important to me," she said quietly. "I...didn't fight for something important once. I'd been hurt, and I didn't want to be hurt again. So I didn't fight, and someone got away with something he shouldn't have and..." She shook her head, frowning again, and stroked the top of Murphy's broad head with her fingertips. "I should have taken a stand. Other people might have gotten hurt because I was too scared and selfish to fight for what was right. But all I could think of was myself, and now I wish..." She laughed suddenly, a quiet bitter sound. "Guilt. The universal motivator."

Kel had gone very still. *Tell me about it,* he urged her silently. *I want to know...need to know....*

"So, where did you get Murphy?"

"A friend of mine who specializes in security systems. Murph's a trained guard dog, so you'll be safe up here with him underfoot. I've got a couple of sacks of dry food, his bed and a choke collar and leash out in the truck. Before I leave, I'll run you through some of his basic commands—

come, stay, attack, seek out…the usual commando stuff."
He laughed at her expression. "He might look like your average house pet, but Murph's military-trained. He spent a year on top secret missions in the Middle East, and about the only thing he can't do is fieldstrip an M-16."

She smiled down at the big dog and got a tail-thump in return. "It'll be like having a squad of marines in the house."

"Better." *I don't have to worry about him looking at you the way those marines would… the way John Harris does,* Kel thought uncharitably. Wondering, even as he was thinking it, just what the hell gave him the right to be this territorial over a woman who, for a muddle of reasons, could never be his anyway.

Nodding slowly, she gazed down at Murphy, stroking his ears. "I saw John Harris today. He… says he ran your name through some computer. But that you're not really working with the U.S. Fish and Wildlife Service, or the special international task force. That no one he's contacted has ever heard of you."

Kel's shoulders tightened. Forcing himself to relax, he laughed casually. "That's reassuring. I'd be a pretty damn poor undercover agent if anyone who had computer access could pull my name out of a government file."

"I told him that. But John thinks there's something… funny about you. Something not right."

"Harris doesn't like me being around you. It doesn't take a genius to figure out why."

"He said you were trying to romance me because you're working with the poachers. That it's your job to keep me preoccupied and unsuspecting, because simply killing me could cause a huge investigation that could jeopardize everything."

"How long have you known Harris?"

Jordon frowned slightly. Kel was still sprawled back against the sofa, looking lazy and relaxed, but there was a sudden watchfulness in his eyes that sent a prickle up her spine. "About seven months," she replied cautiously. "Why?"

"That blood you saw in the back of his truck last week... Are you sure it was bear?"

"Of course." She frowned. "Well, not technically, I guess. I mean, I presumed it was bear because I found the fur at the same time. I didn't run a sample or anything." Her frown deepened, her gaze searching his. In the space of a few words, he'd changed, suddenly becoming every inch the cool undercover government agent with something on his mind. "That's an odd thing to ask."

"Can you test it? If I can get you a sample?"

Jordon paused, eyes narrowing slightly, her mind measuring and estimating as she thought about her answer. "I...could. I do tests on eagle blood, checking for contaminants, stress factors and so on. So I have what I need." She looked at him evenly for a long moment. "But I'd have to know why."

Kel paused for a heartbeat. "One of our agents was killed four days ago. They found his body hidden under a pile of brush up near the end of Lamehorse Canyon. He'd been shot."

"Oh my God, Kel." Jordon felt herself pale.

"His name was Jimmie Two Shoes—you may have seen him hanging around town. A tall skinny Native kid."

"I think I met him once," Jordon whispered, feeling numb. "He and John Harris were in the Rusty Nail Café and I had coffee with them. He...he seemed really nice. And very young."

"He was," Kel said tightly. "Too damn young. And I want to find out who killed him."

Jordon stared across at him, hearing an undercurrent of cool, deadly threat in his voice that made the hair along her arms prickle. "Why are you asking about the blood in the back of John's truck?"

Kel looked at her for a long moment. "The body had been moved, Jordon. Jimmie had set up a meet with someone near Hanging Rock Ridge, arranging a pickup of bear pelts and gallbladders and so on . . . the usual. From what I can tell, he met his contact all right, but then something went wrong. He was shot twice, at close range, by someone who knew what he was doing. Then his body was hidden in Lamehorse Canyon. Whoever did it probably figured no one would find it up there."

"Who . . . ?"

"Hikers. They were in the upper watershed area checking soil erosion where there's been some preliminary logging. They found him just at the edge of the clear-cut, under a pile of brush. Whoever put the body there came in from the top, following the old logging roads over the crest of Lamehorse Mountain and down into the valley."

"It could have been anybody." Jordon's face felt stiff. "I can't imagine why you'd think John might have anything to—"

"Jimmie's body was moved by a four-wheel drive truck, Jordon. Harris drives a four-wheel drive, and you said there was blood in the back of it. I'm not saying he was involved, but I wouldn't be worth my take-home pay if I didn't check it out."

He was right, Jordon thought. And yet the thought repelled her. "I've known John for as long as I've been working up here. He hates poachers almost as badly as I do. He'd never—"

"Money can be a hell of a temptation for almost any man," Kel said matter-of-factly. "I'll get a sample of that blood and bring it to you—tomorrow if I can."

"You don't really expect to find any, do you? It was almost a week ago that I saw it, and it's been raining almost nonstop ever since."

"Chances are I can find enough of a residue for you to run a test on it, even after all this time."

Jordon swallowed. "I'm not equipped—or qualified—to do forensics testing, Kel. This is way out of my league."

"All I want to know is if it's bear blood or... not."

Or human, he'd been about to say, Jordon realized with a cold chill. "My God," she whispered, staring across at him. "Do you know what you're saying?"

"Yeah." His face was hard, his eyes as cold as glass. "I'm saying that someone killed a friend of mine, and I intend to find out who it was."

She had a nightmare that night, one filled with evil and blood and men with cold eyes, and she awoke a little after four with the sound of her voice echoing in her ears, shivering and chilled. Pulling the blankets more tightly around her, she rolled over and realized that Murphy was standing in the bedroom door, ears pricked, looking at her intently.

"It's okay, Murph. I just had a nightmare."

At the sound of her voice, he relaxed perceptibly, his broad tail wafting gently as though to tell her he understood. He walked across and gave the blankets a nudge with his nose, then yawned widely and jumped up onto the bed.

"Murphy!" The dog was worse than Stuart, simply walking in and taking over. "Shouldn't you be standing guard or something?"

Murphy obviously had other ideas. He turned a couple of times, then lay down with a sigh, giving his tail a thump or two in acknowledgment before settling his head on his paws and closing his eyes.

"Some watchdog you are," Jordon muttered, giving the blankets a ferocious tug to get her share. Almost instantly she could feel his body warmth seeping through and she smiled in spite of herself. There was something comforting about having his warm, furry rump tucked against hers, and she realized that she felt safer than she had in weeks. Those big bat-wing ears would hear an intruder long before she did, and anyone foolish enough to break in would be in for a very unpleasant surprise.

Still smiling, she snuggled under the blankets and closed her eyes. Kel Stuart had very much the same effect on her. He irritated her half to death at times, and yet there was something about him that made her feel almost protected.

From outside threats, anyway, she amended with a sleepy grin. Because there were other times when she felt *anything* but safe with Kel Stuart.

There had been those few minutes in the bathroom tonight, for instance. That had, frankly, caught her by surprise. In fact, she'd been surprised that he'd turned up again at all. She'd figured that after that episode at the creek a week ago she'd never see him again. The way he'd gone charging off, filled with anger, had seemed pretty final.

Yet it had taken no more than a look tonight, and they'd both known what was going to happen. It had been almost inevitable, as though the fact he'd come back had been an important decision in its own right. A question asked, an answer given.

Where it was going to lead, she had no idea. There was a tiny part of her that kept telling her it wasn't fair to Kel to let things go on like this. That she was just using him to mend what Alec Davies had all but destroyed two years ago. They hardly had any kind of a future—she was up here only as long as the study lasted, and when World First pulled the plug on her she had no idea what she'd be doing. Or where. And Kel didn't seem to be the type who'd take well to being tied down with a wife and family. No one who went into the dangerous, lone-wolf kind of work he did would.

So what did they have to look forward to? Three or four months of companionship and good sex? If, she reminded herself thoughtfully, it *was* good. If it weren't, it wouldn't be Kel Stuart's fault, she was pretty certain of that—he didn't strike her as the kind of man who'd have any problems satisfying his woman.

Hardly the stuff great love affairs were made of, she thought grumpily. Although there were worse things than spending the summer playing at being in love with a man like Kel. As long as neither of them got reckless and actually started mistaking it for the real thing.

She smiled again, thinking of the few minutes they'd spent in each other's arms at the door tonight when he'd left. Again, she hadn't expected it to happen. They'd walked to the door together and had said good-night and she'd stood there, shivering in the cold night air. He'd turned without warning and had slipped his hands into her hair, angling her face up to his, and had kissed her with deep and satisfying thoroughness.

He'd stared down at her afterward, his eyes dark and almost hard in the cold silver of the just-risen moon, and there had been a heartbeat of time when she'd thought he was going to shove her away from him and stalk off into the night, filled with the same anger he'd displayed before.

But he hadn't. And after a moment the anger in his eyes turned to something she could have sworn was bitter despair. The kind of look a man might have gazing on something—or someone—he knew he could never have.

You're a strange man, Kel Stuart, she advised him, letting herself relax down into the first layers of sleep. I don't know what your secret is, but it can't be worse than mine. And maybe, one day, we'll trust each other enough to share. . . .

Chapter 7

"I don't like this, Stuart. I don't like it at all." Harris was pacing in front of the fireplace in Kel's room at the Caribou Lodge. "You're going to get yourself killed. Or worse yet, you're going to get someone *else* killed."

"I'm not going to get anyone killed," Kel told him calmly. "No one knows who I am except for you, Jordon and the RCMP. As far as anyone else is concerned, my cover story is that I'm up here on vacation, recuperating from a bad divorce, doing a little fishing, taking some time-out."

"And dabbling in the black market."

"Open to the possibility. I'm just asking around if someone can help me find a couple of record-book big horns or a grizzly."

"Out of season, and with no license," John muttered unhappily.

"I want whoever killed Jimmie Two Shoes."

Harris's troubled face darkened. "Yeah, that's bad. He was a good kid."

Kel watched the other man closely. He had nothing to go on, no real proof that Harris wasn't as squeaky-clean as he was supposed to be, but old habits die hard. Until you had proof to the contrary, you never trusted anyone.

Except he was beginning to suspect that his feelings about Harris had a hell of a lot less to do with business than they did with Jordon Walker. Kel had to smile a trifle grimly. He'd come up here with the idea that Jordon belonged to *him,* and although the reasons had changed, the truth was that he still felt that way. And Harris was circling altogether too close.

"Okay," Harris finally said sourly, "I'll start casually passing the word around that I think you're up to no good. But if it gets you trouble you don't want, I don't want to hear about it. I've got enough work without having to track down *your* body."

"Tell me about the Murdoch brothers."

"The Murdochs?" Harris glanced up, looking suddenly uneasy. "What about them?"

"That's what I want you to tell me."

Harris shrugged. A little too casually, Kel thought. "They and their old man live up on Ghost Creek. They do a little trapping in the winter and work at odd jobs in between. Bud was a feller with Kalumet Lumber before he got too close to a chain saw and tore his leg all up."

"Mention them around town, and people get real quiet. Why?"

"Rumors, mainly. I wouldn't put much stock into them."

"What kind of rumors?"

"Things happen to people who cross the Murdochs—let's put it that way. Houses burn down, dogs get shot, trucks get run off the road...nobody can ever prove anything, understand, but most people up here stay clear of them on general principles."

"Think they could be the ones taking shots at Jordon? That Bronco she's driving looks like Swiss cheese."

"If they are, they're not doing it on their own—neither of them are bright enough to do something like that without help."

"Such as?"

Harris shrugged again. "Loggers, probably. Feelings are running pretty high against those tree huggers Jordon's working for. All the cutbacks in the logging industry in the past few years have meant bad unemployment around here. Between that and the Native land claims, this area's a tinderbox. People are scared. And Jordon's right in the middle of it."

"Killing Jordon isn't going to save the forest industry," Kel said with real irritation. He could sympathize with the frustration and very real fears of the men and women facing the destruction not just of their livelihood, but of an entire way of life. But violence wasn't the answer. Better forest management, better public relations, better communications . . . hell, there were a hundred ways to get the message across without starting to kill people.

As someone had killed Jimmie Two Shoes.

A stab of anger jolted Kel out of his brooding. "I want your people keeping an eye on her. If I stay too close, I'll be putting her in more danger than she's already in."

"Good idea." Harris didn't bother keeping the satisfaction out of his voice. He met Kel's gaze across the fire, holding it steadily. "It's none of my business, I guess, but I'd be a lot happier if you stayed away from Jordon permanently. She's been hurt pretty bad. And she doesn't need to be hurt again."

"Taking a hell of a lot for granted, aren't you?" Kel asked with deceptive softness. "Far as I can tell, she's old enough to make up her own mind."

"I'm warning you, Stuart," Harris said in a low voice. "Don't mess with her."

"Or . . . ?"

"Or you just might regret it." Harris's face was hard.

"I'll keep it in mind," Kel told him mildly.

Harris turned and walked to the door, pulling it open. He looked around at Kel as though to add something, then thought better of it. The door closed behind him with a solid bang, and Kel looked at it thoughtfully for a long while.

Then, forcing himself to relax, he walked over and pulled the screen on the fireplace open to toss another log onto the flames. Getting into a territorial dispute over Jordon Walker wasn't why he was up here. Finding Jimmie Two Shoes's killer was.

He still hadn't managed to get close enough to Harris's Ministry truck to scrape a blood sample out of the back. He hadn't gotten any closer to finding out who was shooting at Jordon. He hadn't been able to track down the men who had terrorized her the other night. He hadn't, in short, done a hell of a lot.

Which rankled him almost as badly as Harris's warning had.

He stared into the snapping flames for a moment or two, then closed the screen and walked back to the big armchair where he'd been sitting when Harris had dropped by unexpectedly. His glass of Scotch was on the table, untouched. He lifted it and took a swallow, savoring the twelve-year-old liquor as it slid silkenly down his throat, and thinking, idly, of Harris's threat.

If it had been a threat.

Thinking, too, of Jordon.

Sooner or later he was going to have to make a decision about her. About whether to tell her who he was, or not to tell her. About whether the chemistry between them was real, or merely some potent mix of mutual fascination and loneliness and maybe a little curiosity. And what he intended to do about it if it was real. About whether, too, to continue his search for the truth about her relationship with Alec, or simply to let it lie.

He rubbed his stubbled face wearily. If he went according to the rule book on this one, he'd take his losses and retreat while he still could.

And the reasons were simple. He wasn't going to like what he was going to find out about Alec, he already knew that. And getting involved with Jordon on anything but a purely professional level was just asking for trouble.

So it didn't make any sense to sit here and tease himself with the idea of getting in the truck and driving the long and occasionally treacherous seventy or so miles to where she was living. To knock on the door of her trailer and invite himself in for the cup of coffee they'd both know was only an excuse. To taunt himself even further with the thought of taking her to bed and making love to her with the desperate need of a drowning man trying to save himself, telling himself virtuously the whole while that he was only doing it for her. . . .

A log snapped in the fire and Kel started badly, his heart rate soaring for the half instant it took him to realize what it was. Swearing, he relaxed again and gave his head a shake, putting Jordon firmly from his mind. He'd deal with that whole complicated mess later. Right now, he had a murder to worry about. . . .

It was Murphy who heard them first.

Jordon was checking the baby eagle she'd found the day before, and was still by the big wire cages she'd had built near the storage shed. The eaglet, just a large round ball of grey fuzz that would have been cute if it hadn't had the temperament of a rattlesnake, was still hissing like a steam engine at the indignity of being handled, and Jordon was nursing a bruise on the back of her hand where the bird had stabbed her with its beak.

Murphy had at first been fascinated with both it and the injured adult bald eagle in the other cage, but he'd wandered off finally, and the last Jordon had seen of him, he was rolling luxuriously in a patch of grass, big feet waving in the air, pausing to snap at the occasional bee that wandered too near.

She had just closed the door to the eagle cage when she heard him start to bark. He was standing facing the road leading up to the trailer, paws widespread and braced, and his barking took on a tone of unmistakable warning as he settled into a deep-chested bay of alarm that made her stomach knot.

Not bothering to wait to see who it was, she headed for the trailer at a sprint even as Murphy's barking became more frantic, and she hit the steps at a dead run and took them in two strides. Wrenching the door open, she bolted for the broom closet where she kept the rifle, her heart hammering so loudly it all but drowned out Murphy's furious barking.

It was only then that she recalled Kel's warning about getting trapped in the trailer—and he was right, she realized in growing panic. The thin walls of the trailer wouldn't stop anyone seriously intent on getting in, and if they decided to smoke or burn her out, she'd be helpless.

Swearing, she scooped up the extra box of rifle shells that Harris had insisted she keep on hand and ran back outside. She could hear the truck now, gears grinding as it came up the last steep incline to the clearing, and she paused just long enough to call sharply to Murphy as she headed for the tall trees behind the trailer.

He looked around and whined, then started into another furious bay of alarm as the sound of the truck got louder.

"Murphy! Come!" He'd be a clear target out there, too intent on protecting her to save himself if they started shooting. "Murph! Now!"

He whined loudly again, looking from her to the road, then he gave one last bark and galloped after her, obedience training winning out over instinct. Jordon had stopped behind a thicket of dogwood where she could see the clearing without being seen herself, and Murphy joined her, hackles up, vibrating with a rumbling growl.

"Settle down," Jordon told him tensely. "Lie down, Murph."

He did so immediately, whimpering a little, and Jordon squatted beside him and slipped her fingers under his collar to hold him still. "You're a good dog," she whispered, as much to calm herself as him. "Just settle down now...settle down."

The truck burst into the clearing with no warning at all, startling Jordon so badly she very nearly lost her grip on Murphy's collar when he lunged forward. But she managed to drag him down, silencing him with one sharp word as the truck roared up and in front of the trailer, spraying dirt and grass as the driver spun the vehicle into a tight curve.

The truck rocked to a stop, engine rumbling, and Jordon swallowed. It wasn't the same one the men from the other night had been driving—this was older, with a roll cage welded over the cab and a heavy-duty front bumper mounted with a winch and spotlights.

Perfect poachers' gear, she found herself thinking, keeping a firm grip on Murphy's collar. He was vibrating with tension, one long continuous growl rumbling through him, and the hair across his neck and shoulders was bristling.

"Hey! You!" The man's voice cracked through the morning heat, making Jordon flinch. Bud Murdoch! "I know you're in there!" He followed it with a string of obscenities, then a harsh laugh. "It'll be better for you if you just *stay* in that trailer," he shouted finally. "'Cause you're going to be next!"

The driver—Rolly Murdoch, probably—gunned the engine a time or two, then the truck started moving, wheeling around in a tight curve. Then, suddenly, the near door flew open and a body came tumbling out. It hit the ground and rolled a couple of times, lying still and twisted.

"You're next!" the voice shouted again. "Just stay outta the woods and mind your own business!"

Murphy was going half out of his mind by now, standing on his rear legs and pawing at the air, his bark just a strangled howl of rage as he pressed his full weight against the collar restraining him. Jordon swore, convinced she could feel her arm pulling from its socket as she struggled to hold on to him, then the truck tore out of the clearing and back the way it had come and Murphy gave a fierce lunge that ripped the collar out of her fingers.

He was gone, just a streak of black-and-tan that was across the clearing and after the vanishing truck like a missile. An instant later Jordon was on her feet and pelting after him, able to see nothing but the figure lying crumpled on the ground in front of her trailer.

It was a man, limp and lying facedown. She skidded to a stop beside him, half-afraid of what she was going to see. Gritting her teeth, she knelt beside him and put her hand against the pulse on his neck, relieved to find it steady...he was alive, at least.

But how badly was he hurt? She swallowed, wondering if she should check him for injuries or just cover him with a blanket, then radio for help. His hair was thick and dark and tangled, caked with blood on one side, and Jordon leaned across so she could see his strong profile, already knowing who it was.

"Kel. Oh, my God, Kel...what have they done to you?"

Murph came back just then, panting hard and caked with mud. Whining, he nudged Kel's unconscious form with his nose, then threw his head up and gave a couple of deep barks and looked at Jordon as though she should be doing something.

But what? Frantically, trying to stay calm, Jordon searched her memory for what they'd taught her in that arduous week-long first aid and survival course that World First had insisted she take. At the time, not realizing how isolated the location was, how alone she was going to be, she'd thought it a little dramatic. But right now, looking down at Kel, she breathed a prayer of thanks.

Bleeding...she had to check for bleeding, then make certain he wasn't going to choke or injure himself further by flailing around if he started to regain consciousness. Then she had to—

He groaned. And then, astonishingly, he rolled over, swearing in a thick, pain-dulled voice. His eyes opened slowly and he gazed at her, then one corner of his mouth lifted very slightly in what might have been an attempt at a smile. "Going to invite me in for a drink?"

Jordon closed her eyes for an instant, relief making her light-headed. "Sure. I guess your friends couldn't stay."

"Hell, I thought they were friends of yours." He tried to laugh but it turned into a groan and he winced, struggling to sit up. "Help me up...I want to be ready for them if they come back."

"They're not coming back. This wasn't personal—you were meant to be a message."

"They couldn't just phone?"

"Will you lie still!" Frowning, Jordon planted her hand on his shoulder and tried to hold him prone. "You could be seriously hurt and—"

"Nothin's broke, if that's what you mean." He groaned. "Bent a little, but not broke. And most of this blood isn't mine...." He poked at his torn, blood-stained shirtfront. "I got a couple of good shots in, but there were too many of them." He grasped her hand and squeezed it gently, then ignored her protests and sat up, teeth clenched.

"Kel—"

"I'm all right, Jory. Come on, help me up...we can't stay out here all day."

In the end, it wasn't as difficult as she thought it would be. He was able to stand on his own, and together they staggered unsteadily across to the trailer and up the three steps and inside, although Jordon didn't release her grip on him until they were in the bedroom. Then she maneuvered him as close to the bed as she could, and he sank down onto it with a groan.

"I should take you into town so you can get those ribs x-rayed," she said worriedly, starting to unlace his heavy hiking boots. "You could be bleeding inside, Kel. Or—"

"Trust me, Jory, it's not half as bad as it looks. They weren't trying to kill me, it was just payback."

"I'm sorry you got caught up in this." She peeled his socks off, then moved around the bed and started unbuttoning his shirt. "Your job's dangerous enough without having those idiots running interference."

"Yeah, well, it comes with the territory." Although how this fit into why he was up here—the poaching, Jimmie's death—was anyone's guess, Kel thought wearily. The Murdoch brothers and two of their friends had ambushed him up by Hanging Rock Ridge and had systematically set about beating the hell out of him. Although, in retrospect, it could have been a lot worse. They could have crippled him and left him to die. Or simply tossed him over the nearest cliff and had done with him.

Jordon was right—it *had* been just a warning. But for his benefit . . . or for hers?

Jordon vanished, then came back a couple of minutes later with an enamel washbasin and a cloth. Sitting on the side of the bed, she proceeded to wash the blood from his face and hair, exclaiming angrily now and again. Her touch was sure and incredibly gentle and after a minute or two Kel let his eyes slide closed, content to lie quietly while she worked over him. He should be getting back to the lodge, he thought idly. Being here with Jordon wasn't only compromising his cover, it could be putting her in danger. But it was nice just lying there relaxed and almost comfortable while she eased his shirt off, letting the weariness and aches and pain fall away under the delicate touch of her small hands.

The pillowcase smelled of her, a feminine scent of shampoo and lotion and sweet female skin, and he found himself watching her as she examined the worst of the bruises on his midriff, loving the silken sheen of her thick hair in the sunlight, the way her neck curved, wondering very idly what it would be like to fall in love with a woman like this. To have her in his life forever. To make love with her. To have children with her...

Hell, next he'd be contemplating that house in the country he and Denise had fought over, the one with the wading pool for the kids and the little garden and the swing in the backyard....

It was only then that he realized her small hands were on the button of his waistband and he watched her through half-closed eyes as she slipped it free, his chest tightening at the evocative touch of her hands. And very suddenly he knew that if he weren't careful, all his newly made good intentions about this woman weren't going to amount to a hill of beans. There was something about her that just made him want to gather her up in his arms and lose himself in her... something he didn't understand... didn't *want* to understand....

Managing a rough laugh, he caught both her hands in his. "I think I'd better warn you before you go any farther... I'm not wearing anything under these jeans."

A flood of pink washed across her cheeks, making her more beautiful than ever. "I'm sorry. I thought you might be more comfortable with them ... off."

"I didn't say I wouldn't be," he teased gently. "I just figured you might want to know what you're getting yourself into."

"I appreciate that," she said with a hint of a smile. "Maybe you'd better leave them on."

"For the time being, at any rate." His eyes held hers for a heartbeat longer than they needed to, and Kel knew she was thinking the same thing he was. Knew, too, that if he was even half as smart as he thought he was, he'd damn well better make sure they *stayed* on.

"Try to get some sleep," she said quietly, pulling a light quilt over him. "The best thing you can do right now is rest. I'll try to get the RCMP on the radio and have them send someone up to get your statement. Then—"

"No." Just reaching out to catch her wrist in his hand took more effort than he realized. "That'll cause more problems than it solves, Jordon. I'll take care of the Murdochs—legally—when this is over. In the meantime, I can't afford to do anything that might jeopardize my cover."

She nodded unhappily, frowning, and Kel smiled and reached up to tap her chin with his bruised knuckle. "I'm as tough as old boot leather, Jory. A few hours' rest and I'll be back to normal. Don't look so worried."

"I *am* worried. These people killed Jimmie because he got too close. They won't think twice about killing you."

"They'll find me a hell of a lot harder to take out than Jimmie Two Shoes," Kel said with quiet deadliness.

"I hope so."

There was something in Jordon's dark eyes as she said it that made Kel's heart give an odd little twist, and he frowned. He shouldn't be teasing himself like this, he told himself. Shouldn't be thinking the unthinkable. They had no future—*could* have no future. And yet... a man could dream, couldn't he? "When this is all over—when I've pulled the plug on this poaching operation and you're finished messing around with your eagles—I'd like to spend time with you, Jordon Walker."

"I'd like that, too."

Her eyes were as warm as a summer's afternoon, and Kel felt that little twist again, tried to tell himself it was probably just a pulled muscle. "And there are some things we have to talk about. Things about me. Things you might not... like."

"About your wife?"

He blinked. "How did you know I'd been married?"

She smiled a little. "A woman knows all the signs. The only question is, are you married now?"

"No." He smiled slightly and ran his scarred knuckle across her lower lip. "Not for a long time now. It was...short, and not particularly sweet. I was looking for something that didn't exist, she was looking for everything I couldn't give her and one day we just called it quits."

She was holding his other hand and she stroked the bloodied knuckles gently. "Did you have children?"

"No. That's one of the things we disagreed about." His voice was rough and Jordon gave him a questioning look. He smiled bitterly. "She wanted them. I didn't. There wasn't a lot of room for compromise."

"Do you think your decision had anything to do with..." She hesitated, frowning as though chosing her words carefully.

"With the way I felt about my brother?" he asked roughly. "It probably had everything to do with it, although I didn't realize it then. By the time I figured it out, it was too late. Denise was gone and I was...used to being alone, I guess. I had a lot of growing up to do. A lot of things to sort out."

"And did you finally? Sort it all out?"

"Some of it. Most of it." All but some of the dirty little corners of it, he thought wearily. All but one or two secrets he might never know the answers to. May never *want* the answers to...

"Do you think you'll have kids one day? If you find the right woman?"

Kel smiled. "Is this going to be an offer I won't be able to resist?" It was strange, thinking about sharing a houseful of kids with this woman. Strange how right it felt.

Jordon laughed. "Would you like it to be?"

It was one of those flippant, off-the-cuff things that people say all the time without meaning anything by it, and yet Kel's stomach tightened.

There was a long, static silence between them, fraught with a thousand possibilities. It occurred very dimly to Kel that he ought to say something to defuse the situation then and there—that he should invent a convenient live-in lover or some other long-term complication that would put paid to whatever was happening between them. That he should just blurt out his real identity and get it over with, quick and bloody and final.

Yet he found himself oddly reluctant to end it. Hated thinking of going through the rest of his life knowing he'd been this close to heaven and let it slip away.... And so instead of answering her he simply reached up and pulled her down and into his arms, and when her lips found his and parted sweetly for his kiss, he ignored the voice in the back of his mind screaming about betrayal and lies....

He kissed her as long as he dared, slowly and deeply, his tongue moving languorously against hers as he teased himself with the thought of saying to hell with it and putting both of them out of their misery by making love to her once and for all. It couldn't be wrong, another voice whispered temptingly. She was as willing as he was and they were both consenting adults and how could anything that felt so right be wrong...she'd never even have to know about Alec....

He sensed the change in her almost at the same time she sensed it in him, although probably for another reason, and they pulled away from each other slowly. Kel's blood was pounding in his temples and he eased a tight breath out between his clenched teeth. "Damn."

Jordon laughed quietly. "You always say the sweetest things when this happens, Kel Stuart."

It made him laugh, as it was probably meant to, and he winced as his bruised ribs gave a silent shout of protest. "And it seems to happen a lot."

"True." She looked at him, still smiling although her eyes were serious now. "You said a while ago that you didn't want any complications in your life, Kel. I should tell you that I'm not sure I do, either. So whatever happens..." She shrugged, letting her gaze slide from his. "What I'm trying to say is that you don't have to worry about this getting serious or anything. I've been living my life one day at a time for the past couple of years, and I've started to like it that way. So we don't have to spend a lot of time worrying about where it will lead. It doesn't have to lead anywhere."

If only he could believe it would be that easy. "These things have a way of getting out of hand, Jordon. I want you—I'm not going to lie and tell you otherwise. But if we make love it is *going* to get complicated. Don't kid yourself. And I don't want you getting into something you think you can handle, then finding out later that you wish you hadn't, that's all. I'm just scared you're going to be hurt. And I don't like the idea that it's going to be me doing the hurting."

"If I thought you were going to hurt me, Kel, you wouldn't have gotten within a mile of me. I was victimized two years ago by a man I trusted, but one thing it taught me was to listen to my instincts. If I'd done that with Alec Davies, he'd never have been able to lay a hand on me. So the only reason you're in my bed right now—albeit innocently," she added with a flash of a smile, "is because I've said it's all right for you to be there." She put her finger across his lips as though to keep him from speaking. "Now get some rest. I'll be in the other room if you need anything."

She left then, leaving Kel lying there thinking about everything she'd said, and everything she hadn't. Thinking about hearing Alec's name—for the first time—on her lips. Thinking about how in God's name he was ever going to be able to make things right...or why he thought he needed to.

He was still thinking about Alec when sleep ambushed him, and he drifted down into it restlessly, wondering if he'd ever know the answers to even half the questions life was handing him.

Chapter 8

Kel slept for hours.

Jordon spent the afternoon getting caught up on paper-work, pausing now and again to tiptoe into the bedroom and check on him. He'd been restless at first, but then he'd fallen into a sound sleep that she figured was exactly what he needed.

She was out at the eagle cage behind the trailer when she heard the shower come on, and a few minutes later, he came out looking for her. He was limping slightly and there was a scrape and a swelling bruise on his right cheekbone, and his left eye looked a little tender. But aside from those and a few bruises on his rib cage, he looked almost normal.

Late-afternoon sunlight glittered on beads of water in his hair, and his broad shoulders were still wet. He'd pulled his jeans on but hadn't bothered putting on a shirt, and as he limped toward her, half-naked and tousled and slightly rav-aged, Jordon wondered if he had any idea how damned sexy he looked—bruises, black eye and all.

He grinned a little lopsidedly, wincing slightly as though he'd forgotten the cut on his lower lip. "I figured you'd gone out to fall off cliffs or out of trees or something."

She had to laugh. "This job isn't all fun and games. How do you feel?"

"Like I got hit by a truck. How long was I out?"

"About five hours." She grinned at his expression. "Feel up to earning your keep? I could use a hand with this thing."

The *thing* she was struggling with gave a loud and very indignant squawk just then and splattered her liberally with ground up meat and fish oil. Jordon gave a sputter of disgust and wiped her face with her arm, trying to keep clear of the young eagle's razor-sharp beak.

Kel winced, but nodded gamely. "Sure. What do I do?"

"Just hold it while I shove the rest of its supper down its ungrateful throat." Jordon grinned at Kel's good-natured groan. "And watch its beak—the wretched thing snaps like an alligator."

Kel put his hands around the baby eagle's fuzzy midsection, turning his face away. "Whew! Couldn't you study something that didn't smell like a garbage scow at high noon?"

"*Eau de* rancid fish," Jordon quipped. "All the rage among the environmentalist set this year." She filled the big syringe with the soupy mix of meat, fish oil and vitamins, then attached the long rubber tube to the end and approached the young eagle again. "It's going to throw a fit when I slide this tube down its throat, so hang on tight."

Kel eyed the syringe apparatus. "You're kidding, right?"

"Trust me, pumping the stuff directly into its stomach beats trying to feed it by hand. Are you hanging on?"

"Yeah," Kel muttered unhappily. "Where did it come from?"

"I found it under a nest over by Ghost Creek." Jordon slipped the rubber tube into the eagle's beak and down its throat so deftly it didn't even have time to squawk. "There were three eggs, which is quite rare. And all three hatched, which is even more rare. The smallest hatchling died in just a few days, then the stronger of the remaining two pitched this guy out." She smiled grimly as she continued to feed the bird.

"Young eagles are textbook examples of survival of the fittest. If two of them hatch and survive, they spend most of their babyhood trying to kill each other. It's quite common to find the remains of a baby eagle under a nest. The strongest passes on those survival genetics to the next generation."

She slipped Kel an amused glance. "Sort of like the sibling rivalry between you and your brother when you were kids. The struggle for attention from the parent is strong in all species."

His smile was bitter. "Yeah. Only in my case the one who got tossed out survived, and the other one didn't."

Jordon looked at him curiously, deftly avoiding the eagle's sharp beak as it made a stab at her hand. "Do you mean that literally?"

"Literally enough. Al had some trouble with a girl, I got blamed . . . the consensus of opinion was that it was time I packed up and got out of town." A muscle pulsed along the side of Kel's jaw, and he stared down at the struggling eagle, his face dark with anger. "I should have stood up for myself, but at the time it was easier to just go. I was tired of being known as the bad seed. Tired of having Al's perfection thrown at me every time I turned around, tired of the fighting, the lies." He looked up at her, his smile ragged. "So I decided that if I couldn't compete with him, I'd leave and be the best at something else. I joined the navy and never looked back."

"And were you the best at what you did?"

He grinned suddenly, the anger in his eyes vanishing under honest amusement. "I guess I did pretty good. Nearly got myself killed a time or two trying to prove it, though, until I realized I could finally stop competing with him.''

"It must be hard being on the receiving end of stuff like that," Jordon said softly. "In my family it was me who was held up as the example of what kids *should* be like—I always got great marks and did well at everything I tried…the usual. My brother and sister must have hated me, I'm sure." She looked at the eagle thoughtfully. "This is a terrible thing to say, but I sometimes felt that during the…well, the trouble I had at college, they were…glad." She looked up at Kel. "I know they weren't—I *know* they love me. And yet…" She shrugged, looking away.

And Kel, chilled to the marrow, said nothing. He knew that feeling. Knew it a little too well, in fact. And found himself suddenly wondering if Jordon's brother and sister lay awake nights, fighting the guilt. Knowing that the satisfaction they'd felt at her fall from grace, however momentary, was going to haunt them to the end of their lives.

Kel must have unintentionally tightened his grip on the young eagle, because it suddenly gave a squawk and started struggling. It shook its head wildly and dislodged the feeding tube, and Kel swore, glad of the distraction. "What the hell are you going to do with this thing? Turn it into a house pet?''

"Presuming I was crazy enough to try, it's illegal to keep wild animals without a special permit." She laughed quietly, giving him a mischievous look. "Mind you, if I were half the scientist I'm pretending to be, I'd have let nature take its course. But…I decided to save its scrawny little neck instead. And *this* is what I get for thanks." She gestured at her fish-drenched shirt and jeans.

"I'll keep it until it's strong enough to travel, then I'll send it down to Vancouver Island. There's a wildlife recovery and rehabilitation center just outside Parksville that specializes in eagles—they take in sick and injured birds from all over North America. They release as many as they can back into the wild, and any that can't survive on their own are kept and cared for. I support them in any way I can. This little guy will be the third bald eagle I've sent them. That's where Black Jack's going, too."

Kel looked at the big full-grown bald eagle in the flight cage just behind them. The bird was sitting quietly on a branch of the dead tree that acted as a perch, the baleful glint in its golden eyes making Kel's neck prickle. "What's his problem?"

"Lead poisoning."

"The eating kind, or the getting shot kind?"

"Both. Coastal eagles ingest lead fishing weights from the fish they catch, and they eat a lot of carrion and wind up taking in lead shot from dead birds and so on, as well. And," she added with anger in her voice, "they get shot pretty regularly. Over sixty percent of the eagle fatalities in this part of the country are from gunshot. The woods are full of trigger-happy cowboys who call themselves 'hunters' who go around blasting at anything that swims, walks or flies."

"And Black Jack?"

"I found him out on Desperation Point with a broken wing and spent three days trying to catch him. He was peppered with shot—someone had blasted him with a shotgun a few times." Her eyes flashed. "Unfortunately you don't have to have an intelligence test to buy a gun in this country."

Kel gave a grunt. Whoever had shot Jimmie Two Shoes hadn't been very bright, either. Killing bald eagles was one thing; killing government agents put a whole different spin on the situation. "Speaking of idiots with guns, has anyone been shooting at you lately?"

"No." She sounded pleasantly surprised.

"Keep it that way," he growled. "Can I let go of this thing now?"

"Not yet. I want to band it." She was already slipping a metal band out of a small envelope. "Okay, tuck him under your arm like this—" she showed him what she wanted "—then hang on to his neck so he can't bite me." After checking that the number on the band was the same as on the envelope, she started gently securing it to the eagle's leg using a pair of pliers.

Watching her, Kel had to smile. She seemed completely oblivious to the fact that she was covered with reeking smears of fish oil and ground-up salmon, or that her sunburned nose was peeling or that her hair was knotted and tangled. He wondered if she ever missed her well-ordered life at college, or if that part of her had simply been put away and forgotten.

"Okay—you can let it go now." She opened the spacious wire cage and stood back to let Kel maneuver the struggling bird through the door.

The instant he released it, the eagle scooted into the far corner and puffed itself up, hissing like a snake. "Damn good thing it's not up to me whether it gets fed again or not." He closed the door and locked it. "How long is Mr. Personality going to be with you, anyway?"

"Just another day or two." Jordon grinned happily at him. "Want to stick around and help?"

"Not on your life. I'll stink of fish oil for the rest of the week as it is." He wiped at a smear on his bare chest. "I'd rather take my chances with the poachers."

Jordon frowned slightly as she dismantled the syringe and hose and dropped them into a bucket of soapy water by her feet. She dipped a cloth into the water and wiped her hands and bare arms, and when she was finished, she handed the cloth to Kel. "You, uh...were going to get a sample of that blood in the back of John's truck and bring it to me. No luck?"

Kel wiped the fish oil from his chest and hands. "I got it." He paused, looking down at her carefully. "I sent it to the FBI. They'll test it and get back to me."

"The FBI?" She got to her feet slowly, her eyes suddenly cool. "I see." She swished the feeding apparatus in the water, then took it out and tossed the water into a patch of weeds. "Afraid I wouldn't tell you the truth?"

Kel looked at her calmly. "The possibility crossed my mind."

"I like John Harris. But I wouldn't lie to protect someone involved in Jimmie Two Shoes's murder, either."

"I said the possibility crossed my mind—not that I took it seriously. I sent the sample to the FBI because technically this case is theirs. And because they have state-of-the-art labs, and I didn't want to take a chance on missing something. And," he added evenly, "because I didn't want to put you in danger. If Harris is involved—and I'm not saying he is—and he found out that you were instrumental in the investigation, it could mean trouble for you. And you seem fully capable of getting into just about all the trouble you can handle without *my* help."

She nodded again, her gaze still speculative. Then she smiled wanly and wiped her hair back from her forehead with her arm. "I think you're wrong about John. But I also think you'd be negligent if you didn't follow up every lead. And I trust you to be fair. Regardless of how you feel about him personally."

Kel fell into step beside Jordon as she headed for the trailer. Fair? Up to a point, maybe, he thought a little malevolently as he prodded the split in his lower lip with his tongue. But if he found out that Harris had sent the Murdochs after him to make the warning about steering clear of Jordon stick, he was going to take it *very* personally.

"Hungry?"

Kel glanced down to find Jordon looking at him. "Depends what you had in mind." He gestured toward the bucket and feeding syringe. "I prefer my salmon barbecued, and I like to eat it with a fork."

Jordon laughed. "You're in luck. Your good friend John Harris dropped off a fresh salmon last night, and there's a charcoal barbecue in the storage shed. Do you want to play gourmet cook, or shall I?"

"I'll do it," Kel said decisively, wanting to take no chances on getting eagle vitamins mixed in with his barbecue sauce. "Besides," he added with a none-too-subtle look at her clothing, "it'll give you a chance to get cleaned up."

"Are you saying I stink?" Her eyes glowed with mischief.

"Let's just say," Kel drawled, dropping a companionable arm around her shoulders, "that you'd stand out in a crowd."

They ate by candlelight, more to save diesel fuel than for any romantic reasons, Jordon told herself virtuously, and drank most of a bottle of surprisingly good wine that she'd bought on a whim the last time she'd been in town. Kel had grilled the salmon to perfection, and Jordon discovered one corner of her garden that the deer and raccoons had missed and was able to retrieve enough young lettuce and tomatoes and herbs to make a green salad. The baby carrots with fresh rosemary and ginger had been a collaborative effort and Jordon, inspired, had created a dessert from a handful of small sour apples and a bag of trail mix that rivaled anything she'd tasted in a restaurant.

They went for a walk later, getting as far as the lake before being driven back inside by the mosquitoes and the chilly mountain air. Then Kel started a fire in the small round wood stove in the living room and Jordon curled up on the old sofa with Murphy at her feet. They sat like that for hours, just talking and laughing quietly as the night drew in around them, filled with the sound of crickets and frogs and the mutter of the fire.

And it was sometime during the evening that Jordon, sleepy with firelight and wine and more relaxed and happy than she had been in too long to remember, started to realize that more was going on than just two people sharing supper and a bottle of wine.

Whatever it was, it had less to do with the wine and the easy small talk than it did with the way Kel would look at her when he thought she wouldn't see, his gaze tracing every detail of her features as though committing them to memory. Or the way her heart would give an unruly little thump every time she'd look at him and their eyes would meet, and there would be a sudden, taut silence that always left her feeling dizzy and a bit breathless, wondering if the dark and slightly dangerous things she saw in Kel's expression were real or merely wishful thinking.

She'd been contemplating this for some time, lost in a fog of warm and vaguely erotic thoughts, when she felt Kel stir beside her. He leaned across to retrieve the nearly empty bottle of wine from the coffee table, then poured half of what remained into her glass and the rest into his own.

Stretching sleepily, she smiled and lifted her glass in a toast. "To a most enjoyable evening, good sir."

"To the Murdoch brothers," he said with a grin, touching the rim of his glass to hers. "If they hadn't taken time out from their busy day to beat the hell out of me and dump me on your doorstep this morning, I'd be in my room at the lodge right now, alone, up to my ears in reports and computer printouts."

"You make it sound as though you're almost enjoying yourself."

"I am." His gaze held hers just long enough to make Jordon's heart give another of those funny little back flips, then he smiled and rested his feet on the coffee table, wincing slightly as he moved too quickly. "Not in any rush to get rid of me, are you?"

Jordon let her eyes trace the strong outline of his profile, musing idly at how comfortable it was seeing him there. "No. But if you want to get back to town tonight, we should leave before long."

He turned his head to look at her, his eyes capturing hers in the soft candlelight, and for a moment neither of them said a thing.

Not that either of them had to, Jordon thought with an inward smile. The words were hanging between them as though written in neon; all she had to do was acknowledge them, and the rest would be a foregone conclusion.

A smile played around Kel's strong mouth, tipping one corner up beguilingly, and his eyes held hers, all smoky and warm. "If you take me into town tonight, it's going to mean driving back up here alone. At night. I don't like that idea at all."

"So it would make more sense if you stayed the night."

"It would seem so."

The silence spilled around them, taut as wire. "If I say yes to the question you're not asking," she said very softly, "is it going to mean what I think it means?"

"Would you like it to?" he replied just as softly.

"I think . . . I might."

Kel smiled. "It only means what you want it to mean, Jory. We talked about complications once, remember."

"I know." Jordon felt her own mouth lift in a responding smile. "But I can't remember what conclusion we came to."

Kel's laugh was lazy, and he reached out to stroke her hair with his fingertips, his touch making Jordon's heart leap. "For the life of me, neither can I." But then, suddenly, some of the laughter left his eyes and he looked at her for a long, silent while, his expression curiously pensive. He turned a strand of her hair between his fingers, the frown wedged between his brows deepening. "I think I'd better stick with the sofa again. For now, at least."

It wasn't what she'd wanted to hear, Jordon realized in frustration. She frowned, wanting to say more—so much more—and not knowing how. She was out of her depth here, she thought disconsolately. Sex and all the male-female politics that went with it had been a mystery she'd never entirely mastered, and now with everything that had happened over the past couple of years, she was more uncertain, more bewildered, than ever.

Did he expect her to simply agree and start talking about something else as though the topic had never come up? Or was he waiting for her to ask him in no uncertain terms to sleep with her? Or was there more to it than that? Some complicated array of signals and rituals that he took for granted that she knew and was waiting for expectantly?

"I wish—" She took a deep breath, looking up to meet his gaze evenly. "I wish I were one of those wonderfully brash women who could simply take you by the hand and lead you into the bedroom. It would sure simplify things!"

Kel's gaze burned into hers and for an instant Jordon thought he was going to toss the wineglass aside and simply scoop her up in his arms and that would be the end of it then and there. But at the last moment he relaxed slightly, his breath hissing between his teeth. "Don't be too sure of that." His voice was rough. "Damn it, Jordon, I'm not trying to pretend to be a saint here or anything—I'm just trying like hell to keep things from exploding until we've both had time to think it over."

"I know." She smiled at him, wondering what he'd say if she told him how many nights she'd lain awake thinking it over. Or how many times she'd found herself lost in thought during the day, her mind filled with wistfully erotic daydreams. She'd have to thank him one day, she mused with a secret smile. Even if things between them never got steamier than the few overheated caresses they'd already shared, he'd given her back something she'd thought had been stolen from her forever.

She sat up a little straighter, pushing the thoughts from her firmly. "I should do the dishes and clean up, I guess. And dig out some towels and sheets, and—"

"They'll keep." Kel caught her wrist as she started to stand up. "This is the first candlelight-and-wine dinner I've spent with a beautiful woman in a long time, Jordon. I don't want to end it just yet."

Jordon had to laugh as she settled back onto the sofa beside him. "You've got a point. I usually grab whatever's handy and eat it while checking my observation sheets or writing up my daily reports or filling in forms of one kind or another. I can't remember the last time I just relaxed with a glass of wine and—" She caught herself, smiling, and looked at him. "Tonight really has been special, Kel. If I'd known you were such a whiz with the barbecue, I'd have invited you for supper days ago. It's been a long time since I've done the candlelight-and-wine routine, too."

Kel chuckled. "I can see where living up here would cut into your social life, all right."

Jordon tipped her wineglass so it caught the light from the candle on the table beside her, and watched the sparkles play along the rim. "It's not just that. I haven't . . . socialized at all since—" She hesitated, then decided to simply say it and get it over with. "It's been two years since I was attacked, and I haven't gone out with a man in all that time. Haven't even spent an evening like this with one."

"Something like that takes a long time to get over." Kel's face was curiously hard-edged in the candlelight, and a muscle pulsed along his jaw as though he were holding back his anger.

"It wasn't being . . . raped that did it. Not directly, anyway. After the trial I started having panic attacks—I couldn't go to a restaurant or a theater, couldn't even walk down a city street a lot of the time. I didn't want to be around people—I kept thinking they were looking at me, saying things about me." She gave a quiet laugh suddenly.

"Pretty neurotic, I know. But I just wanted to be left alone."

He turned his head to look at her, his eyes curiously shuttered in the flickering light. "What happened at the trial?"

A chill walked across Jordon's shoulders. "I got raped again," she said bluntly. "In public, this time. It happens all the time, of course. My lawyer told me that probably ninety percent of all the rapes that occur never get reported because the women involved know that even if it *does* go to trial, the nightmare is only starting."

"So the man...involved...got off?"

"The man *involved* was practically lionized. By the time it was over, he was made out to be the poor innocent victim, and *I* was the guilty one."

Kel reached across and slipped his hand over one of hers, braiding their fingers, and Jordon held it tightly. "It was my own fault, of course. I did everything wrong right from the beginning, so I shouldn't be surprised at how it turned out."

"What do you mean, it was your fault?" The pressure of his hand increased just slightly.

"I...did everything you're not supposed to do." Jordon stared down at his hand, running her fingertips across his knuckles. They were bruised and slightly swollen from his fight with the Murdochs and she found herself thinking of that night in the lab. Of how, had she fought, a few bruised, cut knuckles might have made all the difference in the outcome of the trial.

"He caught me so by surprise that I didn't fight, for one thing. And it was over so quickly, I didn't... I was in shock, I guess. It never occurred to me to...to scratch him or hit him or something. To leave marks." She swallowed. "If it ever happens again, I'll make damn certain I antagonize the man to the point where he hits me just so I have something to show at the trial."

Kel swore under his breath, one short, savage oath that made Jordon blink. His face was hard and almost cruel in the fluttering candlelight. "Are you telling me he got away with raping you because the jury wanted *bruises?*"

"Partly. The primary point in his favor was that I didn't report it right away. That night—the night it happened—I just wanted to crawl into a cave and pull it in after me. After he drove me home, I—"

"He drove you home?" Kel's voice made Murphy look up in alarm from where he'd been napping in front of the wood stove.

"I know it sounds bizarre," Jordon whispered. "I—I knew him, you see. And it all happened so fast, so unexpectedly, that I just…froze. He told me quite calmly not to bother reporting what had happened, then he drove me home as though nothing *had* happened. Even walked me to the door of my dorm and gave me a little kiss on the cheek. I…." She closed her eyes.

"Jory?" Kel's voice was soft. "We don't have to talk about this if—"

"Yeah. I do." She took a deep breath and opened her eyes, looking at him quite calmly. "I do, Kel. It's…not for you. It's for me."

He didn't want to hear the rest of it, Kel told himself numbly. Didn't want to have to sit here and pretend he knew nothing about it, didn't want to have to watch the pain in her eyes as she relived the nightmare, all the while knowing it had been Alec's fault.

And his, too, maybe, he thought dimly. If he hadn't let Alec get away with his tricks and lies right back when they'd been kids, maybe he could have stopped all this. Maybe Alec would have had a chance. Maybe…

"I wish I could have been there for you." He heard the words, and only then realized they were his. "I'd have killed him, Jory," he said very softly. "I swear I'd have tracked him down and killed him." And for the space of the time it took to say the words, Kel knew he meant it. And it scared him, how easily he said the unsayable, thought the unthinkable. He stared down at his own hands, at the bloodied, scarred knuckles, and shivered.

"So he just walked away that night."

"I should have called the police and had him arrested," she said raggedly. "Every woman knows that. But I didn't. I was so stunned that it had happened at all that after a while I actually started to doubt it *had*. I can't explain it—heaven knows, I've tried often enough. To the police, to my lawyer, to the court, to my parents...but the very idea that Dr. Alec Davies had raped me was so preposterous that my mind just wouldn't accept it."

Even braced for hearing Alec's name, Kel felt his gut twist. He drew in a deep, calming breath and forced himself to relax.

"All I wanted was a long, hot shower. Then I took everything I'd been wearing down to the laundry room and washed it all. It wasn't until the next afternoon—just before I was supposed to go to Davies's class—that I knew I had to report it. The thought of going into that room and facing him...I couldn't do it. So I called the police."

"And they arrested him."

"Eventually. The fact it actually got as far as the courtroom was more a function of my lawyer's wizardry than anything I did or said. I didn't have a mark on me to prove he'd even touched me. The medical exam proved only that I'd..." She paused and looked down at their braided fingers. "That I'd had sexual relations with a man in the previous twenty-four hours. But, as the medical examiner pointed out, that didn't prove anything. I was a healthy, normal twenty-six-year-old woman...."

"But damn it," Kel blurted out in exasperation, "didn't your word count for *anything?*"

"Davies was an esteemed and highly respected doctor of biology at an equally esteemed and highly regarded university. He was married, had a family. He was up for a promotion. He had a ton of character witnesses, all of them stuffy and pedantic and very, very establishment. He knew six dozen other influential types, from politicians to a judge, all of whom were willing to vouch for his character.''

"And then there was you.''

"And then there was me. The teaching assistant. Young and reasonably attractive and, if you believed Alec Davies, willing to do anything to make sure I got my degree. Including trading sex for a good recommendation to the department head. Or failing that, blackmail.'' Bitterness ran through the words like ice water. "I'm not even sure my lawyer believed me. I know no one else did. The media had a field day with it, of course.''

That was an understatement, Kel thought. He'd watched tapes of those news reports.

"After a while," Jordon said softly, "I started to doubt what had happened myself. I started thinking that maybe I *had* done something wrong, that maybe I'd let him think—'' She shrugged. "Even my parents and my sister and brother doubted me—I could see it in their eyes. My dad asked me one day if I was *sure* I'd never given Davies any wrong ideas. And my brother thought that maybe I'd just misinterpreted the whole thing.'' She gave a sob of laughter. "Misinterpreted! How in heaven's name can you *misinterpret* rape, can you tell me that?''

Kel swore wearily, rubbing his eyes with his free hand, and wondered how in God's name she'd ever gotten through it. Doubted by everyone she knew. Everyone she loved and trusted. Small wonder she'd headed up here into the middle of nowhere just to get away from them all.

"I think, in a way, that was the worst part. The attack itself was over in no time . . . but what happened afterward went on forever. The university board called me in a few weeks afterward and asked me—politely—to drop the charges against Alec. When I refused, they pushed a little harder. When I still refused, they suggested I continue my doctoral studies elsewhere.''

Chapter 9

The expression of betrayal and hurt in her eyes made Kel feel sick. Alec, something whispered, Alec did this. Just like he used to when you were kids, hurting, lying, betraying....

"And that's when you quit," he said roughly.

"I didn't have any choice—they circled the wagons and shut me out. If I hadn't quit voluntarily, they'd have found some other way to get me out. There are a dozen ways to get rid of a doctoral candidate who doesn't toe the party line. And being known for accusing your committee chairperson of rape can make serious inroads in your educational aspirations." She managed a fleeting smile. "And even if I *had* gotten my degree, then what? No university in the country would have taken me into their research program—there'd always be the worry that one of my colleagues would look at me the wrong way and I'd have *him* up on charges. And getting work in a private or industrial lab would have been as difficult."

"And all this just because you stood up for yourself."

"Universities take care of their own. But I must have upset someone, because Davies *was* brought in front of a review board and they never did give him his precious promotion. I think they believed more of my story than they'd ever admit in public."

Kel had his teeth gritted, anger licking through him. Anger at Alec, at himself, at the college for sacrificing Jordon to protect one of their own.

And it was only then, when something wet splashed onto the back of his hand, that he realized she was crying. He swore under his breath and reached for her even as she started to turn away.

"Oh...damn!" Jordon tried to laugh but a sob broke through and she swallowed with a gulp, putting her hand up to hold him off, knowing if she tried to speak she'd burst into tears.

"Jordon..." His voice was just a purr and she shook her head, chin wobbling treacherously as she tried to get to her feet. "Come on, Jory," he murmured, slipping his arms around her. "It's all right, sweetheart. It's all right."

She'd intended to make a run for the bathroom where she could hide out until she got herself back together. But he gave her a tug that pulled her off balance, and in the next instant she'd fallen back onto the sofa and into his arms and then running away didn't make any sense at all.

"Damn, damn, *damn!*" Her voice was muffled as she turned her face into the curve of his throat, valiantly fighting the tears. "This wasn't supposed to happen! Not anymore."

"Why not?"

"Because I'm over it, that's why! I haven't cried in over a year." Which wasn't true. She awoke in tears sometimes, crying in her sleep over things she couldn't remember later. And sometimes during the day she'd find herself crying over nothing at all.

Kel's fingers tightened on her shoulders. "You have a right to *hurt*, Jordon. A man raped you—a man you trusted. He stole something from you that no one is ever going to be able to replace. You can be hurt. You can be scared!"

"I *am* scared," she whispered brokenly. "I try not to be. I tell myself I don't have to be. Not anymore. But it's there all the time. And I just can't seem to shake it off."

"I know, Jory," he whispered. "I know. But it's going to take time. You're just going to have to give yourself time."

"But how long?" She squeezed her eyes against the tears, feeling one or two escape and trickle down her cheek. "I'm so tired of it! I just want to be normal again. I want to feel good when a man looks at me. I want to be able to get dressed up and wear high heels and not feel cheap and on display. I want to be able to be alone with a man and not be afraid. I want to be able to make love with him and not always be thinking of—"

"Rape doesn't have anything to do with sex," Kel growled. "And it has even less to do with making love. It's just about violence and power and control. You know that."

"Rationally. Logically. But—"

"No 'buts.' When the time's right, Jory, and when the man's right . . . everything will be fine. Trust me."

She didn't bother answering. He didn't understand, of course. How could he? How could he possibly know the paralyzing terror that gripped her whenever she thought of being in the lab that night with Alec Davies? The nightmare of being powerless and alone, of knowing there was absolutely nothing she could do. . . .

She shivered and turned her face against Kel's throat, forcing the images out of her mind. "I hope so," she whispered. "Oh, God, I hope so. . . ."

He dreamed about Alec that night. Dark, abstract dreams filled with anger and resentment, and he awoke two or three times to cast them off, only to find them waiting for him again when he slipped back into sleep. And when he awoke the final time, it was like coming up out of deep water, his breath tight, heart hammering, groping for air.

Swearing under his breath, he rolled onto his side angrily, kicking his feet free of the tangled sheet, and realized he wasn't alone.

Jordon was lying on top of the blanket beside him, wrapped in a flannel work shirt, watching him silently.

"What the hell . . . ?" Half-asleep, he scrubbed his fingers through his hair and raised up onto his elbow.

"I had a nightmare. I—" She swallowed, looking cold and miserable. "I was scared to try to go back to sleep. And I didn't want to be alone. I didn't mean to wake you."

"You didn't." No need to ask what her nightmare had been about. Alec was haunting them both tonight. "You're cold."

"I'm all right." She sat up, shivering so badly that Kel could see the spasms run through her. "I should go back to—"

"Stay." He caught her wrist without even thinking about what he was asking. Knowing only that he didn't want to spend the rest of the night alone. That she was cold and frightened, and that he could warm her. That they could warm each other.

"Kel, I don't know if—"

"Just to sleep, Jory," he said softly, wondering as he said the words if he meant them or was just trying to reassure her. Or himself. He had a feeling that he was asking for more trouble than he could handle, but ignored it. He wanted, just for a while, to feel her in his arms.

"All right."

He lifted the blanket and sheet and then, magically, she was there with him, sliding into his waiting arms without hesitation. Laughing, he hugged her against him. "You're frozen!"

"I didn't mean to stay so long," she whispered, nestling against him like a stray kitten seeking warmth. "I was going to make some tea, but I ... I just needed to know there was someone else here tonight. Someone ... safe."

It occurred to Kel, rubbing Jordon's flannel-clad back to warm her, that he'd been called worse things. But it also occurred to him that *safe* wasn't the first word that would come to mind if he had to describe his motives right at that moment.

Because in the brief minute or two that she'd been cuddled up against him, he'd realized two things: first, if she was wearing anything at all under the flannel shirt, it didn't amount to much. And second, his intentions—however honorable a couple of minutes ago—were deteriorating with ominous speed.

It was insane; there were no two ways about it. Making love to Jordon Walker was *not* an option. But...hell, there was something about having a half-naked woman in your bed at two in the morning that put a whole new perspective on things!

Even rigid with cold, she was as supple as a seal, not a wrong curve or angle on her. And it would have been difficult to miss had there been one, he thought with fatalistic calm, trying to keep his hands within the prescribed boundaries of what might be reasonably called her "back." Trying to get warm, she'd snuggled up against him as close as she could get and had tangled her long legs with his and he could feel her moist breath tickle the hair on his chest, tried *not* to feel the silken thigh tucked between his more intimately than she probably realized.

Bad idea, he advised himself philosophically. He should have put her under a scalding hot shower, then found her a blanket and a hot-water bottle and put her back to bed. *Her* bed. Because having her in *his* bed was going to cause some serious complications in about three minutes flat if she didn't quit wriggling around like ... that.

He swallowed, teeth gritted. "Still cold?"

"Uh-uh." She hitched herself a little closer, sighing contentedly. "You're nice and warm."

Hot would be a more apt description, Kel thought. He took a deep breath and tried unsuccessfully to ignore the way she fit in against him, belly and thighs tight against his. He could feel the pressure of her breasts against his chest, the heavy flannel shirt no more a barricade than silk gauze, and in spite of himself he ran his hand slowly down her back, trying to ascertain if she was half as naked under it as he suspected.

To his satisfaction, he detected a faint ridge of elastic that indicated she was wearing—at the very least—a pair of briefs. She'd quit wriggling around by then to his intense relief, and he managed to convince himself that it would be possible—if he tried very, very hard—to actually go to sleep.

And for a while it almost worked. In fact, he may have dozed once or twice, half dreaming. And then Jordon moved and he was wide-awake again. He lay there unmoving for what seemed like an eternity, each second dragging into minutes as he tried desperately to think of how he was going to capture Hollister's poachers and Jimmie Two Shoes's murderer and what he was going to do with his life after this was over... thinking of anything that would distract him from the woman in his arms.

He was so busy trying to distract himself that he didn't even know for certain when he first realized that she wasn't asleep. And that something had changed.

She was no longer shivering, for one thing. And although she was still lying pressed tightly against him, he could sense the tension in her slender body, could hear a slight unsteadiness in her breathing. He moved his hand slowly, experimentally, down her back, letting it rest on the upper curve of her bottom, and felt her shiver lightly.

And knew, with unsettling certainty, that in spite of everything, things were suddenly getting complicated.

"I'm keeping you awake, aren't I?" Her quiet voice startled him slightly.

"No," he lied.

"Would ... that is, do you want me to leave?"

"No." His arms tightened convulsively. He swallowed, wondering where this was going to lead. And what the hell he was going to do when they got there. "Are you comfortable?"

He swore he could feel her smile. "Very."

"Good." There was no way he could stop his body from responding to the warmth and closeness of her, and finally he stopped trying, deciding there was little point in even attempting to hide the effect she was having on him.

She flinched very slightly and he heard her breath catch. But she didn't move away. And then, so gently that at first he wondered if it was just wishful thinking, she moved—not away—but against him. And the soft groan he heard was his own.

She didn't say anything. Didn't make any more indication than that slight acknowledgment of her own body that she was even aware of what was happening. Just as gently, he flattened his palm against her lower back and increased the pressure of his hand, letting her know what he wanted without hurrying her. The whole night—how far this was going to go, how far he dared take it—was going to be up to her.

Another shiver ran through her. "Oh ... Kel...."

"Don't talk."

"But—"

"Don't say anything." His voice was rough. "No words, Jordon. Let your body tell you what you want ... and then let it tell me."

Her breath caught on what might have been a moan, and he felt her fingers flex against his chest. And then, tentatively, she drew the fingertips of her left hand across his upper chest. A pause, then down his ribs, too lightly to be a real caress but at least it was a start. She let her hand rest on his waist, and then, as though drawing courage from the fact he didn't seem to be in any hurry, she ran her palm back up to his chest.

He smiled into the darkness above her head, thinking idly, that if he made it through the night without losing his mind completely he should be up for some sort of award.

Although before he got carried away with his own heroism, he reminded himself ruefully, he'd better have a good look at exactly what it was he was doing. And his motives for doing it. If he made love to her—taught her how to love again, to trust, to enjoy the magic of her own body... in short, gave her back everything that Alec had stolen from her—was he doing it for her, or for himself?

Because it was damned easy, when lying in bed with a mostly naked woman, to rationalize just about anything.

And then Jordon's warm mouth settled on his chest and she started slowly kissing him, gentle biting little kisses punctuated with tantalizing swirls of her tongue, and he lost track of his own argument.

Lying there unmoving while she caressed him with her mouth and teasing fingers was the most difficult thing Kel could remember ever doing.

He ached to gather her into his arms and plunder that sweet little mouth with his and ease himself between her thighs and down into the heat of her. Ached to run his hands around the taut curves of her bottom and then up under the shirt to caress her belly and thighs and breasts. To lower his mouth and capture her nipples between his lips and suck them until they hardened, to slide his hand between her legs and touch her *there* and caress her and tease her until she was so crazed with need that Alec's memory would be no more than a fleeting shadow.

And knew he didn't dare.

Her caresses were more certain now, and as she curled around and settled her mouth over one of his nipples he groaned again, squeezing his eyes closed. He wasn't going to last. It had been too long...and there was no way he was going to be able to hold out for as long as she'd need....

Her mouth was moving again, up to his shoulder, his throat, along his jawline, across to brush against his lips, the touch of her tongue like silken flame. Kel's heart was thundering like a runaway train, and he was having trouble breathing, his body so on fire that it hurt just to think about it. And yet he managed to lie very still as she kissed him again and again, and ran her fingers across his cheeks, up into his hair.

"Kel...?"

Slowly he opened his eyes and found her face only inches from his, her eyes heavy-lidded and smoky. "Are you sure?" His voice was just a ragged whisper. "You have to be sure, Jory. I can quit anytime you want—but only up to a certain point. Beyond that—" he swallowed convulsively "—if you say no, I might not be able to stop. I can't make any promises, sweetheart."

"Don't say anything. Just show me...." She let her mouth linger on his, caressing his lower lip with her tongue, and slid her leg between his and moved provocatively against him.

It took more control than he even thought he had not to strip her out of that damned shirt and make love to her then and there, the kind of fast, hard-driving lovemaking he needed and wanted. Instead, he simply kissed her, gently at first and then less so, moving against her, caressing her through the shirt.

And then she was moving against him, touching him, begging him to hurry in a breath-caught little voice so filled with need that just the sound of it nearly pushed him over the edge. He growled something and released her long enough to reach down and strip off his briefs, then he grasped her hips with both hands and pulled her against him and eased her onto her back.

Trying not to hurry, he slipped his knee between hers and drew his thigh up, opening her for him, pressing himself against the welcoming softness of her through the moist cotton of her panties and hearing her gasp at the eroticism of his touch.

But then, dimly, he realized that something was wrong. Her smothered, rapid breathing held more panic than passion and her movements became suddenly jerky and uncoordinated. Instead of caressing him, guiding him, her hands were planted firmly and desperately against his chest, pushing him away.

Swearing thickly, he lifted himself away from her. "Jory... Jory, it's okay. It's all right. I won't—"

"Don't stop!" It was a ragged cry, torn with tears. "Please, Kel, don't stop! I'll be all right in a minute... please!"

"Jory...Jory, don't." He caught her hand as she tried to touch him.

"If you stop now, I'll never have the courage to try again," she begged. "Please, Kel—I need to learn not to be afraid. It's all right, I swear it! I'll be fine as soon as you—"

"Damn it, Jory, if I make love to you like this, I'll be no better than the man who raped you in the first place. I want to make love *with* you, not *to* you."

"But if I can't with you, then I'll never be able to!" She was sobbing now. "Damn it, Kel, I *trust* you, don't you see? That's why I know I'll be all right if you'd just—"

"No way." Kel shook his head, holding her firmly away from him. "You're trying to talk yourself into doing something you don't want to do. My God, you're so scared you're shaking!"

"But you want to!"

He managed a bark of hoarse laughter. "That's got to be the understatement of the century! But *want* doesn't cut it, Jory. The man who raped you *wanted* you. You've got to want back, understand? You've got to be able to lose yourself in the wanting. To forget all the ugliness and the fear. Until you can do that, you're just pretending.''

"Well, then, damn it, let me pretend!" She was getting mad now, Kel realized. Desire and frustration and fear had coalesced into pure anger, and the glint in her eyes was anything but promising. "There must be eight hundred sex-starved men in these damned mountains who'd make love to me without a second thought, and I have to choose the *only* one with a conscience!"

It would have been funny, Jordon thought, if she weren't so mad. And embarrassed. Although the anger was at herself, not at Kel—who was, after all, only being the gentleman his mother had obviously taught him to be. The gentleman every woman in the world dreamed of—until a time like this.

"I'm giving you carte blanche to make love to me, for crying out loud, and you're acting as though I'm asking you to do something life-threatening!"

"What the hell kind of a man do you think I am?" Braced on one elbow, he glared down at her. "Do you think I'm so hard up for some action that I'd make love to a woman who's scared half out of her mind to get it? You must have a damned low opinion of me, lady! How the *hell* do you think I could do that to you?"

Too embarrassed to hold his angry stare, Jordon tried to roll away but Kel held her firmly. "I want to make love to you more than I've wanted anything in my life before, Jordon. But you have to want me just as badly—it has to be all or nothing."

"But I do." It was just a whisper. "I do, Kel. It's just that . . . something happened. I don't even know what. One minute you were making love to me and I couldn't think of anything else, then—it just stopped." She shivered, unable to even describe the black mass of fear that had unexpectedly enveloped her when she'd felt his weight, his presence, bearing down against her, blotting out the moonlight, smothering her. . . .

"I should have known I wouldn't be able to go through with it. I—I shouldn't have put you on the spot like this." She sat up, unable to meet his eyes. "I don't blame you for being mad. And it'll never happen again, I swear."

He caught her by the shoulder as she started to turn away. "I didn't say I didn't want to sleep with you, Jory." His eyes captured hers, lazy and warm and just a little dangerous.

"But—"

"Learning to trust can take a while," he said very softly. "And you have to start somewhere."

Jordon felt a rush of such love for him in that instant that it took all her willpower not to simply fling herself into his arms. Instead she shook her head firmly. "It wouldn't be fair."

"Come on, Jory. I thought you trusted me."

"I do," she replied uncertainly. She shouldn't stay, she knew. It wasn't fair, taunting him with everything she wasn't able to give him. But she thought suddenly of going back to her own bed—it would be cold by now, and still haunted by the remnants of her nightmare—and she shuddered. "Just for a little while?" she whispered. "Can you just hold me for a little while?"

"Come here," was all he murmured, tugging her down into the warm nest of sheets. "Turn around and snuggle down—that's it." He fit her in against the curve of his body until they lay cupped together like spoons, and wrapped his arms around her, banishing the cold. "You're safe, Jory." He braided his fingers with hers and squeezed them gently. "You're safe here."

Safe. Smiling, Jordon let her eyes slide closed, enveloped in the delicious male warmth of his body. He was still naked, and it was impossible for her to ignore the fact that he was also still very aroused. But she was glad he didn't bother trying to hide the fact, comfortable enough with his own sexuality to accept the natural consequences of this kind of intimacy without embarrassment or apology.

It made being here easier. And even though their attempted lovemaking had resulted in nothing but mutual frustration, she felt happier than she had in months. Love and sex and all the related complexities had somehow lost many of their more sinister overtones in the past few minutes, and she found herself thinking sleepily that for the first time in almost two years the overwhelming sensation she felt was utter contentment.

She was almost asleep when she felt Kel's mouth browse lazily along the back of her neck and she smiled, loving the erotic touch of his lips and breath. She was warm and drowsy and it was wonderful to just relax into the physical sensation of being held against an acre or two of warm, naked male flesh.

"Nice," she murmured, stretching like a stroked cat. "That's nice...."

Kel's breath tickled the side of her throat, his mouth moving slowly from the hollow under her ear down to her shoulder, then back again. And it was only then that she realized he'd undone the top two or three buttons on the old shirt she was wearing. He drew the tips of his fingers lightly down the warm skin between her breasts and Jordon's breath caught slightly.

"Why don't you tell me about your eagles," he murmured against her ear. "How long do they live, for instance?"

"What on earth are you...talking about?"

"Eagles," Kel whispered. "Talk to me, Jory. How long does a bald eagle live?"

"About...ten years...maybe." His fingers were on the next shirt button, and Jordon found it difficult to think about eagles and concentrate on what Kel was doing at the same time.

"And how much do they weigh?"

"Kel, you can't possibly be interested in—"

"But I am, Jory," he murmured. "Concentrate now...."

Concentrate. She was trying to concentrate on the seductive touch of his fingertips on the swell of her breast as he eased the next button free. "N-nine pounds, on average. Their bones are hollow...but you know that. A female bald eagle can have a wing spread of close to eight feet, and... Oh, Kel...." She had to fight for breath as he slipped his hand inside the open front of the shirt. "What are you...doing."

"Touching you," came the murmured reply. "Keep talking, Jory. Don't think about what I'm doing. Just keep talking."

"I...it...oh..." She swallowed, trying to remember what she'd been saying as his fingertips drew lazy spirals on her breasts, touching without really touching, more a promise than an actual caress. "They h-have more than seven thousand...feathers. Bald eagles have been clocked at two...two hundred miles an hour in a full dive, and they can strike with twice the force of a rifle b-bullet.... Kel...!"

"Mmm?" Kel pressed the flattened palm of his hand gently on her lower belly and she drew in a deep, shuddering breath.

There was no point in hurrying her. If she felt rushed or pressured into pleasing him, she'd freeze up again, her own needs forgotten as her mind took over, filling her with its terrifying memories. The secret was to make her forget...forget Alec, forget her fear, forget everything but the hunger burning within her.

He didn't even know when he'd decided to try again. Perhaps it had been listening to her trying not to cry as she'd lain in his arms that last time. Or perhaps it was just knowing that it had been Alec who had made her like this. Alec—his own brother—who had set these demons loose in her mind.

He couldn't do anything to change that, Kel thought painfully. But he could do this...he could make her feel loved and desirable and wanted again. The healing wouldn't be complete in just one night, but it would be a start. And maybe, in some small way, it would repay some of what Alec had done.

She was still telling him about eagles, he realized, her voice unsteady and distracted. But he was hardly listening, concentrating instead on the last shirt button. It was well below her navel and he rested his scarred knuckles on the tantalizing warmth at the juncture of her thighs and proceeded to slip the button free, hearing her breath catch.

Gently he trailed his fingers up her body to the base of her throat, feeling her shiver, and then, slowly, not wanting to startle her, he slipped his hand under the shirt and started caressing her full, firm breasts.

She gave a startled little gasp and completely lost her train of thought, her discussion of feeding habits wandering off into nonsense as he ran his finger lightly around one swollen nipple, teasing it.

"They m-mate for life," she stammered. "Did I s-say that?"

"Mmm. I read once they mate in the air."

"Yes." He could hear her swallow, knew she was fighting to concentrate on what she was saying and not on the gentle motion of his hand as he caressed her breasts slowly, the nipples so aroused and sensitive that the slightest touch made her tremble. "They...ummm...grip each others' talons and m-mate while... Oh, Kel." She moved against him with a soft moan as he drew his hand down the sweep of her belly. "They...you're making it hard to think clearly...."

"You're doing just fine. How do they mate?"

"In f-free-fall," she managed to get out. "S-sometimes they fall for hundreds of feet, locked together and— Oh! Kel...!"

"Trust," Kel breathed against her ear, feeling her tremble at the first questing touch of his fingers. "That's what it's all about, Jory... just falling free. Letting go..."

And that, in the end, is exactly what she did. The desire they'd whetted earlier had only been abandoned, not satisfied, and her body responded to the temptations he was offering like a drought-ravaged flower to the promise of rain.

His skillful touch ignited a heat within her so urgent, so fierce, that after a while she didn't even bother questioning it, didn't bother worrying that it wouldn't last, didn't bother anticipating the moment when desire would turn to fear and she'd push him away. For as long as it lasted, she wanted it—the teasing touch of his fingers, his mouth, his lean body moving, moving evocatively against her.

She didn't know whether it was her or Kel who eased her panties over her hips, but when she finally kicked them off impatiently it was with relief. She didn't want to be encumbered by anything that would keep him from her. She was on fire, and when he finally eased strong, gentle fingers into the liquid silk between her thighs she gave a moan of delight. Gratified that her fear had held off long enough to let him take her even this far, she shuddered against him and moved her hips helplessly, whispering his name in encouragement.

There was a moment—only a heartbeat, really—when she felt a little tremor of doubt. But then his teasing touch found the hidden spot it was seeking and everything simply exploded in a shattering, bright-edged uprush of pure physical sensation that took her so completely by surprise that she cried out, half in wonder and half in disappointment that it was going to end....

Except, to her even greater surprise, it didn't. Not right then, anyway. His deft caresses became more intimate and more demanding until her entire being cried out for the release he finally gave her. And the whole while he just cradled her against him and whispered things to her, and not once—not even for a second—was she afraid....

There was, Kel thought a little smugly, a certain amount of satisfaction in doing things just right. Especially when you were a man, and the thing you'd just done right was give your woman the kind of pleasure he'd just given Jordon.

It was still shivering through her, tiny aftershocks that he could feel run along her body like tremors through rock, and he knew—if he wanted to—that he could bring her there again.

But there could be too much of a good thing. Even this. The whole point had been to show her she could enjoy this kind of release without fear, that the magic was still there. It wasn't just physical release he'd been bringing her, but emotional—the kind of letting go he sensed was the key to everything.

She turned in his arms to face him and he groaned, his own body so vitally ready that even the touch of her was agony. Giving a breathless laugh, she entwined her legs with his, moving against him. "More," she murmured against his mouth, her tongue caressing his lips, teasing him. "I want more...."

"Jordon..." It was another groan as she moved against him lithely. Much more of this and it was going to be all over.... "Jory, I can't. I don't have anything with me...and unless World First took this particular hazard into consideration, too, and stocked your first-aid kit with some kind of protection, it's too big a risk."

There was a chuckle in the warm darkness, the fleeting touch of her hand, gentle yet insistent. "They didn't, but it doesn't matter. I've been on birth control for nearly two years, ever since..." Her lips moved delicately across his chest, teasing him. "I've been having problems—nothing serious, just stress related things. So my doctor put me on the Pill. I always thought it was ironic when the *last* thing I wanted to do was...this." She touched him again.

Kel groaned softly. Dimly, the thought no more than a flicker of awareness through his mind, he realized he'd never

considered that part of it. Not the fact that she was on birth
control now—but that she hadn't been before. That those
brutal, hurried few minutes on the floor in Alec's biology
lab could have resulted in a child...his brother's child.
Thank God for that mercy, anyway; thank God she hadn't
wound up pregnant....

And then the thought, the fleeting brush mark of anger,
was gone as she caressed him with her body and suddenly
there was only this woman and this moment, the past oblit-
erated by the tender, gentle touch of her hand. "You mean
this...?" he asked softly, pressing himself gently between
her thighs.

"Kel...!" Her voice caught. "Make love to me," she
whispered, trying to draw him over her. "Kel, you're driving us both crazy."

"Not like that." Gently he resisted her pull. How he'd finally figured it out, heaven alone knew. It was just one of
those insights that hit him like a bolt of lightning and left
him wondering how he'd been so damned stupid not to have
seen it in the first place. It wasn't making love that frightened her—it was being trapped under a male body, held
captive by his weight, his strength, pressed down and
smothered. "Like *this.*"

Jordon gave a startled gasp as he rose to his knees, lifting
her with him, and as he settled her over him so she was
astride his thighs, her eyes widened. "Kel...!"

"Trust me." Grinning, he pulled the quilt around them,
and then he slipped his hands under her smooth little bottom and lifted her slightly as he rocked against her.

"Oh..." It was just a little breathing of sound and she
went very still, her gaze locked with his. And then, very
slowly, she smiled. "Yes," she whispered as she slipped her
arms around his neck. "Oh, yes..."

And then, miraculously, she eased herself over and
around him, sheathing him in the hot, wet silk of her body.
There was no hesitation, no last-minute doubts—she sim-

ply let the weight of her own body do it all, encompassing him slowly and wondrously. Kel's control finally broke and he gave a harsh groan and arched under her, thrusting upward to meet her cocooning warmth and filling her urgently, and he struggled to hang on . . . hang on! And, even more miraculously, managed to do just that.

Time seemed to stand still for the next while. Or if it passed, it passed so slowly that Kel didn't notice. Nor had he any reason to care. Seconds, minutes, hours . . . they had no meaning or relevance beyond that point. And as time collapsed into itself, unheeded, so did space until the only thing of consequence in the entire world was the two of them, locked together as intimately as only man and woman can.

The erotic whisper of flesh on flesh, the sound of her breathing, unsteady and urgent, the feel of her hot slippery body encompassing him... Nothing else mattered. He made no attempt to hold her, just letting his hands rest on the flare of her hips, guiding her, pacing the rhythmic thrust of her pelvis, and—freed of constraints or fear—she finally just let herself go.

There were a few moments when Kel doubted he was going to be able to wait for her. She was as lithe and strong as a young panther in his hands and he concentrated on the flex of muscle in her lower back as she moved, the velvet of her moist skin . . . anything to keep from losing that final bit of control.

But then her movements became erratic and suddenly more intense and she whispered his name in a tight voice. Gritting his teeth, Kel responded to the urgency in her voice. Clasping the backs of her thighs to support her, he lifted more fully onto his knees and started moving powerfully and rhythmically within the taut heat of her body.

He was vaguely aware of Jordon's moan of pleasure and then she was moving in concert with him, strongly and hungrily, each flex of her hips taking them both nearer the edge. And then, abruptly, she gave a soft, startled little cry and stiffened against him, her thighs clamping around his.

And in the next heartbeat it was all over. He had a fleeting thought that it would be nice to draw it out a while longer, but then it got away from him and he stopped even trying to hold back. Two strong thrusts of his hips, three, and reality simply ceased to exist.

Except for the realization, hovering like a specter at the edges of his mind, that the price for escaping these mountains now—and this woman—was going to be far greater than anything he could ever have imagined.

Chapter 10

It would be dawn soon.

It was cold and clear, the sky the color of skim milk, and Kel shivered and pulled the quilt closer around him. He'd wakened almost half an hour ago and had slipped out of bed, too restless to sleep and not wanting to disturb Jordon, and had come outside to watch the sun rise.

And to think.

He watched his breath crystallize in the cold, damp air and wondered idly if it wouldn't be better for both of them if he just got dressed and left now, without even saying goodbye. She'd be hurt for a while, but she'd get over it. And him.

But the thought of leaving chilled him even more than the cold morning air. His body still tingled from her touch, imprinted with the memory of every sweet inch of her. He knew her by heart. Every curve and indentation, every hidden delight, every secret part of her... knew it and had reveled in it for most of the night.

And each time with her had been special and unique. Once the trust between them had been forged, she hadn't held back a thing, giving more of herself than any woman he'd ever met. Her lovemaking had transcended the mere physical to envelop him in a tidal wave of emotions he was still trying to sort out. She had reached out and swept him up into a place he'd never been before, had never dreamed of being before, and if he felt a little shaky this morning it was just because of the intensity of what they'd shared.

And . . . the guilt.

It hadn't started out that way. There had been times during the night when he'd gazed into her eyes and had felt something tight and constricting fall away, something he hadn't even known was there until it was gone. And other times when he'd ached to tell her he loved her, not knowing if it was true but wanting desperately to put words—any words—to the turmoil of feelings spinning through him.

But all that had faded in the past hour or so, leaving a sour lump of guilt lodged in his gut.

Damn it, he had to tell her.

Couldn't tell her.

The thought of what it would do to her made him half-sick and he swore and sat down on the top step heavily. Wearily he rubbed his stubbled cheeks. How in God's name had things gotten so complicated?

All he'd wanted to do was find her and confront her about Alec. He hadn't intended to fall in love with her.

The word made him wince. Love? Hell, he wouldn't know love if it knocked on his door and invited itself in for a drink.

His mother had loved him. And his father had, too, in his own way—although there hadn't been much left over for him once Alec had been born. But that had been a long, long time ago.

Had he loved Alec? Once, maybe. It was hard to remember anything but the anger and resentment and jealousy.

And Denise? He'd been looking for something with Denise that he'd thought, at the time, had been love. Looking back, he could see that they'd both had their own ideas of what "love" might be, and had been disappointed at not finding it. They'd blamed each other for the loss of the dream, but who, really, had been at fault? They'd been the next thing to kids, and hadn't known a damned thing.

So he hadn't had a lot of experience with love. He felt something for Jordon, that was certain—something strange and frightening and wonderful. But was it love?

He'd never find out, he reminded himself grimly. He could not continue this relationship without telling her who he really was, and when he did that, she'd be gone.

He lunged to his feet with a savage oath and went back inside. Jordon was awake, although barely so. She squinted at him drowsily as he walked across to the sofa bed and he had to smile in spite of himself, loving the way she looked, all tousled and warm and flushed.

Her mouth lifted in a slow, welcoming smile. "Come back to bed. It's still early...."

"Not that early." He sat on the edge of the bed and leaned over to kiss her. Her mouth was soft and familiar, and as her lips parted under his he felt his stomach tighten with expectation. "I should leave...."

"Can't." She slipped her arms around his neck, grinning wickedly. "Your friends just dumped you off last night, remember? You don't have any way of leaving until I'm good and ready to let you go." She let her mouth rest against his, caressing his lips with her tongue. "And that could be awhile, Kel Stuart."

Kel groaned, laughing. There was a familiar heat in his lower belly, and his body was reacting to the taste and scent of her in ways that could only mean trouble.

"And speaking of your *friends*—how are all your bumps and bruises this morning?"

"Forgot all about 'em," Kel murmured, letting his mouth linger on hers. "Everything seems to be working just fine...."

"Yes." Her lips curved against his. "I can tell."

"Oh, you noticed that, did you?"

"Mmm." She smiled sleepily. "Difficult not to. Question is, do you plan to just lie there talking about it, or come back to bed to *do* something about it?"

"I kind of figure that's up to you. Are you in a talkin' mood, or a—"

She whispered something that sent a shaft of raw desire through him and he growled something back that made her breath catch, her eyes already growing smoky with need. And then he was pulling the covers back and sliding into the warm bed with her and she was waiting for him, so ready that he'd pressed himself between her welcoming thighs and deep into her body in one easy, long movement that made her arch under him with a low moan of pleasure.

"I think you answered my question," Kel growled, kissing her long and hard and thoroughly. "And I never was much of a talker...."

He'd worry about the right and wrong of it later, he told himself. It was a little late right now to be taunting himself about things he *shouldn't* be doing—not while Jordon was moving like that and touching him like that and whispering those urgent little pleas that set him on fire...not yet, he promised himself. But soon...soon...

It was a stolen day.

In spite of his best intentions, Kel never did leave. It wasn't that he actually made a conscious decision not to— it just got later and later and then pretty soon it was dark again. And then Jordon decided to have a shower and Kel decided to join her and one thing sort of led to another and they wound up in bed...again. Pleasantly tired, they both fell asleep, and when they woke up it seemed silly to get dressed, especially when making love again seemed like an eminently wonderful idea, and the next time either of them looked at a clock it was nearly midnight. And *much* too late, they agreed solemnly, to do anything as crazy as making that treacherous drive into town.

"I think I should spend the night," Kel told her quite reasonably. "That road's pure hell after dark."

And Jordon, smiling as she drew him down into her arms, could only agree.

But by the next morning, Kel finally knew what he had to do.

There were no choices anymore. No easy excuses. No options. He had to leave—the valley, the job, Jordon. All of it. For the first time in his life he was going to leave a job half-finished; Hollister was going to have to find someone else to find Jimmie Two Shoes's killers. Because if Kel stayed, he was going to break Jordon Walker's heart. And not even bringing a murderer to justice was worth that.

The question was—what the *hell* was he going to tell her? The truth? He'd picked up a handful of medals during his various tours of duty—including a Purple Heart and a couple of commendations for bravery—but he wasn't sure he had the guts to tell her.

That left lying.

And the fact that he was going to spend a lot of the rest of his life avoiding his own eyes in mirrors, and waking up with the cold shakes, and dreaming of soft skin and laughter in the night . . . well, that just served him right. He'd justified this whole "mission" by telling himself that he had to know the truth, but he realized now that the truth had been the *last* damned thing he'd wanted to know.

What he'd *wanted* was for her to tell him that Alec had been innocent. That the rape had never happened. That Alec had not grown up into a monster. That he—Kel—had no reason to lie awake nights racked by guilt for the sins of a brother he'd all but abandoned two decades ago.

So this trip hadn't been about Alec at all, it had been about himself. And there was some sort of obscene justice in the fact that he'd gotten himself into this mess and would be paying for it for a long time to come.

He was thinking about this all the way back into town, wondering if he was going to have the courage to face Jordon again before he left, or just go. Quick, clean and brutal.

He'd barely had time to say goodbye to her this morning. One of Peterson's young RCMP officers had come by the trailer a little after eight, ostensibly to ask directions although Kel suspected that Peterson had ordered his men to check on her whenever they were in the area. It had made sense for Kel to catch a ride back to town with him, although he was starting to wonder if he'd just taken the easy way out. Again. Joining the navy had been a way out; he'd just walked away from Alec and all the trouble he caused, leaving his father to deal with it as best he could.

Which wasn't good enough, he realized now. Alec had always been able to boondoggle their father. What Alec had needed was someone to pull him up short every time he tried to get away with one of his stunts, to disbelieve the lies, to demand that he face his own responsibilities. Someone, in short, to turn a spoiled, manipulative, arrogant child into some kind of decent human being before turning him loose on an unsuspecting world.

"You want to go to the lodge, or come back to the station with me and file a complaint against the Murdoch boys?"

Kel gave himself a shake. "The lodge will be fine," he said hoarsely. "I'll drop by later to talk about filing charges."

Except he wouldn't. One more thing left incomplete. One more hornet's nest he'd stirred up and would leave for someone else to clean up....

He swore softly and rubbed his face with both hands. He'd call Hollister first. Tell him to get someone else in here, someone trained for the job. Then he'd pack his things and hire a plane to take him to Vancouver. He'd write to Jordon from there, he told himself wearily. A letter was the coward's way out, but it was better than just running out on her with no word at all. And better than staying and ruining her life.

It was one of those days when it was impossible to get anything done. Even the simplest task seemed too complicated to deal with, and Jordon finally just gave up and went home. But even *that* proved to be more difficult than she'd imagined when she got so lost in a daydream that she missed the turnoff to her trailer and wound up fifteen miles down the wrong logging road.

Shaking her head, she turned the Bronco around sharply, sending Murphy skating off the seat and onto the floor with a yelp. She apologized to him profusely, then headed back the way she'd just come, wondering how long the symptoms were going to last.

And how—in the few weeks she'd known him—she'd managed to fall so completely in love with Kel Stuart.

It had come to her sometime during the night, cradled in his arms and listening to the deep, slow beat of his heart. Until then she hadn't given much thought as to why she'd wound up in bed with Kel—it seemed fairly straightforward, after all. The man was just about perfect in every way you looked at it: handsome in a rough-hewn sort of way, gentle yet strong, honorable, trustworthy, heroic... not to mention giving off enough raw sexual energy to light up half the country.

She'd thought that's all it had been. That, and simple trust. And the tenderness she'd sensed more than actually seen in him, the awareness that he would never do anything to frighten or hurt her.

But it was more. Much more. The feelings she had for Kel went beyond simple trust into an intensity of emotion she'd never experienced before. She smiled. She'd always hoped to fall in love one day, but had never imagined it might happen this soon. Or this effortlessly.

As she wheeled the Bronco into the clearing where her trailer was, Murphy spotted the green truck parked in the shade of an old arbutus tree and gave a bark of alarm. And Jordon groaned. The last person she wanted to see right now was John Harris!

He was out by the eagle cages when she drove up and he smiled when he saw her. Jordon managed an unenthusiastic smile in return and held the door open for Murphy. The big dog galloped over to where John was standing, bristling and growling, and John gave him a distasteful look. "I see you've still got the mutt."

"If you'd stop being so antagonistic, he probably wouldn't bark at you all the time." Impatiently she started unloading her gear from the back of the truck. "He never barks at Peterson or...at other people he sees all the time."

"Does he bark at Stuart?"

The question sounded innocent enough, but Jordon looked at him sharply and found him watching her with a speculative expression. "No," she said with precision. "He does not."

"I need to talk to you. About Stuart." He tucked the heavy brown envelope he was holding under his arm, then picked up her camera bag, ignoring Murphy's rumble of warning, and fell into step beside her as she walked toward the trailer. "Something's come up I think you should know about."

Jordon had to bite back an impatient reply. Why did men always have to act like such idiots when there was a woman involved? One good jolt of hormones, and even the most rational, practical-minded ones turned into lunatics, pawing the ground and bellowing and showing off. "Whatever it is, I either know it, or I don't *need* to know it."

"Oh, I think you'll want to know about this."

There was something about the way he said it that sent a little prickle of alarm down Jordon's spine. "What's this about?"

"Let's go inside. I could use a drink. And I think you're going to need one, too."

Jordon had her mouth open to tell him she was in no mood for games, then changed her mind and unlocked the door instead, not saying anything as she walked up into the cool interior of the trailer. It was just as she'd left it that morning and she blushed slightly, remembering how she and Kel had made love at the kitchen counter not five hours previously. They'd started out making coffee and toast, but before long they'd been in each other's arms and Kel had lifted her against the counter and had made love to her then and there, oblivious to bubbling coffee and scorching toast.

John followed her in, and Jordon dumped her climbing gear in the corner, realizing that bits and pieces of discarded clothing still festooned the living room, lying where they'd been dropped during the previous day. She gathered up a bra and a pair of lacy briefs from the floor beside the sofa, then picked up a pair of jeans from the hallway, hoping she wasn't blushing half as badly as she suspected as she stuffed the incriminating evidence into the laundry hamper by the bathroom door.

It was only then that she realized that the bedroom door was wide open, the unmade bed clearly visible, and it took all her willpower not to rush across and close the door. It didn't mean anything, she reminded herself. There was no indication from the rumpled sheets that she hadn't spent the night alone.

For that matter, there was no reason why her sleeping arrangements should be of any concern to John Harris. "You said you had something to tell me."

"Mmm." He tapped the big envelope against one palm as though testing its weight. "How well do you know Stuart?"

Kel had asked almost the same question about Harris not long ago, Jordon found herself thinking. She met John's eyes evenly. "Let's cut to the chase, all right? I know you don't like Kel—he doesn't like you a whole lot, either—but if you've been snooping around trying to dig up some dirt on him just so I'll—"

His eyes and mouth seemed suddenly harder. "All right, if that's the way you want it. I was hoping to break it to you more gently than this, but..." He pulled out a plump file folder held closed by an elastic band. Pulling the elastic off, he held the file toward her. "I suggest you sit down before you start going through this. You're not going to like what you find."

Again a prickle of alarm shivered down Jordon's spine. She looked at the folder, tempted to tell John to put it back in its envelope and get out. She didn't want to see what it contained. Didn't want to know any more about Kel than she already knew—that he was kind and loving and gentle, and that she loved him utterly.

"I'm not interested in going through Kel Stuart's dirty linen," she said angrily. "There's nothing you can tell me that will change how I feel about him."

"Read the file."

She stared at it mistrustfully, then watched her hand reach out to take it as though it belonged to someone else. Not saying anything, she walked stiffly to the small table under the window that she used as a desk. Clearing a space, she put the overstuffed folder on the table in front of her and looked at it. There was nothing to be afraid of, something whispered at her. If she'd told John the truth—if she truly loved Kel—then there was nothing to fear. Nothing that would change how she felt. Nothing....

But opening the file—actually reaching out and turning the pale cover back—was the hardest thing she'd ever done.

The folder was dirty, smudged by fingerprints and coffee rings, the corners dog-eared, and it was tattooed with doodles and phone numbers.

She knew John was watching her. Knew also that she was being silly. And in the end, she reached out almost defiantly and opened the folder.

And came face-to-face with herself.

It was a photograph—not a very good one, she couldn't help noticing—and it took her a moment to realize it had been clipped from a newspaper. Her hair had still been long then and a glossy sweep of it had fallen over one eye as she looked over her shoulder and straight at the camera, lips parted in a pose that could only be called alluring.

Except her mood that day had been far from alluring, she recalled with a chill. The photographer had called something to her, something designed to make her look around, and what the camera *didn't* catch was her telling him succinctly and in no uncertain terms to go to hell. The photo had run on the front page of both the early and late editions, just one more bit of ammunition for the defense.

There were other photos under that one, all clipped from newspapers and the small local glossy news magazine that had nearly doubled its sales on the strength of its sensationalistic and often lurid coverage of the story.

"What is all this stuff?" Jordon looked at John impatiently.

"I found it in Stuart's room at the lodge."

"So he has a file on me. He's working for the government—he probably has files on *all* of us." What he'd said hit her finally, and she looked at him sharply. "What do you mean, you *found* it? What were you doing in Kel's room?"

"Looking for something that would tell me who the hell he really is," he said evenly.

"That's break and enter."

"There were no other files, Jordon. Just that one."

"So what?" But she did reach out and start riffling through the papers again. There were dozens of clippings, some just short updates on the trial, others entire sections torn out of newspapers. And she forced herself to handle them without flinching, the lurid headlines leaping out at her. College Prof And Teaching Assistant In Love Nest Spat. Department Head Shoo-in Says Beautiful Coed Lover Crying Wolf! Campus Beauty Having Second Thoughts— Was It Love, Or Rape?

Shuddering slightly, she hurriedly glanced through the rest. There was some straightforward explanation. He'd no doubt had one of his research people collect the information after she'd told him about Alec—probably just standard procedure for the kind of work he did. It didn't mean anything.

"The report stapled to the back of the folder—read it."

Swallowing a wild urge to tell John Harris what he could do with the file, report and all, Jordon flipped to the back cover. There was an official-looking paper stapled to it, and she glanced over it incuriously. Then abruptly she stopped and went back to the beginning, reading more slowly.

It was a report, all right. On her.

Or, more correctly, on what she'd been doing since the trial: the three months she'd holed up in her parents' house to lick her wounds, the two months in Hawaii, the three part-time jobs, the six months she'd spent working on the large-mammal breeding program at a major zoo. And finally, her acceptance of the eagle study with World First.

It summed up by confirming the whereabouts of the subject under investigation—her—and that the investigator, having found the subject as he'd been hired to do, was closing his file and was attaching an itemized bill for expenses. The figure was well into four figures.

Someone had gone to a lot of trouble—and a lot of expense—to find her.

"I don't understand." Her voice sounded thin. Almost frightened. "What's this all about?"

"Look at the envelope," John said quietly. "Look who the report was sent to."

The envelope was stapled to the back of the report and it took Jordon a frustrating moment or two to get it free so she could read it. And when she did, it made no sense. She read it a second time, then a third, staring at the name on the envelope as though it were written in some indecipherable language. *Mr. Kel S. Davies,* the envelope read.

Not Stuart.

Davies.

"He's Alec Davies's older brother." John's voice sounded as though it were coming from very far away. "He was in the Middle East during the trial—he used to be some Special Forces type with the navy. He retired a few months ago and came back to the States, and eventually he started looking for you. He hired that private investigator, and... you know the rest."

"I don't believe it. This... there's some sort of mistake." She felt cold and detached, as though she'd wake up in a minute and discover it had all been some bizarre and unsettling dream.

"He's not with the Fish and Wildlife Service—or any other government agency. I had my suspicions all along, but every time I ran a check on him, I'd come up empty-handed. So I decided to try a little old-fashioned detective work. I went through his things last night and found that file. Then I did some more checking. And that's how I found out his real identity." He looked at her intently. "He came up here looking for you, Jordon. He's probably been the one shooting at you, too—trying to scare you into trusting him. Into letting him get close so he can—"

"What?" She looked up at John. "So he can what?"

He shrugged, looking slightly uncomfortable. "I don't know. Hurt you, maybe. Frighten you."

She thought, fleetingly, of lying in Kel's arms just that morning and gazing into his eyes and seeing, for just a moment, what she thought might have been love. Thought of how gentle he'd been, how patient. . . .

And all the while, she'd been sleeping with the man whose brother had raped her.

"Get out." She swallowed and closed the file folder. "Go away and leave me alone."

"Jordon, I—"

"Get out!" She drew in a ragged breath. "I'll take care of it, John. Now, please—just go away."

He left, although not very happily. Jordon sat at the table until she heard the truck drive away, and then, abruptly, she bolted for the bathroom and was violently and horribly sick.

It was late by the time he got back to the Caribou Lodge, too late to even bother with supper before he finished packing up his things. There was a small plane waiting to take him down to Prince Rupert, and from there to Vancouver, but the local airport shut down for the night at eight sharp and if he didn't make it by then, he'd have to wait until morning.

He was thinking about this as he jogged up to the second floor where his room was. If he couldn't get out of town until tomorrow, it was going to be one hell of a long night.

As it was, it had been a long day. He'd gotten through to Hollister about noon, and the ensuing shouting match had lasted a good half hour. Then he'd gone down to the RCMP detachment to turn over his investigative files and reports, and then had spent a futile hour or more trying to track down John Harris.

And the whole while, all he'd been able to think about was Jordon.

Swearing wearily, he unlocked the door to his room, then kicked it closed again behind him. The drapes were drawn and the room was dark and he made his way gingerly across to the bed to turn on one of the lamps. The glare made him squint and he swore again and tossed his leather jacket onto the bed. His suitcase was lying open where he'd left it, half full. All he had to do was grab his shaving gear and clean out the dresser drawers, and he'd be on his way.

He didn't even see the figure standing in the shadows by the fireplace until he glanced around the room to see if he'd missed anything—and found himself looking right at it.

"What the—!" He was reaching for his revolver at the same instant he realized who it was, and he caught the movement awkwardly. "Jordon!"

She smiled faintly. "Bad nerves? Or a bad conscience?"

Something was wrong. Her voice, the cool, controlled way she was looking at him, made every instinct click into high gear. He looked at her carefully. "What are you doing here?"

"I see you're leaving." She gestured toward the suitcase.

He winced inwardly. Swearing, he raked his fingers through his hair. "Look, Jordon—I hadn't wanted to tell you like this."

"I'll bet you didn't."

The cold spot on the back of Kel's neck—the one that warned him when he was heading into an ambush—was prickling, and he looked at her closely. Her skin looked dry and hot, as though she had a fever, and her eyes were unnaturally bright.

"I've been called back to Vancouver." It wasn't quite a lie—Hollister *had* ordered him to come in for debriefing. "I was going to call you...." That wasn't a lie, either. Quite.

Jordon laughed, a tinkling, airy laugh that made his scalp prickle. "Were you, Kel?" The laughter vanished from her mouth and she started walking toward him, her expression intent, eyes locked with his. "Although, when I think about it, maybe you were, at that. After all, just *sleeping* with me wouldn't accomplish much. Sure, I'd be hurt when you disappeared with no word, but I'd get over it. The key was making sure I knew who you were. That's where the *real* hurt would come in—making damn good and sure that I *knew* I'd been bedded by Alec Davies's big brother.''

For half a moment, Kel felt, literally, as though he'd been punched in the pit of his stomach. The blood drained from his face and he had to fight to catch his breath, seeing—for the first time—what she was holding in her hands. "How...how the hell did you get that?"

Jordon smiled slightly. She dropped the folder at his feet and it burst open in an avalanche of paper. "Does it matter? I didn't go snooping through your things, if that's what you're worried about. I may be an easy lay, but I draw the line at invading someone's privacy."

She said it with deliberate crudity, her eyes holding his as though daring him to deny it, and Kel felt sick. "My God, Jordon..." He put his hand toward her. "Jory—"

"The only thing I can't figure out is why." She was looking at him seriously, as though honestly curious. "I can't believe you went to all this trouble just for personal satisfaction. So I figure it's got to be either blackmail—although for what, I have no idea—or you're up here as a favor to Alec. Is this his way of getting even? Sending big brother up to seduce me and break my heart?" She turned and strolled across to the fireplace, then looked around at him.

"Or are you up here all on your own? Was it curiosity? Did you want a little of what Alec had? Or was it just that old sibling rivalry again—the need to be bigger and badder and better than he is?"

Kel swallowed, the blood pounding in his temples. "For the record," she went on companionably, "you are. Although the comparison's hardly fair. Alec was too rushed to bother with skill or finesse. The entire thing lasted all of five minutes, and I was too surprised to pay much attention to the finer points of his lovemaking...if that's what you want to call it. By the time I realized what was happening it was more or less over.''

It was like a scene from his worst nightmare, Kel thought numbly. He'd fantasized a dozen times, a hundred, how to tell her, yet nothing had prepared him for this. There wasn't anything he could say that would make her believe he didn't mean to hurt her, he could see that; could tell by the pain in her eyes that any hope he'd ever had of trying to explain, of trying to work things out between them, was hopeless.

The only thing he had left to give her was the truth. ''I know I have a hell of a lot of explaining to do, Jordon,'' he said softly. ''And I know you've got every right to hate my guts right at this moment, but I—''

She moved so quickly that she nearly got past his guard, but twenty years of training brought his hand up just as she swung an open-palmed blow at his face. He caught her wrist easily in his hand and held it firmly, looking down into her furious, upturned face. ''That won't solve anything,'' he said hoarsely. ''If taking a shot at me will make you feel better, you can do it later. First, we're going to talk.''

''Talk?'' She wrenched her arm free and spun away from him, her voice rising. ''You think *talk* is what I came here for? I just wanted to drop off your file, Mr. Davies. You spent a lot of money for the information in it—I figured you'd want it back.''

She stalked across to the door, but Kel was after her in the next heartbeat. He caught the door with the flat of his hand just as she was pulling it open, and it slammed closed again so violently that the entire wall shuddered. ''You're not going anywhere until we talk this out!''

''I don't have anything to say to you, and I can guarantee there's *nothing* you have to say that I'd be interested in hearing! I don't know what sick little prank you and your brother had planned, but it's over!'' Her voice was shaking with fury. ''Get away from this door or I swear I'll call Peterson and have you up on rape charges just like I did Alec.

Only *this* time, mister, I'll make it stick if I have to perjure myself to do it!"

"Alec is dead, damn it! He shot himself six months ago."

The words cracked through the room and Jordon recoiled as though he'd struck her, going so pale that her eyes looked like wide pools of ink. She took an unsteady step or two and dropped into one of the armchairs, one of her hands pressed against her lips. "My...God."

"I thought you knew," he said hoarsely. "It wasn't until a couple of days ago that I realized you didn't. And by then..." He raked his fingers through his hair again and swore disgustedly, feeling old and tired and so sick of the whole damn thing he wished he could just walk out and put it all behind him. Except he couldn't. There was no way out. Not now. "His wife left him not long after the trial, taking the kids with her, and he started drinking. Things went from bad to worse, he got fired...I guess he figured there wasn't anything left to live for."

Jordon was as still as stone, dead-white, her eyes closed, and Kel eased his breath out between gritted teeth. "I thought you knew," he repeated wearily. "It never occurred to me that someone wouldn't have told you."

"No...one told me." Her voice was barely audible. She looked up at him, her eyes filled with anguish. "I...my God, all those times I wished him dead. But I never...even after what he did to me, I never really..." She hugged herself tightly. "I thought if he died, I'd feel something. Relief. Happiness. Vindication. But...I don't feel anything." She looked up at him again. "I don't feel anything."

"There's no reason you should," he said raggedly.

"That's...why you came after me."

"That's part of it."

"Part?" Some of the color had come back into her cheeks and she slowly got to her feet again. "What's the rest of it?"

"I don't know."

Jordon looked across at him, still feeling slightly numbed with shock. Kel's face was ravaged in the firelight, cheeks hollowed, deep lines bracketing his mouth. He looked as though he'd just aged ten years and she found herself wondering what he was thinking. His eyes gave nothing away. They were watchful, almost wary, and they never left hers.

"You bastard." She said it softly, never taking her eyes off him. "You really think it's going to be that easy, don't you. That you can drop the news about Alec on me and then waltz out of here as though that explains it all."

"Jordon—"

"*Why!*"

"I don't know why!" He wheeled away from her, fists raised, his voice a cry of anguish. "Damn it, I don't know! It was all clear once, but after I got up here, after I met you, it just…" He shook his head, looking around at her. "I just know that after Alec died, I needed answers—and you were the only person who could give them to me."

His words—too easy, too glib!—went through her like flame and she felt a sudden surge of anger that was so strong it actually frightened her. She struggled to control it, realizing she was actually shaking with fury. "Answers? How the *hell* could I give you answers when you never even asked the questions! Is that what you were looking for in my bed—answers?"

"Damn it, Jordon…" His voice was ragged with what she could have sworn was pain. "I don't know why the hell I came looking for you, all right? I got stateside in time to bury my brother, and I needed to know why—all I had was a scrapbook full of newspaper clippings and the transcript of the trial, and what my father told me. He blamed it all on you—hell, Alec was so perfect in my old man's eyes that nothing could have made him think otherwise. But I—" He struggled with it, as though not wanting to say the rest.

"I've blamed myself for every wrong step Alec took since we were kids," he finally said in a low, hoarse voice. "He was *my* responsibility after Mom died—any trouble he got into was my fault. I grew up with that hanging over my head, and I hated it—and him—so bad I could taste it! When I left home and joined the navy, I thought it was over. Then when Dad contacted me about the trial . . ." He shuddered, pacing now, not even looking at her. "It was as though he was blaming *me*—as though if I'd been around to keep an eye on Alec none of it would have happened. I . . . I went a little crazy. I told him Alec was going to have to fight this one without me. I didn't even go home for the trial."

She didn't want to hear any of this, Jordon told herself calmly. She didn't give a damn about Kel Stuart Davies's excuses or explanations . . . and yet there was something that kept her there, silent and waiting. Something about the pain in his eyes. The anguish on that lean, handsome face as he paced the firelight like something restless and caged.

"Part of me wanted Alec to be found guilty. I *wanted* it! It seemed like perfect justice. Payback for all those years when we were kids and I got blamed every time he got into trouble. But this was one time when little Alec Davies was going to have to face the music on his own because good ol' Kel wasn't going to be around to take the heat."

A muscle ticked along the side of his jaw and he glanced sidelong at her, his eyes sultry with anger. "I figured he was innocent. Alec was capable of a lot, but I honestly didn't think he could do something like that. But that just made it better. It made me smile every time I thought of him on the stand, finally being made to pay—and the irony was, it was for something he didn't even do." He gave a bark of harsh laughter, but his eyes, when he looked at her again, weren't laughing at all. They were haunted eyes, and the expression in them made her shiver.

"When he got off, it didn't surprise me. Just the old Alec Davies charm at work. It had never failed when we were kids and I figured it was as potent as ever. Then . . ." He swal-

owed, staring down into the flames. "Then six months ago
got word that he'd holed up in a ten-dollar-a-night motel
on the edge of town with a quart of cheap bourbon and a
gun he bought off some kid for twenty bucks. The maid
found him the next morning. He'd put the barrel in his
mouth and—" He braced both hands on the mantel and
leaned heavily on his outstretched arms, eyes squeezed
closed.

"It wasn't your fault." The words were out of her mouth
before Jordon even realized she'd been thinking them.

They surprised Kel almost as badly as they had her. He
lifted his head slowly and gave her a quizzical look.
"What?"

"I said, it wasn't your fault." She rubbed her arms, shivering slightly in spite of the heat in the room. "But more to
the point, it wasn't mine, either. You didn't come up here
looking for answers at all. You just wanted me to admit that
I'd lied at the trial. You wanted Alec to be innocent so you
could blame his suicide on me." She stared at him defiantly, seeing by his eyes that it was true. "Is that why you
slept with me? To see if I really *was* as easy as everyone
said?"

"That didn't have a damned thing to do with Alec!"

"It had everything to do with Alec! He's the reason
you're even up here."

"But he wasn't the reason I made love to you, lady," he
grated. "That was just between you and me. Hell, I know
it wasn't right—but it just all fell apart once I met you, Jordon. Once I realized what Alec had done to you, I... Hell,
I don't know. I felt responsible in a way. As though if
I'd—"

"*Responsible?* Was that all it was? Just charity?"

"Damn it, Jordon, quit twisting everything I say!"

"I'll bet you convinced yourself that you were doing me
a real favor. A week ago I was scared if a man even got close
to me, but now—thanks to you, Dr. Feelgood—I'm almost

cured. Maybe I should nominate you for a Good Citizen
ship award.''

She turned and stalked toward the door. ''You don't giv
a damn about me, Kel, don't kid yourself. I was just you
do-good project for the week.'' She paused to look aroun
at him. ''But for all your excuses and your lies and your ra
tionalizations, you're no better than Alec was. The onl
difference is that when *he* raped me, he didn't pretend it wa
anything more than what it was. At least he didn't make m
fall in love with him first!''

The expression on Kel's face in that moment—had sh
cared—would have been worth all the pain. He went a
white as ashes under his tan, the torment flickering acros
his face so real that she turned away abruptly and walked t
the door, unable to look at him. There was no satisfactio
in her victory. They'd both struck mortal blows, and al
though she may have gotten in the last hurtful word, his ha
wounded deeper.

She hadn't even reached the wide curved staircase lead
ing down to the main floor of the lodge before her eyes fille
with tears. And although she fought them valiantly as sh
strode across the lobby and out the front doors, by the tim
she'd reached the parking lot they were streaming down he
cheeks.

It was only then—when she pulled open the door on th
Bronco and Murphy shoved his broad, furry face into her
worriedly, giving her cheeks a swipe with his tongue—tha
she realized she hadn't returned the dog to Kel. And, for on
heartfelt moment, she didn't care. She wrapped her arm
around his neck and sobbed into his thick fur and Murph
rested his chin on her shoulder and whimpered softly, a
though understanding exactly how a broken heart felt.

Chapter 11

She didn't remember the two-hour drive back to her trailer. Didn't remember ripping off her clothes and getting into a pounding hot shower. Didn't remember crawling into bed—and thinking that it had never before felt so big and empty and cold.

She kept seeing Kel's face—the haunted anguish in his eyes as she'd turned and walked out, the despair, the grief. It had all been too real to have been feigned. Whatever hell he'd put her through, he'd been right there with her.

And maybe that's what made hating him so hard.

And she tried—she tried! Up and down all night, pacing the moonlit corners of the trailer, she tried almost desperately to work up the rage that she knew should be there. But it eluded her, leaving her feeling more sad and weary and despairing than angry.

Even the shock of finding out who he was had worn off finally. When she'd gone through the file that Harris had brought her, it had sickened her—not just the lies and betrayal, but *who* he was. It was as though Alec himself had

stepped back into her life, bringing with him all the horro
and the outrage.

But now...? She cradled the mug of steaming chamo
mile tea between her palms, trying to draw warmth from i
Now there was nothing but a gaping, bland emptiness. And
oddly, the worst part was knowing the real reason he'd mad
love to her.

Revenge would have been preferable. Revenge she coul
have understood. Could have handled. But pity...?

And it was only then that she realized she was crying.

She didn't even hear the truck pull in late the next morr
ing, too busy swearing at the balky generator to notice any
thing else. It was only when she saw something move fror
the corner of her eye that she realized she wasn't alone.

Turning her head, she saw the tall figure looming throug
the doorway of the shed and was in motion in the next in
stant, spinning away from the generator and snatching u
the rifle in one move. "Don't even think about coming an
closer!"

The man stopped dead, his eyes narrowing as he looke
at the rifle pointed at his belly. "Do you know how to us
that thing?"

"You're damned right I do. And unless you've got par
you don't mind losing, you'll stay right where you are."

A smile brushed his mouth. "You must be Jordo
Walker. Kel told me about you."

"Yeah? Well, Kel Davies is no friend of mine, so don'
count on that keeping you alive. Who are you and what d
you want?"

"I'm Trey Hollister. And I came up here looking for you
And," he added, the smile widening, "to see how my dog'
doing."

That should have been the first clue that she was in n
danger, Jordon realized. Instead of tearing the stranger's le
off, Murphy was bouncing around like an overgrown pup

whimpering with excitement, tail windmilling. Hollister gestured toward him with a nod of his head. "Do you mind...?"

Jordon shook her head, taking the rifle off him, and watched as he hunkered down and started rough-housing with the shepherd. Murphy applied a liberal swipe of wet tongue to the man's face, eliciting a sputter of protest, and after a moment or two more, Hollister got to his feet, wiping his face with his sleeve. "How's he been working out?"

"He's been wonderful." Jordon smiled, watching Murphy nudge Hollister's hand with his nose. "Kel said he was worth his weight in marines, and it's true. I'm going to miss him."

"No rush—keep him as long as you need to. My boy missed him pretty bad for a few days, then Linn—my wife—found a stray kitten on the beach, so poor old Murph's all but forgotten."

Jordon had to laugh, liking this tall, dark-eyed man almost at once. In spite of the fact he looked every inch a Barbary pirate, she found herself thinking, his dark hair long and wind-blown, the flash of gold in his right ear unmistakable. He had a reckless smile and dangerous eyes, and he made her think of Kel....

"What can I do for you, Mr. Hollister?" she asked abruptly.

"I'm looking for Kel. I figured you might know where he is."

She managed a rough smile as she walked by him and out the door of the shed into the sunshine. "You know, you really ought to be more careful about your choice of friends. Davies is gone. He left last night. I have no idea where, and no interest in knowing."

He followed her at a thoughtful distance. "So...you know who he is."

"I know who he is. And *what* he is." Jordon managed another rough smile. "Biologically impossible, of course—and an insult to Murphy's ancestry. But you get my point."

"I don't imagine my word counts for much, and I doubt you're interested in hearing this, but—for what it's worth—Kel Davies is a hell of a good man. He didn't come up here to hurt you. In any sense of the word. He just needed some answers."

"So he said." Jordon turned her face to the sun for a moment, eyes closed, then looked at Hollister. "If you know why Kel came up here, then you know what his brother did to me."

"Yeah." His face darkened with anger. "I know. But don't judge Kel because of that. Alec Davies was cold and manipulative and spoiled rotten—he'd been raised as a child prodigy, given everything he wanted, and he just figured the world was his plaything. If he wanted something, he took it—right and wrong meant nothing to him. Ethics and morality and rules applied only to other people. *Lesser* people. He was too brilliant and gifted, too damned superior, to have to live according to the rules set by mere mortals. That was all right for people like Kel. But not for him."

"I'm not really interested in this, Mr. Hollister. I'm sorry I can't help you, but—"

"Did he tell you how his old man broke down at the funeral and told Kel that it should have been *him* that had died, and not Alec?"

Jordon stared at him. "You can't be serious."

"I'm dead serious. His old man figures it was Kel's fault that Alec killed himself—that if Kel hadn't run off to join the navy, if he'd stayed in touch, if he'd come home during the trial…" He gave his head an angry shake. "Like I said, Kel came here looking for answers. Except I figure the ones he found weren't the ones he'd expected." Hollister was silent for a moment. "Sometimes," he said carefully, "a man has to tear his life apart to get it back together."

And where had she fit in, Jordon found herself wondering. Had she been part of the tearing apart, or part of the healing? She abruptly shook her thoughts off. "You're going to have to excuse me now. I have work to do."

"The damn fool's gone in alone."

"What?" Not even wanting to, Jordon found herself stopping and looking around. "What do you mean?"

"I mean he's gone after whoever killed Jimmie Two Shoes."

Jordon just looked at him. "You're crazy. He doesn't even work for the Wildlife people—it was all just a long complicated story he concocted to—"

"He didn't concoct it, I did." Hollister's face was grim. "I run a high-tech antiterrorist security business, and my men get hired by various government agencies when people with specialized training are needed. Technically, Kel was working for me. At first it *was* just a cover story, but Jimmie Two Shoes's murder changed all that. Kel was up here to find you all right, but he was also trying to find who put a bullet through one of my undercover agents. And to bring down that poaching ring that's been making your life miserable for the past six months."

He was telling the truth, Jordon could see it in his eyes. And for some silly reason that didn't make any sense at all, it scared her.

Even telling herself that she didn't care—that it was none of her business, that Kel could look after himself just fine, thank you—she felt her heart turn over. She rubbed her bare arms, looking up at the mountains. "I hate to tell you this, but your agent's flown the coop. We had a . . . discussion, I guess you could call it. Last night. He was packing to leave when I turned up, and I can guarantee I didn't say anything that would have made him change his mind."

"He didn't go." There was something in Hollister's voice that made Jordon look around. "He intended to, all right— he called me last night and told me all about it. Then early this morning he left a message with my people saying that he'd changed his plans. That he was following up a hot lead. He said some guy by the name of Harris had got hold of enough evidence to put paid to the poachers—and whoever killed Jimmie—once and for all."

"Harris? John Harris?"

"That's right. Kel said he was meeting him this morning, up around someplace called Lamehorse Canyon. He asked for backup—FBI, FWS, border patrol, the works. He must be on to something hot...." He shook his head, looking worried. "He left the Caribou Lodge around seven, and no one's seen him since. And I have a bad feeling. A real bad feeling."

She didn't care, Jordon reminded herself savagely. If Kel was out there playing superagent, it was his business. She didn't have anything to do with it. "I'm sure he'll turn up," she said shortly, turning to walk back to the trailer. "And if you and Peterson and the FBI and the FWS and the border patrol and whoever else you've got out there looking for him can spare a *moment* of time, you might think about catching a poacher or two while you're at it!" The anger she felt was hot and all-encompassing, and she didn't even bother fighting it. It felt good just to be feeling *something* again other than numbed misery.

"Hey!" He took a running step or two after her. *"Hey!"*

"What!" She turned and glared at him. "I don't know where Davies is, all right? So why don't you just go and find someone who gives a damn!"

Hollister just looked at her for a long moment, his eyes shrewd and a little too speculative. "I've got thirty men coming in later today, but it could be too late by then. I need to get up to Lamehorse Canyon—now—and I need you to tell me the quickest route. That's all I want from you, Jordon—just a map and some directions."

"Hire a guide, Mr. Hollister. The town's full of men who know their way around these mountains better than I ever will."

Hollister stared at her for a hard moment, then swore between his teeth and wheeled away. "If he comes through here, tell him to get back to the lodge and *wait* for me. And tell him that report he was waiting for came in from the FBI labs this morn—"

"Report?" Jordon's voice snapped through the cool air. "The blood sample? The one in the back of John Harris's truck?"

Hollister looked around at her sharply. "*Harris's* truck? You mean the same Harris who—?"

"Yes." Fear tightened Jordon's throat and she swallowed, fighting it down. "What did the report say?"

Hollister paused, as though trying to decide how much to tell her. "The sample was human blood. A-positive."

"And—" She had to swallow again. "And Jimmie Two Shoes's blood type? What was it?"

Hollister's face was grim. "A-positive."

Jordon closed her eyes, feeling numbed and cold. John Harris. Kel had been right all along. And Kel was meeting him.... "He's walking into a trap."

Hollister's oath was savage. "I've got to get up there. Now."

"But it wouldn't make any sense for him to go up there on his own. Not after calling you. He'd wait for you, wouldn't he? He wouldn't just go charging up there alone."

"He would," Hollister said grimly. "He's ex-Special Forces, used to working alone. Problem is, he's not thinking clearly. He isn't doing this because of the job, he's doing it because of you."

"Me?" It was an indignant yelp.

"You. The man's in love with you, haven't you figured that out yet? And a man in love does crazy things!" He sounded as though he'd had some close personal experience with the phenomenon, and wasn't very happy about it.

"You're the crazy one if you think—"

"Hell, I doubt he even knows it himself yet. But he's up there right now walking into a trap because of it. Because he figures he owes you, maybe. Because he knows the eagles are important to you—and saving them, bringing the poachers in, is one way he can make it up to you ... hell, a hundred reasons." He looked at her evenly. "But they're all about you. And it scares me. Because he figures it's all over between you, that it's all gone wrong, that he's got nothing left to lose. And that makes him reckless."

Something cold walked down her spine. "What do you mean ... reckless? I thought he was good at this sort of thing."

"One of the best. But he's doing it for all the wrong reasons. He's not trying to bring these guys to justice because it's his job, he's doing it for you. He's being a damned *hero.*" He made the word sound like an obscenity.

And maybe, Jordon thought uneasily, for men like this it was. "But ... he wouldn't do anything stupid. Would he?"

His one look told Jordon everything she didn't want to know. Her stomach was a knot of ice. "You said you wanted a map."

"I need to get up there without being seen."

"But you can't go up there after him alone!" Jordon stared at him in disbelief. "My God, you *are* as crazy as he is!"

"Look, I know you figure you don't owe him a thing—and maybe you're right, I don't know. But damn it, he's a good friend of mine. And he's in trouble."

"Because of me," Jordon said sarcastically.

"Because of me." Trey turned away, his voice rough. "Because I helped him find you in the first place, even though I knew it was insane. And because when it all started to fall apart and he came to me two weeks ago, wanting out, I talked him into staying."

Jordon looked at Hollister's broad back, her heart giving an unruly thump. "Two weeks ago?" she asked very carefully. "He said he wanted to leave two weeks ago?"

"Yeah." He looked around at her. "He said he'd found out all he needed to know—I figure he meant he'd found out the truth about Alec. And he said it was starting to get complicated...that if he stayed, you were going to be hurt." He let his gaze slide from hers almost guiltily. "Anyway, I talked him into staying. So if it's anyone's fault he's out there playing hero, it's mine."

Two weeks ago. Right after that afternoon they'd spent at the creek. When she'd asked him to make love to her and he'd pushed her away and had stormed off like a man possessed.

It was a small thing. Just a detail, really. But somehow it seemed very important.

"If you can draw that map for me, I'd appreciate it." He sounded subdued. "I've got to call Peterson and tell him what's going down. And I want you to hightail it for town—all hell's going to bust loose up here, and you're right in the firing line. If I *do* get Davies down alive and he finds out I let you get hurt..." He grinned suddenly, looking boyish in the morning sun.

He strode across to his truck and rummaged inside it, then walked around and spread a map across the hood, his radio in one hand. Jordon watched him for a moment, then turned and walked into the trailer.

She felt very calm all of a sudden. It would be the easiest thing in the world to just let him go. To tell herself it was impossible, for too many reasons to count. To convince herself that she didn't want him—didn't love him—and that what they'd had for that too-short time had counted for nothing at all.

She could do that all right. He was Alec Davies's brother, and it would be easy to find all the right excuses.

The hard thing would be to damn well take a chance. To fight for what she knew in her heart was true.

The small automatic pistol that Kel had insisted she keep for added protection—against all her vehement protests— was in the cupboard where he'd left it. It was unloaded, the six clips lying beside it on the top shelf, and she loaded one into the pistol as he'd taught her. Tucking the gun into her jacket pocket, she slipped the extra clips into the other pocket, then added a box of cartridges for the rifle. And it occurred to her a little grimly that for someone who hated guns and knew nothing about playing cops and robbers, she was faking it pretty damned well. Then grabbing up the rifle she went back outside.

Hollister was talking into the radio when she came out and he watched her walk across to her Bronco. He finished barking orders into the radio and leaned through the window of his truck to pull it back into its cradle. "Do you have that map for me?"

"A map is useless in this part of the country. These mountains are crisscrossed with old logging roads and hunting trails and game trails—half of them have never been mapped, and the other half aren't where the maps say they are anyway." She pulled the Bronco door open and slid behind the wheel. "Grab your things and get in. You need four-wheel drive and extra-high suspension where we're going—you'll take the transmission out on that truck the first set of serious ruts you come to."

"No way." He shook his head firmly. "Uh-uh. I'm not taking you up there. It's too dangerous."

Jordon shrugged and started the engine. "I'm going up there to find Kel, Mr. Hollister. Are you coming with me or not?"

"Look, lady," he bawled, "you can't just—*hold it!* Damn it, stop!" Jordon braked sharply and he glared at her.

All right, all right," he growled. "Hang on while I grab my ear." It took him only a minute to transfer the duffel bag— nd Murphy—from the back of his truck to the Bronco, and rhen he slid into the passenger seat he gave her a faintly peculiative look. "You love him, don't you?"

"I do, Mr. Hollister," Jordon said with a sigh. "God help ke, I do."

He was dead.

Not literally, perhaps. But close enough to it that quib- ding over *how* dead wasn't going to make a hell of a lot of ifference.

The point was, he'd run out of luck about the same time e'd run out of ammunition, and whoever had come up be- ind him with that M-16 assault rifle had known how to use

.

He was bleeding. Bad. He'd torn up part of his shirt and ad tied it over the hole in his shoulder, but that probably vasn't going to be what killed him anyway.

Exposure would do that. Or maybe the sea. Each wave hat crashed into the wide mouth of the cave seemed to pile little higher on the jumble of rocks between him and the vater, and he didn't have any more strength to drag himself o higher ground.

If there was higher ground. They'd tossed him down a issure in the limestone cliffs and into a cave that faced open vater, and although the cavern mouth wasn't entirely sub- nerged, it well could be at high tide. The rocks around him vere slimy with seaweed and algae, telling him all too raphically that if he didn't move he was going to drown as he tide came up... except he couldn't move. His ankle was roken, by the feel of it. And he was still so groggy from the low on the head he couldn't think straight... just knew that ie had to pull himself into the back of the cave where it was iigher. Out of the path of the incoming tide... Move... *Aove...!*

* * *

"I don't like this one little bit." Hollister shaded his eye and stared up at the pale wall of rock soaring above them. "You're wide open up there, Jordon—anyone with a rif and scope can pick you off like a target at a country fair!'

"I'll be fine," Jordon assured him, wishing she felt eve half as confident as she was pretending to be. The truth wa she was scared to death, and she had to keep her hands ou of sight so Hollister couldn't see them shaking. "Kel cam up here—those are definitely his truck tracks. And the *know* he's up here or they wouldn't have done that." Sh nodded to the huge fir tree lying across the narrow loggin road, blocking it completely. "They don't want him gettin out—or reinforcements coming in."

"Kel could have done it himself," Hollister said grimly "To keep them penned in while he cleans them out."

"And cut off his own retreat?" But the minute she sai it, Jordon knew the answer. He'd come up here knowin there was no retreat—he'd either come out victorious, or h wouldn't be coming out at all. "This logging road only goe one place—Lamehorse Canyon. It ends at an old deserte lumber mill just above the cliffs. At least it *used* to be de serted." She gave Hollister a pointed look. "It's completel isolated except for this road—the only other way in or ou is by helicopter. It would be a perfect place to set up poaching base."

"You'd think someone would have stumbled across it b now."

"This is John Harris's territory up here—he'd just file hi reports saying there was no activity in the area, and who' question him?" She didn't even try to keep the anger out o her voice. "Besides, no one ever comes up here. The whol coast is riddled with caves and undersea caverns, and ther are blow holes and fissures in the cliffs. When the wave wash into the caves, air is forced out the fissures and i makes all sorts of eerie groans and whispers. Then when th waves pull back, air is drawn back *into* the caves—it's as though the mountain is alive and breathing. The local Natives and old-timers won't come near the place, and it's too isolated to interest anyone else."

"I still say it's too risky."

"If we go in together, we're going to be twice as easy to spot. If we split up, we can come in from two different directions and odds are *one* of us will find something to tell us where Kel is. And to warn him about Harris."

Hollister's face was hard. "Damn it, Jordon, you're not trained for this kind of thing. You have no idea what you could be up against."

"I know what I'm up against." Jordon checked her climbing gear, then slung the heavy coil of rope over her shoulder. "These people will kill me as soon as they look at me. But it's too easy to back off when things get rough, Trey. Too easy to just say 'I can't fight anymore—let someone else take care of it.' I did that once, and I'll never do it again. These people are destroying the wildlife up here, they killed Jimmie Two Shoes and now they're trying to kill Kel." She managed a grim little smile. "If I don't go in there—and if Kel gets hurt—I'll never be able to forgive myself."

"Like I said—people in love do crazy things." He gave his head a shake and swore under his breath. "I don't know how I can stop you, short of chaining you to this damned tree. So just keep your head down, okay? Peterson and the others will be here in a couple of hours and this whole thing is going to blow wide open. Make sure you're not in the middle of it when it does, because the bean counters in Washington get real unhappy when civilians get hurt during operations like this." The worry in his eyes belied his rough tone. "And if you find Davies, tell him that he's ordered—*ordered*—to pull back and wait for the cavalry."

"If I get into trouble I'll send up smoke signals." She grinned at him, trying to ignore the cold, stark terror clutching her heart. "If you find him first, tell him I love him." In case I can't, she nearly added. In case...

"Tell him yourself," he growled. "And no heroics, understand?"

He was still alive.

Kel grinned groggily and wiped the sweat from his face. Beyond him, where the floor of the cave sank below the water but was still sheltered from the pounding surf, the rightful landlords of the cave were in full-voiced residence. Sea lions. Fifty or more, Kel estimated. They ranged in size from tiny pups to two massive bulls who had spent the past half hour roaring lazy insults at each other from opposite sides of a dry rock that lifted above the water. The majority seemed to be cows, fat and sleek, some of them nursing pups, some floating in the heaving swells that washed in with every wave, some simply lying on the rocks asleep.

Jordon would love it, he found himself thinking with a weak grin. Even the incredible, mind-numbing stink of sea lion and rotted fish and tidal debris and animal waste wouldn't faze her. Five minutes down here with them and she'd have them all cataloged and named and would be setting up camera angles and trying to figure out how to band the young ones without getting eaten alive in the process.

A wave broke noisily on the rocks beside him, splattering him with oily spray, and he swore thickly and forced himself to sit up, to drag himself a couple of feet farther toward the higher end of the cave. Part of him wondered why he was even bothering to prolong it—he was drifting in and out of consciousness as it was and if he passed out again, he'd probably drown. If he didn't bleed to death first... or freeze. It was just a matter of time.

And the worst part was that he wasn't going to get a chance to tell Jordon he was sorry....

* * *

"Don't move, or you're dead." Something gave Jordon
a sharp jab between the shoulder blades again and she
closed her eyes, trying desperately not to panic. "Well, well,
well," the voice behind her said with a cold laugh. "I always said we were going to have a party one day, you and
me."

Rolly Murdoch. A scream clawed at her throat but Jordon refused to give in to it, lying unmoving on the flat rock
overlooking the logging camp. What in God's name had
happened! She could have sworn that she'd been in the clear
as she'd made her way down here. That no one could have
seen her slipping through the trees and undergrowth....

"Get on your feet." He jabbed her with the rifle barrel
again.

"Rolly?" Jordon wet her lips, daring to glance over her
shoulder. "You don't want to take me down there and share
me with Bud and the others, do you?"

"Nice try, but I ain't that stupid." Rolly gripped her upper arm and dragged her to her feet, his smile cruel. "You
can't offer anything I can't just take, Jo-Jo. And takin's half
the fun."

She thought wildly of just wrenching away from him and
trying to run for it. But the rifle in his hand made her hesi-
tate just a heartbeat too long and then Bud and two others
were there, and it was too late. Rolly gave her a brutal shove,
and together they stumbled and slipped down the rocky
hillside to the camp.

It was John Harris she saw first. There was a group of
people standing near a collection of vehicles to one side of
what had once been a bunkhouse, now mostly fallen in. He
stared at her in shock, then sprinted across the clearing toward her.

"Why did you bring her here!" Harris looked frightened
and pale, his skin clammy with sweat, and he stepped between her and Rolly. "I told you to leave her out of it,
Murdoch!"

"I found her spyin' on us from up on them rocks." Rolly gestured with the rifle. "And I thought *you* said you could keep her from snoopin' around up here."

"Damn it, Jordon, why couldn't you just stay away!"

Harris moved toward her and Jordon recoiled. "Don't you touch me! You killed him, didn't you! You killed Jimmie Two Shoes."

"No! I never knew anything about it, Jordon, I swear! Not until it was too late. I never even knew they'd used my truck to move his body until later. And by then—"

"Shut up, Harris." Bud Murdoch looked hot and angry. "I don't like this. I thought you said no one knew about this camp, and suddenly we've got *two* of them up here! Something's wrong."

Two? Jordon looked at him, her heart racing. Who was the other one? Kel? Hollister?

"I told you," Harris said quickly. "I tricked Davies into coming up. I knew he was on to us and—"

"On to you, you mean," Rolly said, jabbing at Harris with his rifle. "He was just on to you, and you led him right up here."

"I just thought—" Harris swallowed nervously. "I mean—"

"That's your problem, Harris—you *don't* think. That's why you were just supposed to do what you were told." Rolly glowered at Jordon. "What are we going to do with her? If we kill her, these mountains are going to be knee-deep in law."

"Not if it looks like an accident." Bud smiled coldly. "All we have to do is make it look as though she fell trying to climb to a nest, and no one will think twice about it." Rolly lifted his rifle slightly and Bud put his hand up to stop him. "No. We want her body to turn up right away so we don't have the RCMP and that bunch of tree huggers she works for wandering around up here looking for her. Just give her a knock on the head and dump her off the cliff."

"No!" Harris stepped in front of Jordon. "You can't kill her. It's gone too far, Murdoch. First Two Shoes, then Davies—"

"Kel?" Jordon's heart quite literally stopped. "What have you done to Kel!"

Rolly smiled. "I shot him. And stuffed what was left down a crack into a sea cave. By the time the water and crabs and birds are finished with him, it'll take the experts a year to figure out who it is. And by that time we'll be long gone." He stepped forward, reaching for her. "And now it's your turn."

And the last thing Jordon remembered clearly, as hands came groping toward her, was the sound of a woman's scream of rage and anguish, and then she was snatching for the rifle hanging over Rolly Murdoch's shoulder....

Chapter 12

It was a scream that wakened him.

Or what he thought had been a scream. He sat up grog-gily, vaguely surprised to realize he was still alive. How long had he been out? Five minutes? An hour?

It was darker now. The crescent of sky and sea visible from the cave mouth was just a dull pewter and the light reflected on the ceiling and far wall had dimmed to almost nothing at all. The sea lions were still there. Kel wondered if they came in to shelter here for the night, realizing, with some regret, that he knew nothing at all about them. And probably never would, he reminded himself grimly, aside from what he learned during the next few hours. Or as long as it took him to die.

He gave his head a shake, trying to clear it. He wasn't dead *yet,* damn it. If the bullet hole in his shoulder hadn't killed him and the fall to the floor of this cave hadn't killed him and the rising tide hadn't killed him ... well, maybe he shouldn't be so quick to write himself off.

Hell, what was a bullet hole and a broken ankle or two? He had a trio of really good reasons to get out of this mess alive—seeing Rolly Murdoch face life for the murder of Jimmie Two Shoes, knock a few of John Harris's teeth down his throat just on general principles . . . and tell Jordon Walker that he loved her.

There was a noise back in the darkness toward the rear of the cave, the sound of what could have been a scuffed footfall, a few falling pebbles. He went motionless, straining to listen, and folded his fist around a piece of driftwood. He didn't have a lot of fight left in him, but he didn't intend to go down without a hell of a struggle. Some of the sea lions were ponderously hauling themselves up onto the rocks, but that wasn't what he'd heard. They moved like sacks of cement; whatever was moving in the shadows behind him was as stealthy as a cat.

Cougar? Surely no mountain cat in its right mind would pick its way down here to hunt. Even if it did manage to snatch one of the sea lion pups, how would it get its kill back up to the top of the cliffs? Unless there was another way into this death trap . . . and another way out.

And then—the sound of it so incongruous, so unexpected, that he simply blinked—there was a short and earthily pungent oath that went ringing eerily around the cave, causing a ripple of concern among the sea lions.

Kel closed his eyes, breathing an oath of his own, torn between relief and numbed bemusement. It couldn't be, of course. That blow to the back of his head must have done more harm than he'd thought, because he was obviously hallucinating . . .

"K-Kel?" Her voice wavered with fear and cold and uncertainty, echoing off stone. "Are you in here?"

"Here." He struggled to sit up, biting back a groan of agony as his ankle twisted awkwardly. "I'm here, Jory."

"Oh my God!" She exploded out of the darkness like a small whirlwind, and in the next instant she was beside him, her face no more than a pale circle in the rapidly fading light, her eyes huge with fright. "Kel...Kel, they said they'd killed you." A sob broke through the words. "They said they'd shot you. That they'd thrown your body in h-here and..."

"They did." His voice was hoarse, but he managed to grin at her as he grabbed a fistful of fabric at the front of her jacket and pulled her against him, wrapping his one good arm around her tightly and burying his face into her sea-damp hair. "I must be dreaming—I never thought I'd see you again."

"You didn't really think you were going to get away from me this easily, did you?" She was trying to laugh, but little hiccuping sobs kept breaking through, spoiling the effect. "Getting yourself killed in action—no matter how honorable the cause—is *not* an option. We'll just work things out."

"What in the *hell* are you doing here?"

"Saying I'm sorry," she whispered, hugging him fiercely. "Saying I love you. Saying that I don't want to lose you." She gave a hiccuping laugh. "I was terrified I wouldn't get a chance to tell you I'm sorry for all the dumb things I said last night."

"I recall saying a few myself," he murmured against her ear. "How did you find me down here? How did you get in?"

"Same way you did—compliments of Rolly Murdoch."

He swore softly. "Are you all right? He didn't hurt you, did he?"

"N-no." She sounded frightened and shaken up, but reassuringly clearheaded. "I hit my head when Rolly shoved me down that crack, but I'm okay." She gave him a hostile look, her eyes flashing in the faint light reflecting off the water. "He's going to regret that. He was supposed to throw me over the cliff so the RCMP would think I'd had a climbing accident. Except when he said he'd killed you, I kicked him in the...well, where I should have kicked Alec when he attacked me, I guess. Anyway, it made Rolly so mad he said he wanted me to think about how I was dying, so he shoved me down here instead. He and Bud are up there now arguing about it. But I doubt Bud's going to climb down here and do it right.''

''They must be getting real nervous if they're willing to risk killing you. Even if they did make it look like an accident, there'd be an investigation and an inquest. And a lot of very suspicious people ready to make trouble.''

''They didn't have a lot of choice,'' Jordon said disgustedly. ''I found your truck at the creek and tracked you as far as the old mill. Except Rolly spotted me.'' She pulled his shirt and jacket gently away from his shoulder, frowning as she checked the wound in his shoulder. ''Trey says the cavalry's on its way—we just have to hang on until they get here.''

''Trey? Trey Hollister is with you?''

''And Murphy. But we split up, and I don't know where he is now. He got your message, though. The FBI, the FWS, the RCMP and about six dozen other alphabet-soup agencies are on their way.'' She let his jacket fall closed and got to her feet. ''That's the good news. The bad news is, they won't be here for hours.''

He nodded, teeth gritted, wondering how many more hours he was going to be able to hang on. And even then ... could Trey find them? He thought about telling her all this, telling her they were on their own, but it was hard just to concentrate on what she was saying let alone making the effort to talk. ''You never did tell me what you're doing up here.'' It was no more than a hoarse whisper. ''Trey wouldn't have brought you. Not voluntarily.''

Even in the dimness of the cave, he could see the flicker of her smile. ''Not voluntarily. But when I realized you were walking into a trap, I had to come.'' She touched his cheek with her fingertips. ''I love you, Kel. And the thought of losing you..." Her eyes seemed very bright and he wondered if she were crying. It gave him an odd feeling, seeing the fear in her eyes and knowing it was for him; seeing the love glowing in every look she gave him, and knowing that it, too, was for him.

He couldn't die, he found himself thinking a little idiotically. Not with this much to live for. A man would be a damned fool to be so close to this kind of happiness and then die and lose it all. He thought of holding her in the night, of loving her...and held on to the thought with a fierce, single-minded intensity.

He realized then that Jordon had slipped out of her heavy denim jacket and was unbuttoning the flannel work shirt she was wearing under it, and in spite of the pain and weakness, he found himself grinning like a madman. "I love your bedside manner, sweetheart."

"You wish," she told him mildly. "If you can think about sex at a time like this, you're obviously in better shape than you look." She worried away at the hem of the shirt for a few minutes, then he heard fabric ripping and saw she was tearing the shirt into strips. "You really got yourself banged up this time, mister. What's the damage assessment besides the rather obvious hole in your shoulder?"

"Left ankle's broken...maybe the leg, too. Couple of busted ribs. Slight concussion."

She closed her eyes for a moment, as though collecting her strength, then nodded, her face grim and businesslike. "Well, I guess we're going to find out if that first aid course I took paid for itself or not. All I've used it for so far is patching up broken wings."

"How did you know I was walking into a trap?" He was asking it more to distract himself than anything else, as she started easing his jacket off his shoulder. "I didn't know myself until it was too late. I didn't trust Harris—hell, you know that—but he still managed to catch me by surprise."

"Trey said the FBI lab report came in—and that the blood in the back of Harris's truck was human. And probably Jimmie's." She shook her head. "You were right about him. And it explains a lot—why every time the RCMP tried to set a trap for these guys, they were never there, how the poachers always seemed to know exactly what was going on. Anyway, when Trey said you'd left a message that you were meeting Harris, I knew right away..."

Kel watched her for a minute or two, feeling something tight pull through him that had nothing to do with the pain or the anger at his situation or even the fear of dying. It was something else, something precious and rare and so achingly perfect it made his chest ache. "You could have been killed," he whispered hoarsely. "Damn it, Jory—you shouldn't have come after me. If you die down here..."

"I'm not going to die down here," she said matter-of-factly. "And neither are you."

"Jory—"

"Shut up, Kel. Just shut up, all right?" Her voice rose with anger, ringing off wet rock, edged with fear. "Now, the tide's coming in—and this whole part of the cave is going to be underwater soon. We've got to get back up to that ledge—it's dry rock up there and we'll be safe. But I can't carry you, Kel. You're too big and you're too heavy. So you're going to have to help me."

He didn't remember much about the next while except the pain—and Jordon's voice, snapping around him angrily as she chivied and harassed him into dragging himself up to the wide, dry ledge at the back of the cave. She did a lot of it herself, one small fist gripping the collar of his jacket as she simply hauled him over the rocks by brute force, swearing furiously at him when he started to black out. And once, when he swore back at her in exhausted frustration, she slapped him soundly, rousing him to full consciousness, and the jolt of anger it had sent through him had been enough to get him that final distance.

He lay there panting, thinking through a haze of pain and dizziness that he should be talking to her. Should be telling her all the things he wanted to tell her... but every time he tried to capture the thoughts and put them in order they eluded him, and finally he just gave up and let himself slip into the waiting darkness.

He awoke with a start, clear-headed. His shoulder was hurting now, the pain raw enough to set his teeth on edge, and his left ankle and leg throbbed steadily. But he was alive. And warm.

And it was only then that he realized the snapping sound he was listening to was a log fire and that the flickering reflections on the walls and ceiling of the cave weren't from the water. Braced for the pain, he sat up slowly and looked around for Jordon.

She wasn't there, but he could see her in the far reaches of the cave, holding what looked to be a torch as she walked back and forth, searching for something. Below her, lying like tiers of logs on the ledges of rock, dozens of sea lions bellowed and barked and squabbled, seemingly undisturbed by the intrusion of their domain.

He checked the wound in his shoulder. She'd rewrapped the dressing she'd put on it earlier, and he realized she'd also roughly set his ankle using flat pieces of driftwood and strips of shirt.

Jordon came back into the ring of firelight just then, carrying an armful of driftwood, her face rived with worry and fear. But when she realized that he was awake, she grinned jauntily. "Welcome to the Hotel *Eumetopias jubatus*. We have running water, air conditioning and fresh fish on the menu if you catch it yourself." She nodded toward the sea lions. "The smell's pretty awful, but the entertainment's free."

"The Hotel Eumetopia-whatus?"

"Stellar sea lions." She dropped the driftwood and set her flaming torch by the edge of the fire. "This and a stretch along the Oregon coast are the only places they stay year-round. I've watched their rookeries from the cliffs, but I never dreamed I'd get this close to them. I'd love to come back and set up a camera and—what are you laughing at?''

"Nothing." Kel reached up and caught her hand, drawing her down beside him. "We're trapped in a half-submerged cave, people are trying to kill us and we're probably going to die of exposure, and all you can think about are how beautiful the sea lions are. You are, bar none, the most fabulous woman I've ever met."

"We're not dead yet," she replied calmly.

"How did you get the fire going?"

She grinned a little maliciously. "Rolly was supposed to search me, but he was too busy groping me to do a proper job. He didn't find these—" She held out a handful of rifle cartridges. "A little gunpowder, a little ingenuity...and we have fire."

Kel's eyes narrowed, thinking about Rolly touching her. "The little weasel's going to pay for that, too," he growled.

She checked the dressing on his shoulder. "How do you feel?"

"Like I've been shot and beat-up and dropped down a hole, but aside from that, I'm great." He looked at her wonderingly, thinking how beautiful she was in the firelight. Her face was dirty and smeared with blood—hers or his, he didn't know—and her hair was wet with sea spray and salt and there were tear tracks in the grime on her cheeks...and she was the most gorgeous, desirable thing he'd ever seen.

"I love you, lady," he told her softly, reaching out to brush a tangle of hair off her face. "I don't know how or why, but I've fallen for you in a big way."

She just smiled. "I know."

"It could get complicated."

"I think it already has."

It made him smile, and he traced the curve of her cheek with his fingertips. "I've been lying here trying to figure out how to ask you to marry me. Thinking of all the reasons why I shouldn't."

Her eyes were huge in the firelight, and she looked only slightly more surprised to hear the words than he was. "Marry?"

He had to smile again. "I guess I'm taking a hell of a lot for granted. But you did say something about loving me the other night. Of course, you could have changed your mind, by now, but—"

"I haven't changed my mind." Her face was calm, almost serene, in the flickering light. "There's a part of me that says I shouldn't love you—that I could never love Alec Davies's brother. That every time I look at you, I'll be reminded of him. That every time I make love with you, part of him will be between us."

She turned her face to kiss his palm. "But there's another part of me that says none of that matters. That if I deny how I feel about you because of Alec, I'm letting him win again. And I'm not going to do that. I love you. And if you ask me to marry you, I'll probably say yes."

"Probably?"

"Ask me and find out." Her lips curved with a mischievous smile.

Kel let his gaze caress her small, perfect features. "It won't be easy, Jory. My dad will never understand. Neither will your family. And when the media finds out, it'll be like the trial all over again. Are you sure you want to put yourself through that?"

"I put myself through this for you, didn't I?" Her gesture took in the entire cave and her soft laugh rippled through the darkness. Below them, the heavy swells washed up onto the smooth rocks and broke lazily, and Kel could hear the occasional roar and bark from the sea lion herd as it settled in for the night.

Jordon gazed at him for a long while, her expression as soft and loving as the warmth in her eyes. "I love you, Kel. If we die down here, I don't even care—because at least I'm with you. If that's crazy, then I'm crazy. And I guess Trey was right."

"I lied to you," he said quietly. "About who I am, why I was here. I followed you and spied on you. I even went through your trailer one day when you were out."

"You were hurting, Kel. Worse than I was, almost. At least I *knew* the truth. If you'd come to me openly and told me you were Alec's brother and what you wanted, I...well, I don't know what I would have done. But I don't think I'd have handled it very well. It sounds strange, but I think it was better this way. I got to know you first. To trust you."

He gave a snort. "And look where it got you."

"I don't care," she whispered, leaning forward and brushing his lips with hers. "I've got you, and that's all that matters."

Kel cradled her against him with his good arm, feeling her body heat seep into him. It was a healthy heat, a healing heat, but he wondered if it was going to be enough to keep him alive until Trey found them. If he found them.

"I wanted you to be guilty," he murmured thoughtfully. "I don't know if I'll ever forgive myself for that. Because if you were guilty of lying at Alec's trial, that meant he didn't rape you. And that meant I didn't have to lie awake nights wondering where I'd gone wrong." He kissed her hair, tightening his embrace as she snuggled against him. "You talk about taking the easy way out—that's what I did when I left home instead of taking on the responsibility of trying to straighten him out. Maybe if I'd quit making excuses for him, if I'd made him face the music when he pulled one of his stunts instead of letting him get away with it, he might have grown up normal, instead of... all twisted-up inside."

"I don't believe that." Jordon sighed, resting her head on his good shoulder and slipping her arms around him gently. "Alec was just…Alec. In a way, I actually feel sorry for him. For a while I thought he'd destroyed my life. Actually, he destroyed his own. Don't let him destroy yours with guilt."

He smiled against her hair. It was strange in a way. The reason she was in his arms at all was because of Alec. Odds were, if it hadn't been for that few minutes of brutality on the floor of a college biology lab two years ago, Jordon Walker would never have come into his life. He'd still be empty and cold and a little embittered, his heart well barricaded. It was unbelievable that anything good could come out of an act of violence like that, and yet it had....

"I love you," he murmured, letting himself drift toward unconsciousness again. "I love you…."

There was no way out.

Swearing uncreatively, Jordon swept her damp, tangled hair off her forehead and stared up at the roof of the cave. She could see the crack in the fractured rock above her that led to the surface. The fissure was long and narrow, and completely impossible to reach, a good fourteen feet above her head. And even if she did miraculously get up to it, there was a climb of what—another eight or nine feet?—up the smooth-sided chimney of rock to the surface.

A drop of twenty feet or more, total. She shivered slightly. It was a miracle she hadn't broken her neck when she'd come down. The only thing that had saved her from dropping onto the rocks where Kel had broken his ankle was that she'd somehow caught a tiny handhold at the lip of the fissure and had hung there, suspended literally by her fingertips, for the two or three seconds it had taken her to get her wits collected and correct her fall.

One more thing to thank Alec Davies for. He'd gotten her interested in rock climbing in the first place. As one of his chosen few from the doctoral program, she used to go out with him and the others once or twice a month, just as a break from the rigors of school. Little had he known her climbing skills would one day get her a job studying eagles, which in turn would get her into a war against poachers, nearly murdered and now entombed in a sea lion rookery with his older brother.

Shaking her head at the bitter irony of it all, she walked back to where Kel was lying by the fire. His skin had a gray cast that frightened her, and he was hot to the touch—too hot. He'd been restless during the night, slipping in and out of consciousness, and he'd started hallucinating near dawn, struggling to get to his feet and shouting at things that weren't there.

She quietened him finally, but he was getting worse by the minute. And it terrified her to think of having to watch him slip further and further away from her and not be able to do anything. To have him die while she raged helplessly...

"Kel?" She wiped his burning hot forehead with a rag she'd torn from her shirt. "Are you still with me?"

"I'm with you, darlin'," he whispered, his voice slurred. He turned his head away from her touch, his eyes feverish, and grinned weakly. "How are you doing?"

"I'm fine." Her voice was tight, but she tried to keep her fear out of it. It wasn't herself she was worried about. "I've explored every inch of this place, and there are exactly two ways out—through that fissure we came in by, or out the cave entrance." She looked down to the half-moon of the cave mouth, the tantalizing crescent of sky and open sea beyond.

There was a heavy surf running and even if you could battle your way through it and the riptides beyond, the water temperature would kill you in a short while. And if a strong swimmer by some miracle did get through the cave entrance and into open water, and did survive getting smashed on the jagged rocks by the relentless, pounding waves, he faced a fifty-foot climb up wet rock to the top, and a seventy- or eighty-mile hike through rain forest to the nearest hospital. . . .

"I've been lying here thinking. . .that I never did ask you to. . .marry me."

"Why don't you wait until we're out of here?"

"No." His fingers caught her wrist in a viselike grip and he held her gaze with a hot intensity. "I want you to know I love you. And that I'm sorry for everything."

"Shh." She wiped a trickle of perspiration from his cheek. "Of course I'll marry you." She bent down to kiss him gently. "But you have to ask me again when we're out of this mess, because you might be delirious and I don't want you accusing me in twenty years that I tricked you into anything."

He gave a bark of laughter that deteriorated into a ragged cough and Jordon's stomach pulled into a knot. "Just hang on, Kel," she whispered, blinking back tears. "Please hang on. I want to marry you and have your family and live with you for the rest of my life. . .so don't give up. Hang on for me. Please!"

"I'll do my best," he whispered. "Any sign of anyone yet?"

She swallowed. "No."

"No one knows we're down here, sweetheart," he reminded her gently. "They could spend years looking for us. . . ."

Years. They didn't *have* years! Kel wasn't going to last even another night. "There has to be some way to let them know." She shivered, dashing the tears off her cheek before Kel saw them. "Poor Trey. He didn't want me coming up here, but I wouldn't let him leave me behind. I said if I got into trouble, I'd send up smoke signals. But—" She stopped dead, her heart giving a thump.

"Jordon? What is it?"

"Smoke signals." She wet her lips, terrified to even voice it in case it wouldn't work. Hating to give him—and her-

elf—false hope. "It's daylight now. If I built a big fire under the fissure and put seaweed on it to make it smoke, the
draft would draw the smoke outside. And Trey might see
t...."

"The wrong people might see it, too. We don't know for
sure what's happened up there, Jordon. That gunfire we
heard during the night may not mean anything."

"I know. But even if the Murdochs do see it, what are
they going to do about it? Come down and put it out?"

"Dynamite would put it out," Kel said quietly. "Or a
couple of mortar shells." She nodded, holding his gaze with
hers, and a moment later he smiled. "Do it," he told her
decisively. "Do it."

She paused long enough to give him a lingering kiss, then
was on her feet picking up the dry driftwood she'd gathered during the night. The ledges and recesses at the back of
the cave were littered with it, collected over thousands of
years of tides and storms, and it didn't take very long for her
to have a blazing bonfire going. It took a couple of trips to
collect enough slippery strands of seaweed to create a proper
smudge, but she stood back a few minutes later and watched
the billowing clouds of smoke with satisfaction.

As she'd suspected, the natural draft created along the
clifftop drew the smoke up the fissure like a well-designed
chimney. It would be visible for miles with luck. If there
wasn't a fog bank up there to hide it, she reminded herself.
If anyone was still up there to see it. If the right people saw
it, and it brought a rescue party down and not a grenade or
a stick of dynamite.

And then, unable to do anything more, she walked back
to the other, smaller fire, to sit with the man she loved and
wait for the rescue that might never come....

"Well, all I can say," Linn Hollister was saying emphatically, "is that it's a darned good thing that when men like

you finally fall in love, you do it with a resourceful
woman!"

Kel grinned lazily, enjoying the banter and the hot sunshine and the smell of barbecuing ribs. He was stretched out
on a chaise on Trey's big sun deck, his left leg—complete
with autographed ankle cast—propped on a pile of pillows
and Jordon tucked comfortably into the curve of his good
arm.

"I can agree with that," he murmured, meeting Jordon's gaze and trying not to smile too broadly. "A resourceful woman is a hell of an asset when the going gets
rough."

To his amusement, she blushed like a schoolgirl. He
teased himself with the memory of making love to her early
that same morning in Trey Hollister's big spare bed. It had
been awkward—the cast on his ankle and the tape on his ribs
and the sling on his left arm kept getting in the way, and
there had been a few pulled muscles and odd bruises and
scrapes to watch out for. But Jordon had been deliciously
inventively resourceful, and they'd managed to spend an
erotic and very enjoyable hour or two pleasing each other.

"I'm serious." Linn paused in her salad-making long
enough to sample the dressing, then added a dash more
pepper and tossed the greens again. "I would have died of
fright down there, let alone had the presence of mind to send
up smoke signals."

Trey, playing chef at the barbecue, gave a disbelieving
snort. "This from a woman who single-handedly out-
smarted a Colombian drug lord and his entire army, and
saved my life into the bargain."

Linn smiled sweetly across the top of the barbecue at her
husband. "As you always say, people in love do crazy
things."

Kel laughed, lazy and relaxed and utterly happy. He and
Jordon had been here for five days now, recuperating in the
warmth of his old friend's easy hospitality. He gazed around

im comfortably: at Trey puttering around barbecuing ribs
nd chicken in bare feet and old cutoff jeans, at Linn look-
ıg beautiful and serene in the early days of her pregnancy,
ɩt their two-year-old son asleep in a nearby chair. Murphy
ʌas stretched out on his side, trying to sleep while a gan-
ding yellow-and-white kitten gnawed industriously on his
ɹil, pretending to be a tiger, and Poe, Trey's pet raven, sat
ın the deck railing, keeping a watchful eye for scraps.

And there was nothing here—not the love, the compan-
ɔnship, the children—that couldn't be his.

All he had to do, Kel reminded himself, was ask.

He turned his head to look at Jordon, his heart doing one
ɔf those silly flip-flops as her eyes met his. He thought,
ɹddenly, of what it had been like waking up this morning
ʌith her tucked into the curves and angles of his body. Of
ʌhat it had been like watching her as they'd made love later,
ʌatching her simply letting go, watching her respond to his
ʌery caress and touch with abandonment and trust. Of
ʌhat it would be like to awaken to her every morning . . .

"How would you like a job, Davies?"

Trey's voice broke the spell and Kel gave himself a men-
ɑl shake, looking up at his friend. "That depends. The last
ɔb you gave me damned near got me killed."

"How would you like to do it full-time?"

Jordon nearly choked on her soft drink.

"You, too," Trey told her bluntly. "The two of you make
ɩ damn good team. I'd like you to come into the security
ɒusiness with me. I keep getting requests from all over the
ʌorld for undercover people who are in touch with envi-
ɹonmental issues. Jordon, your background makes you a
ɹatural."

"Are you *crazy?* We barely made it out of there alive!"

Trey gave a cavalier shrug. "But the job got done. Rolly
Ⅿurdoch is facing life for the murder of Jimmie Two Shoes
ɩnd your *attempted* murder. Bud's going down for twenty
ɔr thirty years for his part in it. John Harris's testimony

broke the poaching ring wide open and resulted in the a
rests of over two hundred people around the globe—once w
got him talking, we could barely shut him up. He had it all-
tapes of conversations, copies of invoices and orders, pho
tographs, dates, names, even addresses and phone num
bers.''

"Did you ever find out why he did it?" Jordon asked.

"Money. It started out small—and because he cared to
much, in a way. He'd look the other way when some u
employed logger took an out-of-season whitetail to feed h
family, and turned a blind eye when local Natives took mor
than their quota of salmon. But then, like it usually does,
got away from him. And before he realized what was hap
pening, he was in too deep to quit. He was the one shootin
at you all this time, trying to scare you into leaving. Oddl
enough, he was trying to protect you."

"And this job you're offering?" Kel put in.

"The black-market trade in illegal game and animal par
is massive, and trying to put a stop to it is like trying to sto
Niagara. And it's not just the poaching that's a problem
Conservationists world-round are in danger every time the
take on an issue. Trained operatives are in high demand
And the two of you, working as a man-and-wife team
would have the perfect cover. What do you say?"

Kel looked at Jordon, who was looking at him. And sav
by her eyes that—after the initial amazement had wor
off—she was clearly intrigued. "There's one little problem
with that," he said quietly, holding her gaze. "The man
and-wife part might be tricky to fake."

She nodded thoughtfully. "How do you suggest we ge
around it? Pretend to be brother and sister?"

"We could."

She nodded again. "Trouble with that is all that siblin
rivalry stuff. It could get in the way."

"Could." He pretended to give it a lot of thought. "Or we could just get married and to hell with faking anything."

"Trey, I need you to help me with something in the kitchen." Linn was already moving toward the sliding door into the house.

"Hell, no," Trey said with a laugh. "History is in the making here—and I don't intend to miss a minute of it."

"Trey!"

"It's all right, Linn," Kel assured her with a lazy laugh. "If I'm going to do this, I may as well do it in front of God and everybody. Jordon, when we were in that cave, you said that if we got out alive—and if I was serious about marrying you—that I should ask you again when we were safe. Well, we're safe. And I'm asking. Will you marry me?"

"You're not having a relapse or anything, are you?" She looked at him worriedly. "Harris gave you an awful crack on the head with that rifle." Kel's eyes started to glitter ominously, and Jordon broke into laughter. "Yes, I will. But only on the condition that we spend our honeymoon somewhere safe and quiet. I'm tired of being shot at."

"Consider it done," Kel murmured, lowering his mouth to hers. "And the job?"

"Let's just see what happens," she said with a quiet laugh. "And handle it one day at a time."

Epilogue

Standing at the front door to the tidy brick house, Jordon took a deep breath. The baby in her arms stirred slightly, murmuring in his sleep, and she smiled down at him. Then, bracing herself, she looked up at Kel. "Ring the bell. It's time."

The man who answered it was stooped slightly, his face lined with time and grief and older than its years. He looked at Jordon for a long while, then simply nodded and looked, finally, up at his eldest son.

"Kel." The one word held more wonder than accusation. More joy than anger. "You're home. At last."

Kel smiled. "There's someone else here you should meet, Dad." He slipped his arm around Jordon and drew her nearer. "Your grandson. Daniel Alexander."

The elder Davies gazed down at the sleeping child with an expression of wonderment, and Jordon felt tears prickle her eyes. "Would you like to hold him?" she asked softly.

"Please." Gentle arms enfolded the baby, held him close. "I think," he said, softly, looking back up at Jordon, "that there's a miracle here somewhere."

And Jordon, slipping her arm around the old man's shoulders and kissing him lightly on the cheek, just nodded. "Oh, yes," she told him, smiling up at Kel. "Oh, yes."

"I'm sorry." Kel's father looked at her evenly, his eyes calm. "For what my other son did to you, I mean. Alec. And for what I did to you. Underneath, I knew he was guilty. But having to admit that..." He shook his head, looking down at the baby again. "Well, a father never wants to let go of his dreams."

"And a grandfather, Dad?" Kel asked gently. "What kind of dreams does he have?"

"Dreams of a family," his father whispered. "Dreams of a son coming home.'

"I am home." Kel smiled. "And my son needs a grandfather."

"And you, son?" Jordon held her breath as the old man's gaze moved up to meet Kel's. "Do you still need a father?"

"I was never very far away. Not really."

"You were always the strongest, Kel. Always the bravest. Alec was quick with his mind, but he...lacked something. That's why I gave him so much of my time, trying to help him. Trying to nurture that lack within him. But I guess I never explained that properly. I let you grow up thinking I didn't love you, when actually I loved you enough to let you go."

And Jordon, watching them, suddenly felt something break from around her heart and fall away, setting that last, tiny part of her free. Kel's eyes met hers across the sleeping form of his son, and he smiled, his eyes clear and happy, the shadows that had been there for so long, gone at last.

And she knew somehow that they'd all come full circle back to this point, hardened and purified by fire, as strong as tempered steel. And that Alec—son to one, brother to the other—had, finally, been put to rest. There were no more secrets now. No more shadowed memories. Just the future, unsullied and bright. And the tall, gray-eyed man—her dangerous stranger—who had stepped into her life and made it whole.

* * * * *

From the popular author of the bestselling title
DUNCAN'S BRIDE (Intimate Moments #349)
comes the

LINDA HOWARD

COLLECTION

Two exquisite collector's editions that contain four of
Linda Howard's early passionate love stories. To add
these special volumes to your own library, be sure
to look for:

VOLUME ONE: *Midnight Rainbow*
Diamond Bay
(Available in March)

VOLUME TWO: *Heartbreaker*
White Lies
(Available in April)

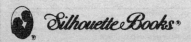 *Silhouette Books*

SLH92

Take 4 bestselling love stories FREE
Plus get a FREE surprise gift!

Special Limited-time Offer

Mail to Silhouette Reader Service™

In the U.S.	In Canada
3010 Walden Avenue	P.O. Box 609
P.O. Box 1867	Fort Erie, Ontario
Buffalo, N.Y. 14269-1867	L2A 5X3

YES! Please send me 4 free Silhouette Intimate Moments® novels and my free surprise gift. Then send me 4 brand-new novels every month, which I will receive months before they appear in bookstores. Bill me at the low price of $2.96* each—a savings of 43¢ apiece off the cover prices. There are no shipping, handling or other hidden costs. I understand that accepting the books and gift places me under no obligation ever to buy any books. I can always return a shipment and cancel at any time. Even if I never buy another book from Silhouette, the 4 free books and the surprise gift are mine to keep forever.

*Offer slightly different in Canada—$2.96 per book plus 49¢ per shipment for delivery. Canadian residents add applicable federal and provincial sales tax. Sales tax applicable in N.Y.

240 BPA ADMD   340 BPA ADMR

Name _____ (PLEASE PRINT) _____

Address _____ Apt. No. _____

City _____ State/Prov. _____ Zip/Postal Code _____

This offer is limited to one order per household and not valid to present Silhouette Intimate Moments® subscribers. Terms and prices are subject to change.

MOM-92   © 1990 Harlequin Enterprises Limited

NORA ROBERTS

Love has a language all its own, and for centuries, flowers have symbolized love's finest expression. Discover the language of flowers—and love—in this romantic collection of 48 favorite books by bestselling author Nora Roberts.

Two titles are available each month at your favorite retail outlet.

In April, look for:

First Impressions, **Volume #5**
Reflections, **Volume #6**

In May, look for:

Night Moves, **Volume #7**
Dance of Dreams, **Volume #8**

Collect all 48 titles and become fluent in

THE LANGUAGE of LOVE

Silhouette®

LOL 492

FREE GIFT OFFER

To receive your free gift, send us the specified number of proofs-of-purchase from any specially marked Free Gift Offer Harlequin or Silhouette book with the Free Gift Certificate properly completed, plus a check or money order (do not send cash) to cover postage and handling payable to Harlequin/Silhouette Free Gift Promotion Offer. We will send you the specified gift.

FREE GIFT CERTIFICATE

ITEM	A. GOLD TONE EARRINGS	B. GOLD TONE BRACELET	C. GOLD TONE NECKLACE
# of proofs-of-purchase required	3	6	9
Postage and Handling	$1.75	$2.25	$2.75
Check one	☐	☐	☐

Name: _____

Address: _____

City: _____ State: _____ Zip Code: _____

Mail this certificate, specified number of proofs-of-purchase and a check or money order for postage and handling to: HARLEQUIN/SILHOUETTE FREE GIFT OFFER 1992, P.O. Box 9057, Buffalo, NY 14269-9057. Requests must be received by July 31, 1992.

PLUS—Every time you submit a completed certificate with the correct number of proofs-of-purchase, you are automatically entered in our MILLION DOLLAR SWEEPSTAKES! No purchase or obligation necessary to enter. See below for alternate means of entry and how to obtain complete sweepstakes rules.

MILLION DOLLAR SWEEPSTAKES
NO PURCHASE OR OBLIGATION NECESSARY TO ENTER

To enter, hand-print (mechanical reproductions are not acceptable) your name and address on a 3"×5" card and mail to Million Dollar Sweepstakes 6097, c/o either P.O. Box 9056, Buffalo, NY 14269-9056 or P.O. Box 621, Fort Erie, Ontario L2A 5X3. Limit: one entry per envelope. Entries must be sent via 1st-class mail. For eligibility, entries must be received no later than March 31, 1994. No liability is assumed for printing errors, lost, late or misdirected entries.

Sweepstakes is open to persons 18 years of age or older. All applicable laws and regulations apply. Sweepstakes offer void wherever prohibited by law. Prizewinners will be determined no later than May 1994. Chances of winning are determined by the number of entries distributed and received. For a copy of the Official Rules governing this sweepstakes offer, send a self-addressed, stamped envelope (WA residents need not affix return postage) to: Million Dollar Sweepstakes Rules, P.O. Box 4733, Blair, NE 68009.

✂

SI1U

ONE PROOF-OF-PURCHASE
To collect your fabulous FREE GIFT you must include the necessary FREE GIFT proofs-of-purchase with a properly completed offer certificate.

(See center insert for details)